BATTLE

To Save The

Soul

Of The

UNIVERSE

The final battle in a ten-million year war.

Book One of the Liberation of Humanity

DUANE C
HUFFMAN

Battle To Save The Soul Of The Universe

For information contact :

https://www.duanehuffman.com

Cover by Denise Worisch

http://dwbookcovers.com/

ISBN: 978-1-7338914-1-7

First Edition: March 2019

10 9 8 7 6 5 4 3 2 1

Special thanks to my daughter Sarah, who painstakingly read my manuscript, edited, and believed in me. And to my other daughters Annette and Lisa who also encouraged and believed in me.

ONE

The evacuation alarm sounded. Katrina promptly stopped reading a translated twentieth-century book about elves and placed it on the reading table. She wished she had a time machine that she could step into, pull a lever, and go back in time and talk to people from ancient Earth. But since time machines didn't really exist, she settled for the next best thing: reading their literature.

"Come on, we have to leave and make it down to the lower level," Katrina said to Anthony, her eleven-year-old brother. He ignored her and continued reading.

Whenever she asked him to do something it turned into a power play, and dad and mom had already lectured him several times about minding her. "If you have a problem with something she tells you to do, just tell us about it when we get home and we'll decide," her dad had told him. But it hadn't helped.

She approached him and reached out to grab the book he was reading, a translated collection of adventures about a detective in nineteenth-century London. He jumped up and angrily walked to the door. "It's just another drill! You know that!"

Outside their apartment, they were greeted by their ever worrying aunt Harriet, a thin, fragile woman in her late thirties. "We've had way too many of these drills lately," she said, holding her anxious hands up to her heart.

Just then, a pleasant sounding female voice came over the loudspeaker. "Please hurry to your assigned lower level emergency shelter. This is not a drill. I repeat. This is not a drill."

"What do you make of that?" Harriet asked, becoming even more alarmed. "They've never said anything like that before."

Katrina, placed her hand on Harriet's arm to calm her and said, "We'll be okay. I'm sure it's just a new type of drill." But she was secretly worried, too. The invasion must have begun. Her father had come home less than three weeks ago from Earth and had warned the city that the Ophidians, an alien race of giant telepathic snakes, and Mega-Corp, the corporation that controlled all buying and selling on Earth, had become aware of their existence. Since then they've had nothing but martial law, curfews, and daily invasion drills.

Everyone was scared. They all knew what had happened the last time humans had fought the Ophidian army. They began the descent down the stairway from their seventh floor. They had been advised not to use the elevators and the stairway became quickly crowded. When the lights blinked, the stairway shook, and the ground rumbled, the people around them became hysterical and began pushing each other in a sudden mad rush to reach the bottom of the stairs, drowning out each other with their nervous, loud screaming.

Several dozen grim-faced guards armed with clubs appeared and pushed the crowd back, quickly restoring order. They then assembled and led everyone in an orderly fashion down the stairs.

"What's going on?" Harriet, in her squeaky voice, asked a busy guard watching the crowd as it passed.

The poker-faced guard said, "All we know is we were instructed to escort everyone in our sector down to the lower levels as quickly as possible and await further orders."

Just past the bottom of the stairs, they walked underneath a large blast door and into a large manmade cavern, built many centuries ago just for this day, with stone walls and a simple dirt floor. The area was well stocked with emergency rations, water, and even weapons that were housed in metal cabinets that Katrina was told would only open if the blast doors shut. There was even an exit door that led into a tunnel that bore through the mountain and came out in the surrounding countryside many miles away.

More rumbling occurred, dirt and a few small rocks and dust rained down on everyone from the natural ceiling. It was obvious to everyone that the rumbling was caused by heavy explosions somewhere on the surface and that the final battle for their civilization's survival had commenced. Soon the rumbling became incessant and many people, including Katrina and Anthony began coughing up phlegm and mucous because of the ever-present dust that now fell from the ceiling.

Katrina tried to engage Anthony and Harriet in conversation. She hoped that by getting them to talk about something--anything--that it might get their minds off their current situation. She herself was worried sick for their dad. He had volunteered against their mother's wishes to be part of the first wave of defense. Her parents almost never argued and always had seemed to happily get along, yet they had argued with loud voices about his volunteering deep into the night.

On this issue, she had agreed with their mother, and she wished for once that their dad wasn't always so eager to prove himself. She feared for him. He would be in the front lines and fighting against the most organized army in the known universe. Anthony acted like their dad was a hero but Katrina was old enough to know that his chances of coming home again were slim.

She tried not to think about that anymore. Her father had always tried to be positive, and he was the heart and soul of their family. *And where was mom?* She bit her lip. She should have been here an hour ago. *Why hadn't she come?* She knew where they would be, and she had promised she would come here at the first alarm.

Her hands shook and she caught herself then, and she realized she was turning into Harriet. She looked to see what Anthony was up to and had just managed to get her nerves under control and work up a small smile when a stern-faced soldier ran into the cavern and said, "We need all available adults and any older children who can use a weapon. Please come with me at once."

Harriet, looking even more worried, turned and gave Katrina a sad look that said, "I'm so sorry," but then abandoned them anyway, leaving them alone with no adults and several dozen younger children. After that, the blast door closed, and her fears returned with a vengeance. Now she really was Aunt Harriet.

* * *

Two thousand years ago, when the first inhabitants of Sanctuary, a city on an alternate Earth in the multiverse, came to this world to escape the Ophidian invasion of Earth they had brought mostly practical, how-to books necessary for surviving in an SHTF scenario. Books of science, literature, and the arts had only existed in softcopy on computer drives and disks. To their good fortune, there were a fair number of teachers among the settlers, and it became their responsibility to educate and keep alive the technical and scientific knowledge that they had grown up taking for granted.

Their ancestors also had the foresight to bring a large number of spare parts and only use the equipment sparingly until such time as they could begin to remanufacture such items again. That hadn't happened for the first several centuries, there simply had not been enough people to provide the necessary manpower to restore a manufacturing society.

The main library of Sanctuary was located in the center of the city and was one of the most popular buildings in the entire metropolis. Hundreds of people came through here every day. The building stood over twenty stories high and went several levels below the ground.

This one building contained, in hard format and softcopy, all of the knowledge and everything that humans had ever accomplished on Earth before the invasion.

When the evacuation alarm first sounded, Emily frowned and rose from her translator's desk in the main library's vault. Most of the information in this level was stored electronically, although there were several thousand volumes of translated printed literature in the main library above her. There were also several thousands of original books brought with her ancestors to this world in the vaults below. Even though the humidity and the storage conditions were ideal, most of that printed literature could now only be handled with the utmost care due to its extreme age.

She was the director of the library and her pet project was to comb the ancient literature, both fiction and nonfiction, for candidate books worthy of printing and housing in the main library above. With limited space and resources, only the best and most important books would become hardbound copies again. She spent many hours a week combing the ancient literature and looking for such gems.   Emily considered staying at her desk, thinking that it's just another drill when the entire floor shook like an earthquake. Alarmed for the safety of her children, she left the library in a rush, now worried sick, and headed for their apartment's emergency shelter where she knew they would be. But before she was halfway there, she ran into several soldiers who told her to follow them at once. "But I need to get to my children," She begged the soldier in charge.

The soldier, a sergeant, sighed. "It's too late, ma'am. The blast doors for all emergency shelters were ordered shut five minutes ago. They won't open now for anyone."

"But they would only shut the blast…." Her mind raced. That could only mean that their military was certain that the city's defenses were in imminent danger of falling. The plan was to shut them as a last-ditch effort for all noncombatants to escape through tunnels into surrounding hills and mountains, then scatter and flee for their lives.

The look on his face only confirmed her fears, *he knew*. "Do you know how to use this?" He asked holding up a military rifle.

Angry now beyond words, knowing that she would never see her children again, she grabbed it, confirmed the safety was on and pulled back the charger. "Just what the hell's going on?"

"The Ophidians have launched their attack… but they're not coming through the cave portal."

"What do you mean?"

Somehow, they managed to get the coordinates of our world, and they have teleported an invasion army just twenty miles or so south of us.

It's a large army with boots on the ground, and it's heading this way.

TWO

With the inevitable threat of an imminent invasion, the leaders of Sanctuary ordered the scientific community to work 24/7 to figure out how to close the cave's portal link to their world. They knew it was possible because their historical records said that within a few weeks after their ancestors had ventured here, it mysteriously closed. And no one knew why, just as mysteriously, a little over a hundred years ago the portal opened up again.

After several weeks of intensive investigative research by the city's best scientific minds, they reluctantly admitted to the city council that they had no idea what the cave was or how to sever the link. Whoever or whatever had created it truly wielded a technology that was beyond them.

The leaders of Sanctuary then ordered their military to blow up the cave and destroy the portal in a desperate move to seal off their world forever. But it hadn't worked, and after the fourth attempt with ever larger explosives, they reluctantly abandoned the idea. Their only hope now lay in defending the pass against the most successful military in the universe.

Sanctuary's military decided on a two-prong approach to their defense strategy. They would build up a massive force on The Sanctuary side knowing that the portal would act as a bottleneck and only allow a small force to pass through at any given time. But the military needed time to lay in their defenses so they asked for volunteers for a vanguard of militia, on the Earth side entrance, whose sole purpose would be to delay any invasion force from entering and using the portal, buying them precious time to build up their defenses.

Of course, everyone in Sanctuary knew it to be a suicide mission but that didn't stop Kyle from volunteering, and to his gleeful surprise they not only accepted his application, but they also placed him in command.

However, when he ran over to the library to tell Emily the exciting news, her response was not what he expected.

"Oh, Kyle…Why,…," She had said, turning pale. When she stood up she knocked her loose research papers and the lavender roses he had just handed her as a peace offering onto the floor. They scattered everywhere, and while he helped her pick them up she growled, "You didn't even think to consult with me first."

He offered her the papers and roses.

"You only volunteered to prove yourself because you weren't born here," she said, snatching the papers from his hands.

"That's not it. I know that some people here will always see me as just a backward hick from Earth and I have learned to accept that. Maybe this sounds crazy, but call it a hunch, premonition from a higher power, or whatever, but I just know I'm supposed to be there. I can feel it."

The sound of tanks and other heavy equipment moving onto the flat grassy plateau brought Kyle back to the present moment. He watched through the powerful scope of his laser rifle with growing alertness as a legion of human-possessed troops advanced up the hill. They were the totally possessed; those poor souls who had their sense of self-sucked out of their minds to be replaced by the identity and will of an Ophidian master telepath. Seeing their blank faces in detail through the scope filled him with a deep sense of remorse. They were helpless pawns. Yet, he knew in a short while he might be required to kill as many of his own kind as he could. He hoped to God he didn't see the face of anyone he had once known.

Finally, the Ophidian army began its advance. Kyle did a quick estimate and knew that his men were outnumbered many times over. It was impossible odds but in spite of this something didn't feel right. Sure, they were outnumbered, but this was not a crushing force. The Ophidians enjoyed crushing their enemies and liked to make an example of anyone who resisted their empire. He had expected their army to be at least three times this size. And where was their air force? They had absolute air superiority, yet there were no aircraft above them. *Why?*

As he counted troop sizes a small convoy of lightly armored buses full of Ophidians with their heads sticking out of passenger windows pulled in behind the front wave of advancing possessed troops. Those Ophidians he knew would be the master telepaths that controlled the troops.

A cold chill raced down his spine and on impulse he felt the top of his head reassuring himself that he was still wearing his thought band. A small pulsing magnetic strip was his only protection against those telepaths from reaching out with their minds even at this distance and turning him and his men into the possessed too.

His orders were to hold this position for a minimum of three days at all costs before falling back. Yet, he and his superiors knew that they would be hard-pressed to hold their position even two. But thank God, they had the secret weapon, their ace in the hole. Everything depended on it performing as hoped.

Before Dr. Perry, Emily's father had been killed he had built upon the simple headband technology and had successfully created a psionic field generator that effectively blanketed an area with a psionic dampening field that performed just as well as a headband but over a broader area. Of course, he had only tested it on a small scale in the laboratory using only a tiny field generator, the size of his fist, but it had worked, blocking all psionic activity over an area of several yards.

Today, they were about to field test a psionic field generator bigger, better and many millions of times stronger.

The device looked everything like a common portable power generator. It fit comfortably inside an ordinary pickup truck. If it worked as hoped, it should block out all psionic activity over an area of several hundred square yards. He had believed in Dr. Perry's work, and he dared to hope that the simple device could turn the tide of battle.

The enemy opened up with their artillery, but their shields held and explosions boomed above them harmlessly raining down bits of dust and shrapnel. Upon discovering that they had shield technology, the shelling soon stopped and the tanks and other heavy machinery began to advance. They were followed closely from behind by a massive wall of possessed troops.

"Wait," Kyle thought. He wanted to make sure the entire possessed force was in range. Just before the tanks encountered their shields, which would allow the slow moving tanks and walking troops to pass through the invisible wall, Kyle turned toward his second in command, a bright young man, Lieutenant Greg. He was a regular soldier and not militia. "Activate the psionic shield on my order."

The soldiers and tanks that had passed through the shield wall began to open fire, and their position became strafed with small arms fire. He turned to lieutenant Greg and gave him a reassuring smile as they both hunkered behind a large boulder. "Activate the psionic shield."

Several seconds later, the Shelling from the tanks and the small arms ceased. It became deadly quiet, and he could hear his heavy breathing. When he peaked around the boulder he saw the blank faces of the possessed soldiers melt away to be replaced by looks of confusion that quickly turned to anger and hostility when their eyes fell upon the Ophidian telepaths riding in the passenger vehicles among them. They brought their weapons up and took aim at the Ophidians. The Mega-Corp drivers quickly grasped what was happening and abandoned the vehicles.

With no hands or feet to operate the passenger vehicles and with the telepathic control over all humans severed, the Ophidians began to slither out of the vehicles as well. But then the formerly possessed troops opened fire and showed no mercy. Within a few minutes, every Ophidian among them was dead.

"Alright!" Kyle gave his young aid the high five. Everyone cheered. The psionic field damper worked even better than anyone had dared hope. Possessed soldiers as far as his eyes could see were now free. He was about to give the order for a full charge at the few remaining regulars and slavers hanging back in the distance when the communications officer, a short, stout, serious-faced man, came up and handed him a slip of paper.

"Sir, urgent message from HQ," the communications officer said saluting.

Kyle returned the salute. "At ease soldier." He glanced at the slip of paper and his mouth dropped. The encoded message said, "Red Alarm! Sanctuary under Siege. Cease engagement and return with the army to Sanctuary at once. Bring secret weapon. Hurry!"

His mind raced. So, the entire battle here was a ruse. The real battle for Sanctuary was about to begin and he was on the wrong world. "Quick," he said turning to Lieutenant Greg. "Give the order to fall back. We leave for Sanctuary at once... And bring the psionic weapon."

He then poked his finger into the chest of the serious-faced communications officer. "Get General Cobb on the tachyon radio and find out what the hell's going on." Thank god for tachyons, thought Kyle. They made inter-world communications possible and it just might have saved Sanctuary.

Ten minutes later, as they began their march into the cave, the communications officer rushed up. "Sir, General Cobb says that the enemy forces outside Sanctuary are considerable and he also says the enemy has complete air superiority. He said to hurry. The city is in grave danger of falling before morning."

"Get back on that radio of yours and tell the General not to despair. Tell him that the secret weapon works even better than hoped."

The communications officer just stood there and said, "I can't sir. All communication is severed. After that last communication, someone began transmitting a block on all frequencies."

Damn, thought Kyle. They marched, double time, all night with no sleep and no stops. They exited the cave on Sanctuary's side just before morning...

THREE

With just a short notice of an imminent invasion, the city had become a frenzy of several million people throwing up security fencing, barb wire, pits, booby traps, and trenches.

However, Emily could see that their last-ditch efforts had been futile the moment she focused her binoculars on the approaching army. The whole valley below appeared black and pulsed like she was looking upon a giant swarm of soldier ants. The sheer size of it amazed her. How did the Ophidians manage to teleport so many soldiers, so quickly? She wondered.

The ground shook from a nearby large explosion, but Emily kept hold of her rifle and even managed to follow up with a well-aimed shot at the enemy helicopter that buzzed overhead. It was a direct hit, but the helicopter's shields successfully absorbed the blast and it flew away unhindered.

There were now hundreds of Enemy helicopters in the sky. They were busy dropping bombs, strafing their defenses and trying to inflict as much damage as they could.

Sanctuary's entire fleet of their small air force had been miles away back at the cave entrance to the portal, and they were just now beginning to return and engage the enemy aircraft. They were having some effect, and she watched gleefully as they pushed back the front wave of enemy attack helicopters, but she could see they were quickly losing aircraft of their own and it wouldn't be long before they were no longer an effective force.

She worried for Anthony and Katrina. She took some small comfort in that at least the evacuation order had been given for all noncombatants. She hoped they were both in the escape tunnels and on their way into the mountains with her sister Harriet.

She worried then for Kyle. She regretted that they had spent their final night together arguing. They should have made love the whole night instead. She wished that she could tell him just one more time how much she loved him.

Heavy machine gun fire erupted as the first wave of the Ophidian army came into range. The electrifying sound of many thousands of bullets whizzing by inches above her head brought her back to the present. All she would have to do is lift her head high out of her fox hole and it would be over. No more worries.

But that was not Emily. She affirmed her resolve to fight to the bitter end by taking with her as many as these possessed bastards as she could. She prayed that she would get very lucky and take a few of those Ophidians too.

She watched with horror as the approaching wave of enemy tanks made quick work of their defenses and within minutes they had plowed an open path. As hundreds of possessed forces rushed towards the city, she opened fire and fought with no mercy…

Katrina, Anthony, and the children waited behind the blast doors. The ground shook again, then the same woman's voice that this morning had told them to come here and wait once more came over the loudspeaker system. "Please begin the evacuation. Everyone, please proceed in a calm manner into the escape tunnels."

There were crates and boxes of supplies and survival equipment stacked neatly onto one side of the cave. Katrina ordered Anthony and the other children to pick up all the emergency rations and survival gear that they could carry. Katrina grabbed a duffel bag that contained survival gear and put on a backpack that was full of food rations. She ordered all the older children to do the same.

They traveled several hours through the narrow tunnels. Some of the younger children were crying. They were afraid and they missed their parents. She and Anthony did their best to console them and put on a brave front, but inside she was afraid too. She understood what was happening on the surface, and she also feared that she'd never see her mother or father again.

The ceiling shook and this time the emergency lighting failed leaving them in total darkness. All of the children, even the older ones, screamed out rigid with terror.

Katrina became angry with herself for not anticipating this and having flashlights ready. She rummaged in the darkness inside her duffel bag, desperately feeling for anything shaped like a flashlight while the children continued to scream.

At that moment, almost in response to her intense desire to find a source of light, her locket began to glow. It was the same locket that the mysterious Fengani priest had given to her father before she was born. A soft blue radiant light emanated from it giving off enough light for her to see the other children. They stopped screaming and crying, and when she held it up; they flocked around her and the reassuring light.

The locket's chain felt icy cold in her hand, like grabbing an ice cube. Not trusting this strange source of light she ordered those children carrying duffel bags to dig out flashlights, just in case. They then continued walking for several more hours more until everyone was totally exhausted and they could go no farther.

She ordered them to stop for the night even though doubts about the wisdom of her decision plagued her. What if the city had already fallen and even now there were Ophidian forces in the tunnels searching. Of course, that would mean her parents were probably both dead. So, she tried not to think about that.

She forced her mind instead to focus on the children's needs for now. She was the oldest in the group and she felt responsible for their well-being. They ate cold rations for an evening meal. Katrina ate crackers and cheese and discovered that she was famished. She wanted more but she resisted the temptation to open another pack. She didn't know how long they would need these rations and she wanted to make them last. They then opened the duffel bags and took out the emergency blankets and camped out for the remainder of the night in the tunnel.

✱ ✱ ✱

"Yes!" Emily shouted waving her fist in the air. Miraculously, through sheer determination of will and luck, they managed to push the possessed assault back and a squad of determined fighters armed with handheld antitank rockets had made quick work of the three tanks that had penetrated their defense sector. However, their defenses where the possessed had broken through were in ruins. Their barbed wire had been cut and pushed aside and those tanks had smashed through their chain link fence. A gaping hole stared at her wide enough for several buses, traveling side by side, to drive through.

The rising sun lit up the battlefield, and in the distance, she saw another fresh battalion of possessed troops at three clicks out marching for this sector. How were they going to stop them? Everyone was exhausted from fighting all night with no rest or sleep.

In the binoculars, she could make out Mega-Corp's regular troops and slaver mercenaries in a camp on a hill over a kilometer away all to themselves. They were holding back. No surprise there. They were going to let the possessed troops do all the dirty work. Their work would begin when the battle was nearly over. They would swoop down like vultures rounding up any survivors for the slave market.

She watched the large mass of possessed troops with trepidation as they marched forward. Their faces were empty without the hint of the slightest emotion. However, their complete blank faces gave her an idea. She remembered her father's theory that the mind control ability of an Ophidian to control the mind of a subject decreased with distance. He had said there was a law in physics for electricity and magnetism, called the inverse square law, and he believed he had uncovered evidence that telepathic forces followed it as well. The formula went, as you double the distance, their power of control dropped to a fourth. For the possessed troops to be completely controlled, then there had to be a cluster of Ophidians somewhere near the battlefield. She used her binoculars to scrutinize the enemy-infested battlefield between her present position and the advancing line of possessed troops. If only she could just find it, they might have a chance.

Her wondering eyes soon discovered a convoy of almost a dozen lightly armored military buses parked a little way off to the side of the battlefield about four hundred meters out looking deserted with no troops or escort. Why would their military park buses there where they could be damaged? And with no escort or guards, that just had to be it. While studying the buses, she watched breathlessly as an Ophidian poked its head out of one of the passenger windows to peek at the battlefield. *Yes! I've got you!*

Now, if she could just get there with a small strike team and take out those buses, their chances of winning this engagement would go way up. They might even survive.

She turned and smiled when she saw a young, grim-faced lieutenant coming her way, "Sir, where's your commanding officer?"

"You're looking at him. Our captain is dead, and we can't communicate with division HQ except with runners, they're blocking all transmissions. Even the tachyon transceiver is out. We're on our own."

"Then I'm giving you an order. My rank is lieutenant colonel in the militia. I need about a dozen of your best soldiers and several of those hand-held antitank weapons that made nice work of those tanks.

"Why?"

I need them to assist me in taking out those buses," she said pointing out to the plains outside the city.

He looked doubtful. She saw she had some convincing to do. He was regular-army and probably didn't relish the idea of taking orders from militia types, especially in a real firefight. "It's where the Ophidians are holed up that are controlling the minds of these soldiers marching towards us," she said.

"And just how would you know that?" he said, still unconvinced.

"Because I saw one stick its head out of a window just a few moments ago. Look for yourself," she said, handing him the binoculars.

He grabbed the binoculars and callously pulled them out of her hand. As he used them and worked on focusing them for his eyes, he said, "Lady, I don't really have time... What the... Your right! The bastard just stuck its head out."

"Well, do I get my team?" She said gleaming.

The lieutenant scratched his head. "OK, you're right. If we can take out those buses, we might just turn the tide." But he looked doubtful and shook his head. "But how are you going to get there? There are four hundred meters of open ground you would have to cross. See those laser cannons and laser pulse machine guns on that far hill?" he said pointing. "You wouldn't make it fifty meters, let alone all four hundred to those buses."

She smiled. "You're wrong. Look again. There is a drainage ditch less than 12 meters out that runs diagonally away from the city and passes to within 20 meters of those buses. Lieutenant, I've been in that ditch with my children frog hunting and it's at least three meters deep and the water in it only comes up to your ankle. We would be completely safe from small arms fire."

He used her binoculars again, Oh yeah, you're right. It does run close to those buses. OK, you get your team, if you can get twelve volunteers."

Less than five minutes later, she and a dozen volunteers hustled through the gap in their defenses. Just before she left, the Lieutenant came over and handed her a submachine gun and a backpack of several round drums of ammo. "Here take this. My compliments."

She put on the backpack and took the submachine gun from him, and then motioned for her team to go.

When they dashed out through the break in the fence, they came under immediate small arms fire. The auto tracking machine guns began to swing their incessant fire towards her team.

But they made it! They were inside the ditch before the machine guns were able to swing over to their location. So far, luck held out and they only suffered one casualty. The poor woman took a bullet to the head and died instantly. The ditch was deep enough and just wide enough that they could run. They moved fast and made it to the closest point to the buses in minutes.

Emily poked a mirror device not unlike a small periscope to see over the top of the ravine without exposing her head to the enemy. The buses were just up ahead and there were no guards.

"Lock and load," Emily said. On her signal, a soldier armed with an anti-tank rocket launcher fired at the closest bus. After the explosion, Emily's team charged out of the ravine and began firing at several large Ophidians slithering out the blown-out windows of the burning bus to escape the heat and flames.

When the next bus exploded, an ear-piercing roar of anger erupted from something inside this bus that cut through the incessant rat-tat of her submachine gun. It was unnerving, but everyone continued firing. Once again, the Ophidians slithered out of the burning bus trying to escape the flames. Many of them were already so badly burned they would have died soon anyway. The air she breathed took on the heavy smell of burning flesh.

As they fired their weapons into the dying Ophidians, thick black smoke poured out of the flaming bus and rapidly coalesced into a single black cloud less than ten meters above them. They were just about to hurry onto the next bus when the black cloud flowed to the ground and solidified into a bipedal creature as tall as a large grown man. It sported black leathery wings, a doglike face, and a naked body covered in a black thick fur. A forked tongue flicked rapidly in and out of its muzzle, and then it roared that same loud roar they had heard only a short time before.

Her team stopped firing to look at this bizarre creature. The soldier closest to it raised his rifle and shot it in the head, but the creature, unscathed, turned its ugly face towards him, raised a claw-like hand and a red bolt of bright light flashed out of it severing the body of the man who had shot it in two.

Upon seeing the creature just kill one of her men, she raised the submachine gun and fired a continuous stream of bullets. But the bullets seemed to travel right through it as if it was not there. She went to move closer then but found she couldn't move her feet. She found herself frozen in position. Somehow this creature was holding her and her men prisoners.

Then she heard the creature's guttural voice inside her head. "How dare you attack and hurt my pets. Do you have any idea of what it feels like to burn to death?" The creature paused. "No...? Let me show you. How about a vivid hallucination? Let me show you what it feels like when your entire body is on fire."

All at once she felt immense pain like she was standing inside a blazing furnace. She looked at her hand and watched her flaming arm as the burning flesh dripped away exposing the bone of her arm. She screamed, "It's only an illusion!" just before she blacked out.

✳ ✳ ✳

Kyle's army reached the outskirts of Sanctuary just after Dawn. The distant sound of gunfire coming from the city's defenses assured Kyle that the city hadn't fallen but the situation was desperate. Sorties of enemy helicopters were flying over the city, strafing and dropping bombs everywhere. The entire grassy plain surrounding the city was covered with dead combatants from both sides.

Kyle hoped and prayed that Emily and the children were together in the escape tunnels and not somewhere in the city.

They advanced until they were within a quarter mile of the city. The regulars and slaver mercenaries, who had until now had held back, attacked Kyle's unit in force. They raised the shield wall, and a soft blue giant transparent half-bubble several hundred meters wide formed above them blocking all weapons.

The shield was taking a heavy beating from continuous fire and the technician in charge told him that at the rate they were being fired upon they would exhaust their power supplies in less than twenty minutes. Kyle ordered the men to work fast on getting the secret weapon powered up. He had his men spread out and prepare to shoot any of the enemy that came inside their shield.

They worked lightning fast. Fifteen minutes later, they were about to flip the switch when a dark, black cloud appeared twenty meters above them. The cloud descended to the ground and transformed into a grotesque creature looking like a demon right out of hell. When the creature raised its hands towards the secret weapon, Kyle guessed its intent and did a quick draw firing his pistol, but the bullets had no effect. It glanced his way and a bolt of red lightning flashed out of its hands striking him in the chest. He flew twenty-feet backward. He landed on his back and the back of his head bounced against a half-buried rock…

* * *

The next morning, after a cold breakfast of more emergency rations, Katrina and the children continued walking through the tunnel that had turned slightly upwards. Several hours later, they reached the end of the tunnel and emerged onto a narrow pass high in the mountains.

They came out on a small plateau. She and the children walked carefully over to the cliff side and peered down. They were above the valley and they could see the ruins of Sanctuary below. Smoke rose in the air marking where the city had once stood. Everything was in ruins. "Oh my," thought Katrina. Tears ran down everyone's faces. Even the younger children seemed to understand that the world they had always known was no more.

She watched the smoke billowing out of Sanctuary and worried for her parents. she considered what to do next. The Ophidians would have slavers looking for survivors. She had learned from her parents that slavers especially prized children. They would assimilate more easily into their new life and would bring a higher price at the slave market.

We must go far, far away and now. She forced everyone to start walking the narrow pass to wherever it would take them, but they hadn't traveled more than half a mile when she saw a cloaked figure just standing in the middle of the path up ahead as if it were waiting for them. The mysterious stranger wore a black robe with the hood pulled up hiding its face. Is it a mountain man? She had heard that there were some people who lived in the mountains preferring the solitude of the high places to the hustle and bustle of the city life. Would he help them escape?

But what if it's a slaver? She became afraid again. She wanted a weapon, but she had none. She realized then that there was probably a small caliber survival pistol stashed somewhere in the duffel bag she carried and she cursed herself for not having the foresight to have taken it out in advance. It was too late for that now. Should they turn around and run?

She motioned for the children to stay while she walked cautiously ahead. Anthony started to walk beside her, but she placed her hand on his shoulder and whispered to him, "No stay here. If anything happens to me, have the children drop everything and bolt back into the caves. Look for other groups escaping. Look for another way out."

They stared at each other. Wiped away was Anthony's sibling rivalry. In its place, she saw real concern for her safety. They hugged, and she reassured him. Then she turned toward the dark figure and advanced slowly with her hands open and up. When she was about twenty paces away she said, "Hello? Will you help us?"

The dark figure pulled its hood off exposing bulbous eyes, a lipless reptilian-face populated with rows of sharp teeth in a menacing grin. A Fengani! Here! "Oh no," she thought. He must be with the slavers.

She was about to turn and tell Anthony to run when the Fengani said, "Katrina, you're safe, relax."

The use of her name put her off guard. "How do you know my name?"

The Fengani stood up on its two legs. "My name is Iaghi." He said ignoring her question. Its whip-like tail swayed back and forth in the air behind it.

"How did you know where to find me?"

"When you used the locket I sensed its use and learned of your general whereabouts. Since you continued to use it, it led me straight to you."

"How could using the locket do that?" She became alarmed again, if this Fengani could sense the use of the locket, then perhaps the Ophidians could as well.

"Your fears are ungrounded. No one but a learned master of the Way can sense your use of the locket. The Ophidians know nothing about you, and I want to keep it that way. I won't let any harm come to you. You're much too valuable. You and the children, please follow me. I'll take you all to Earth where you will be safe."

"Earth? But what about my parents? I want to find out if they survived and escaped."

The Fengani looked at her with his black bulbous eyes. "They are both alive, but they are prisoners."

Prisoners? "Do you have the power to help them?" she asked almost pleading. Was that sadness she saw in those eyes?

"I'm sorry, I cannot. We're not yet ready to reveal our true powers to the Ophidians or the abomination that controls them. I'm taking a big risk in just helping you. But you're far too important. You don't yet know your true destiny. Please come at once. We must go. Soon these hills will be crawling with slavers looking for escapees."

Wow. Talk about a leap of faith. This reptilian alien with his threatening grin and a total stranger just asked her to trust him with her life and those of the children. But then again, what choice did she truly have? She knew nothing about these hills. They had no destination and no idea where to go. Where were the other groups of escapees? She decided she would have to trust him for now. But on the first opportunity, she was going to dig out that survival pistol out of the duffel bag and arm herself.

She motioned to the children to come up and they all followed the Fengani. "Where's he taking us," Anthony asked coming up beside her.

"To Earth. He said he was taking us to Earth."

✳ ✳ ✳

Oh, my head! Kyle Thought. But then the pain meant he was still alive. Soft, gentle fingers massaged his head. *Who could that be?* When he opened his eyes, he looked into Emily's dark eyes. He grasped her hand.

She sighed with relief, "Thank God! You're awake. Can you stand?"

He examined his body for pain. "I think so. What happened?"

Some of your men told me you tried to take on the same creature that captured me. He knocked you back and you hit your head on a rock. Fortunately, your skull doesn't seem fractured, but you may have a concussion."

Remembering then what happened, his face lit up with alarm. "The psionic field damper!"

"The creature destroyed it," Emily said stroking his hair. She helped him to stand. They were part of a group of about two hundred prisoners confined inside a chain-link enclosure. Mega-Corp's human guards wearing Mega-Corp uniforms stood menacingly outside. "How did we get here?"

"We're prisoners, the remnant of Sanctuary's army."

Kyle squeezed Emily's hand. "Do you know if the children got away?"

"I'm not sure, but the evacuation order was well under way when I was captured."

So, this is how it all ends, Kyle thought. The last free human city was now destroyed.

Later that afternoon, a group of senior Mega-Corp officials approached their compound and announced that the empire had something special planned for them and they would be marching in the morning through the portal to Earth.

FOUR

hree weeks after the destruction of Sanctuary, Kyle, Emily, and several hundred fellow prisoners walked under guarded escort wearing heavy shackles and chains into a small, sand-colored village.

The local citizens came out and stared at them looking gaunt and dressed in rags. The buildings of the village needed to be painted and many of the roofs were missing shingles and sagging from dry rot. The wispy looking children simply stared at them as they marched by with vacant, hungry eyes.

Kyle and Emily had their first hot meal that night since becoming prisoners. He almost refused to eat it. It certainly didn't look appealing, but his mind kept being haunted by the frail village children with hungry eyes. There was no doubt in his mind they'd be very happy to be served this. So, he forced himself to eat it. It was a tasteless gruel, but at least it was hot, and he did enjoy the sensation of a full stomach for a change.

The heavy chains clamped to Emily's ankles were causing blisters and Kyle put a salve on them to ease the pain and keep out infection. "How does that feel?" He asked.

She smiled wanly, and she held her head up as she tried to appear strong. But Kyle knew that it was a front. Her incessant worrying for the welfare of Katrina and Anthony was taking its toll. She'd become short, snappy, and hardly slept. It was eating away at her insides like a fruit maggot inside an apple. Everything inside her was becoming rotten.

* * *

The next day, more prisoners entered the village. Emily interrogated them in turn as they entered the prison yard hoping to learn anything she could on the whereabouts of their children. No one knew anything about Katrina or Anthony, but she did learn that the Ophidians had ordered bands of slavers to capture everyone they could find. They wanted none of the citizens of Sanctuary to escape. They wanted all human resistance to cease once and for all.

Two days later when more prisoners arrived, Emily saw a tired and haggard looking Harriet marching in with a group of ragged women and children.

Emily ran to her. She was concerned for her sister and frantic for news, but a disheveled Harriet looked at her with dead, unfocused eyes. She inspected Harriet's, torn, dirty garments. "Oh, Harriet," she thought. What have these bastards done to you? None of the women in Emily's group had been molested, but she could see clearly by locations of the rips on these women's clothes and dead expressions on their faces that the women in Harriet's group had been much less fortunate.

Finally, as if coming out of a trance, Harriet suddenly recognized Emily. She reached out, clung to Emily like a drowning person to a life raft, and sobbed on her sister's shoulder for a very long time.

When Harriet finished crying, Emily discovered that she had been crying too. It was obvious to her that poor Harriet was hanging on to her fragile sanity by a thread. She delayed questioning Harriet about

Katrina or Anthony. They just talked instead for almost an hour reliving mutual fond memories of better times and circumstances.

As they talked, Harriet began to smile, and the inner light and warmth gradually returned to Harriet's eyes. When Harriet seemed to be almost back to her old talkative self, she risked asking the question that had been on the forefront of her mind, "Do you know what may have happened to Katrina and Anthony the day of the attack?"

Harriet's eyes became distant as she tried to remember. "I remember… when the evacuation alarm sounded…. We all went down the stairway together…" Harriet paused. "…And we had made it down into our assigned emergency shelter. We were all together behind the open blast door when a soldier came in and commanded all the adults who could fire a weapon to follow him. I left them in charge of some younger children and I remember looking back as I went up the stairs. Sometime later, perhaps an hour or two, I broke away from my station during a respite in the fighting to check up on them, but the entire building was gone. Our building had taken a direct hit. There was nothing left but rubble. I think it was before they ordered the blast doors closed. I'm so sorry…."

Emily's heart sank. Her children must have certainly been killed. She left Harriet then too upset to ask any more questions. She had more but she thought could wait and that she could ask them to Harriet after she had some time to absorb what she had just learned.

But that was not the case, for that same afternoon. Mega-Corp helicopters landed in the village and a team of Mega-Corp soldiers inspected all the prisoners and took any who were wounded or appeared weaker and loaded them into the helicopters and then took off. Unfortunately, they also took Harriet and loaded her into a copter before Emily could even say goodbye.

After that, despair and anger seeped unhindered into her soul. She had not been there for Harriet or her children. She blamed herself and she began to have vivid nightmares where she dreamed of her children and Harriet undergoing all sorts of torture and physical abuses.

She became completely withdrawn and refused to eat. Her misplaced guilt turned towards Kyle severing her relationship with him. She couldn't understand what she had ever seen in him. How can he go on as if nothing happened? She stopped caring about herself and no longer cared whether she lived or died.

FIVE

The propeller of the overloaded cargo-copter struggled to take off and it made a mournful roar as it worked to generate the necessary lift.

Harriet stood crammed tight against the many strange men and women in the back of the cargo hold. The gagging strong smells of fear, sweat, urine, and excrement were almost overpowering. If she had anything in her stomach, she would have lost it.

She looked around hoping to see someone she knew, but all she saw were terrified strangers staring back at her. Many were indigenous to Earth, and they all had hopeless eyes inside resigned faces of doom. Her nose began to itch, and she frantically struggled to reach it, but with her hands and feet securely bound in heavy chains, her efforts proved futile.

Harriet was on the cutting edge of hysteria, and she began to feel her mind slip away again as it had during the march out of Sanctuary. But this time just before she snapped and lost all sanity, her feelings shut down. She felt nothing.

For the first time in her life her mind, not burdened with needless fears, began working with poignant clarity. She made a quick mental assessment of her dire situation. She briefly entertained the possibility of escape, but the fantasy soon died. She knew she would never have the necessary courage to try even if an unlikely opportunity presented itself.

She didn't know how long this respite from her emotions would last. They might return with a vengeance at any moment. With no real hope of escape or rescue, and nothing to do but think, she began to replay her life from its beginning to each defining moment that had led to her present circumstance.

Each summer in her youth she and Emily tagged along with her parents' scientific summer-expeditions to Earth.

She still blamed herself for that fateful day years ago when her and Emily while away from camp out exploring on their own a band of slavers, from out of nowhere, attacked and grabbed Emily. Instead of trying to make it back to camp and warn everyone that slavers were about, frightened for her life, she remembered running frantically through the wilderness driven by sheer terror. She ran deep into the wilderness across rocky terrain and hid. Too frightened to move any farther, she remained in her little hiding place until the next morning. When she did make it back to camp, she had discovered that both her parents had been killed by the same group of slavers when they had gone out looking for their missing children.

Yes, she had always been afraid, afraid to fail or succeed, even afraid to try; that is why she had never formed any lasting relationships. In truth, her entire life had been one fear-filled situation after another. *I am a hopeless coward.*

Her candid thoughts then turned to what kind of future fate might have in store for her. She remembered what Emily had told her about her experience as a slave. It didn't sound all that bad. Other than the heavy manual labor she had mentioned, she also had said that the food and living quarters where she lived had been very acceptable, and as long as you stayed in line and didn't cause trouble you were treated fairly. If her destiny was to become a slave, she might as well try to make the best of it.

At that moment the copter made a turn and headed due south. Many of the indigenous captured slaves in the cargo hold began to wail and moan like they were being taken to slaughter. "What's wrong," she asked in universal, the native language of Earth, a young wild indigenous woman dressed in animal skins with feathers stuck in her hair.

She began to cry. "They're not taking us the slave markets, they're taking us to their snake temple," she said in anguish.

Harriet strained her neck and managed to get a peek out of the port window. She glimpsed a large pyramid-shaped structure, many stories higher than the surrounding forest canopy off in the distance. It certainly looked impressive, blazing white in the sunlight.

"What's the problem with that?" Harriet asked. She had never heard of this snake temple.

"It's where they make their possessed or worse. You enter it as a human and if you come out, you are a mindless slave."

The thought of having herself turned into a mindless possessed soul totally under the control of an Ophidian master-telepath thawed her emotions and they returned with a vengeance. She began to shake uncontrollably with sheer terror.

When they landed, several dozen armed Mega-Corp soldiers removed their shackles and escorted them in double file towards the large pyramid. A twelve-foot-high security fence surrounded the rectangular compound. Guard towers armed with machine guns stood at each corner. Even if she could somehow muster the courage, escape was impossible.

They were taken to the front entrance of the large pyramid where they entered a narrow hallway. Inside, the hallway walls were covered with pictograms of a bipedal creature with a long dog's snout and black, bat wings.

As they walked, she felt a shifting not unlike she felt when she walked through the portal in the cave that connected Earth and Sanctuary. She had no idea where she was, but she was sure she was no longer on Earth. That had to be a portal that she just walked through.

The hallway made a turn and then opened into a large central chamber, where a feeble light coming from two black candles burning atop two candelabras on either side of a black stone altar was the room's only source of light. In the dim light, the shadows seemed to move. *What?* She realized to her horror that the chamber was full of large Ophidians. "My God, there must be hundreds of them."

Their guards marched them to the front of the altar and then lined them up into three tight rows. Harriet stood in the middle of the second. Now that everyone was in a group, she estimated that there were about two hundred slaves altogether.

An Ophidian, much larger than the others, slithered from out of the shadows from the other side of the altar. It wore a headdress adorned with many multicolored beads and about a dozen braided leather strands that dangled about a foot down its face, each ending in a black stone and a small white feather.

This was interesting. She'd never heard of an Ophidian wearing anything. This certainly made it unique and she watched as the other Ophidians moved out of its way and bobbed their heads and lowered their eyes as it passed them by.

The large Ophidian moved to the front row of slaves and began to take interest in the first slave, a terrified young man. It brought its face down to his and began swaying its head slowly back and forth. The young man stopped shaking and the Ophidian stopped swaying. They both stared into each other's eyes. Finally seeming satisfied, the Ophidian moved to the next slave and a possessed soldier lead the now catatonic young man away to the right. The scene was repeated with each slave in line. Sometimes they were escorted to the right and sometimes to the left. It's dividing us into two groups, she observed. *Why?* Sweat rolled off her face. She wanted to bolt and just run, run, run. But her feet refused to move. They were no longer under her control. She was bound to where she stood, but without chains. She surmised it must be something that the Ophidians were doing with their minds. *How are they doing that?*

The giant Ophidian was working on the second row now. Soon it would be her turn. Please don't turn me into a possessed soul she pleaded to a nameless god. Her heart beat hard inside her chest. Afraid it would soon burst all together only added to her fears.

When the Ophidian with the headdress stood before her, it began swaying its head back and forth just like with the others. Its large glowing yellow eyes with slit pupils burned into her. She wanted to look away, but her head and her eyes no longer obeyed her commands. Feeling naked and exposed, she felt the creature's presence penetrate her mind. The pain…burning… was almost unbearable. Her head felt like the creature had just ripped open the top of her skull and had poured boiling acid onto her brain. She so wanted it to stop; She felt its parasitic presence moving around inside her head, examining her. *For what purpose?*

After a seeming eternity, it left her mind and moved on to the next person in line. and she found herself being escorted to the left. She breathed a sigh of relief for she still had her own mind and she was not possessed.

When the sorting was over, only a single woman now remained at the altar. She had not been sorted into either group but had been moved up to the altar instead. Harriet recognized the woman to be the same indigenous woman who had told her about the snake temple.

The Ophidians now approached and crowded around the altar. Their yellow eyes seemed to glow as if they were on fire and she sensed that they anticipated something as if it was their birthday and they were examining their presents. Harriet felt a cold shiver down her back, and she sensed that something really bad was about to happen.

Uncannily, the tongues of the Ophidians who gathered around the altar began to dart in and out of their mouths in sync and their heads swayed in unison like a large percussion marching band slapping rhythm and moving in time with each other. Their eyes concentrated on the woman standing in front of the altar. Harriet's ears began ringing; all she could hear was a loud high-pitched hum. The woman undressed in timely sync with their swaying and then stretched herself out on the altar.

The tempo of the bobbing snakes increased. The buzzing in her ears became even louder. She found her mind succumbing to the hypnotic effect of the snake ceremony. Suddenly the loud buzzing noise turned into words and she heard ..."Lord master Draka come... over and over."

At that moment, a dark cloud materialized above the altar. The rate of their chant quickened "Draka...master, come...."

The black cloud shrank in size and solidified. Harriet now looked upon the ugliest creature she had ever seen. Never in her worst nightmare, had she encountered a more terrifying beast.

It was bipedal and stood up about the height of a man. Its body was covered in black fur, and it had long leathery, black wings. Its face was shaped like a dog's with large pointy ears, looking just like the Egyptian god of Anubis, in person. It had snout full of razor-sharp teeth with a snakelike tongue that darted in and out of its mouth rapidly as it tasted the air.

The creature stepped up to the altar. The ugly creature began chanting in a deep and resonant baritone voice in a guttural language she'd never heard before. "Evunga Narunga Evunga Narunga... Evunga Narunga..." Then the creature spread its wings as if it was preparing to fly. Instead, it transformed. Where one moment it appeared solid and physical in form, the next its bodily dimensions expanded threefold and its body became translucent and Harriet could see through it.

Harriet looked with pity on the woman restrained on the altar afraid of the unknown and what was about happen next, and… she aged!...aged decades before her eyes. And then just turned into dust and disintegrated. *"Oh my…"*

Her eyes glanced again at the creature, and it seemed darker and more pronounced.

What she had just witnessed happen to that poor woman was *not* going to happen to her. Finally, in the end, she found the courage that had always eluded her. She fought like a wild animal with everything she had, and she pulled with all her strength against her invisible bonds. She was of the mind to chew her legs off with her bare teeth if it would do any good. Miraculously, she moved her foot! But before she could take that first brave step away from the altar and this madness, the Ophidian with the headdress focused on her and took control of her body once more freezing her again in place. She was now beyond terrified. Tears streamed down her face. The Ophidian with the headdress moved to her and began to coil its body around her and its forked tongue darted rapidly in and out of its mouth, touching different parts of her body each time. Then it brought up its face to hers and began to sway again as it did before. The Ophidian brought its face very close to hers again and they stared at each other for a moment. Then the Ophidian moved its head back and began to open its mouth wider than Harriet had thought possible. My God! It's eating me! Her heart beat inside her chest, with a large thump, thump, thump. She pulled and tugged at her mental bonds with everything inside her. But it was no use. She simply couldn't move. She screamed when its mouth slid over her head and…

SIX

Modern San Diego, the slave trading capital of Earth, stood on top of the ruins of pre-invasion San Diego. This modern city had a surrounding black Nano-carbon wall that was ten feet thick and rose over 100 feet into the air. Thanks to this wall, no slave had ever escaped from this city.

Slaves were brought here and auctioned off by Mega-Corp to all alien species that were on good trading terms with them. After the slaves were sold, they would be transported to former Ecuador and hitch a ride on the space elevator up to the Ophidians inter-world portal in synchronous orbit. Once there, they would be teleported to their new owner's home world.

This was the city that Kyle and Emily entered three weeks after leaving the small sand-colored village.

Kyle walked beside Emily who shared a wrist chain with him. He had tried often during the march to New San Diego to engage her in a conversation hoping to bring her out of her foul mood, but she only responded with grunts and growls. He knew that he was losing her. The light was now all but gone from her eyes, and she was looking gaunt from lack of sleep and hardly eating. Whenever he tried to engage her in conversation she would just remain silent pushing him away. Her depression had gained a very firm grip on her soul.

✳ ✳ ✳

Emily's dark, angry thoughts turned to Kyle. How could he act as if nothing had happened? Their children were either dead or captured, and they took away poor Harriet just after getting reunited. Nothing he could say would change that. Why does he keep trying to talk? It bugged her that he kept trying. Doesn't he see that nothing matters anymore?

Their guards escorted them directly to a holding area and a large cage inside an enormous amphitheater, which was crowded with aliens waiting for the bidding to open. Kyle and Emily's group, the last remnant of Sanctuary's army, were off to the side. They weren't for sale as they had already been promised to Mega-Corp and some experiment they wanted to perform. They were just here for the formalities.

Standing in front of the large alien audience brought Emily's mind out of the internal hell of guilt and anger she had created. Her Hatred of the Ophidians and Mega-Corp fueled her. Her eyes lit up and her old, stubborn self returned.

The audience wanted to see a ragtag assembly of disheveled and broken humans, destitute and forlorn. But she held her head up high and told her comrades to look proud when the guards made them form into a parade and march in front of the masses of aliens in the packed stands. She transformed into that same young girl that Kyle had first liberated so long ago, and those same words came back to him when they had first met. ... *"My spirit will never be broken."*

After the parade, they were escorted to the side of the amphitheater where they were to stand and watch their fellow citizens be auctioned off one by one before the Mega-Corp auctioneer could commence the bidding. When he motioned for the first slave to be brought up she jumped up, raised a clenched fist above her head and

39

screamed the word …FREEEEE…DOM…. She did it again, and again. Each time more of the men and women prisoners joined her until they were all screaming at the top of their lungs the word FREEEEE…DOM…

The Mega-Corp guards stood by idly confused as if waiting for orders on how to proceed. The crowd of aliens in the amphitheater went wild with anger. They continued their chanting and even the citizens in line to be sold joined in.

Meanwhile, the captain of the guard, a human, came over and began wailing his leather whip at her and Kyle, but they worked together as a team and used the chain attaching them together as a shield to ward off most of the blows. Finally, another guard came up from behind and shot Emily with a stun gun knocking her unconscious. Kyle stopped shouting and held an unconscious Emily in his arms.

Her brave demonstration of defiance reignited his waning love for her and he sensed their inner connection once more. Yes, this was the wonderful Emily he had fallen in love with.

When a guard took out his Billy club and began to approach them, most likely to make an example of her and Kyle, the other prisoners gathered around them wearing angry, determined faces making a human shield. The guard looked at them and seeing open hatred in their eyes and sensing their defiance, he wisely backed off and walked slowly away.

Later, after Emily woke up from the effects of the stun gun, she and Kyle spent the entire night talking and repairing their damaged relationship.

The next morning, Kyle, Emily and the rest of their small group of prisoners were taken to an experimental facility where they learned from the guards that their memories would be erased and supplanted with new ones to serve the needs of Mega-Corp.

While they stood in single file outside the facility waiting their turn, Emily and Kyle silently held hands just enjoying being alive and together for the last time.

Kyle walked into the space elevator that would take him to the teleportation portal in Earth's synchronous orbit. He no longer remembered any part of his former life. His new synthetic-memories told him he had volunteered to fight for Mega-Corp's foreign legion to escape from unrequited love. His false memory told him her name was Morgana. Warm memories of the sweet smell of her blond hair against his face caused his heart to pang.

The group of men and women with him were all thinking about their implanted pasts hoping to forget names and events that had never really happened. He recognized no one in the group that boarded the elevator with him, just nameless faces, except... for a pretty, dark-haired woman in the back. She stood out in his mind. She seemed different, surer of herself. He had the strange feeling he'd seen her before, but where? He couldn't quite place her...

SEVEN

Iaghi led the way along the narrow mountain pass. Katrina carried the youngest child, an exhausted six-year-old girl named Jan. As she walked, she wondered how Iaghi was going to manage to transport them back to Earth when the portal was across the valley and was now occupied by many thousands of Ophidian soldiers.

She had a sudden insight. Perhaps there was more than one portal. Sure, why not. She was just about to ask Iaghi about her theory when she felt a sudden resistance as she tried to walk, and she had to push forward like she was walking into a strong wind, only there was no wind, and then just as quickly it was gone. "Did you just feel that?" She asked Anthony.

"Feel what?"

"Like it just got much harder to go forward."

He shrugged. "I'm tired and my feet are killing me, but it didn't feel any anything."

Perhaps she had imagined it. But when she looked to her left out into the valley below, where five minutes ago they had looked at the smoking ruins of Sanctuary, the smoke was gone and so were the ruins. The valley looked pristine like there had never been a city at all.

She picked up her pace until she walked beside Iaghi. "We're on Earth, aren't we?"

The Fengani turned toward her and gave her that threatening grin again. "Very perceptive of you, yes, we're on Earth. I've just teleported us here."

She looked back to take a quick head count to make sure everyone was still following. "But, there was no portal. How did you manage it? Do you possess some form of magic?"

He chuckled. "No, there's no such thing as magic, just technology. However, much, much, more sophisticated and advanced than anything your people or the Ophidians possess."

She pushed Jan, who was fast asleep, up higher onto her shoulder. "How come I could feel it happen, but Anthony didn't."

"You've used the locket. He stopped in midstride to stare at her with those reptilian eyes of his. "By doing so you have begun to awaken your attunement. Your mind and senses are already operating at a higher level."

Attunement? She wasn't sure she liked the sound of that. "Earlier you said you sensed my use of the locket. I don't understand. I didn't try to use it, it just lit up. It's never done that before."

"You were frightened and in mortal danger for the first time in your life. You panicked when the lights in the tunnel failed. The locket felt your fear and it responded accordingly." His eyes lit up like he was trying to make a point. "You must understand the locket will do everything in its power to protect you. It's much more powerful than anything you can imagine."

He had just talked about it like it was alive, even sentient. She grabbed it and studied it in her fingers and gave it a cursory examination. As always, the deep blue crystal felt icy cold. She turned it over in her hand and examined its back and saw the familiar zodiacal symbol of Leo. Until yesterday, she had always considered it to be just a pretty trinket. How could an inanimate object be sentient?

She remembered the story her father had told her about a Fengani priest giving it to him as a gift for her just before she was born. "You're the same Fengani that gave my father this locket. Aren't you?"

Iaghi ignored her question and simply started walking again.

She took his silence as an affirmation. "Why me? Why am I so special? I've done nothing to earn this."

"Yes, you have. You simply do not remember your past life. But you will. Your soul and the locket's are already bound to each other. Now that you are reunited it will not allow itself to be separated from you, not even for a few minutes. You don't yet realize your importance." He laughed again. "Do you remember even once you or your parents of removing the locket from around your neck?"

Funny, come to think of it, he was right. They had never removed it. Not even once. Even when she was very little, and she felt the strong need to always wear it. "I don't understand…"

"Your soul and the locket's are one."

He picked up the pace and she sensed that their conversation was ending, but she had a million more questions to ask. How could she be one with an inanimate object? And why did the Fengani have it in the first place?

She was just about to vocalize that question when as if reading her mind, Iaghi said, "Please enough questions for now. You need to think about and absorb what you have just learned. Your questions will best be answered later when you are ready for more," he said turning and walking away.

Later that day they were joined by several more dozens of Fengani and they all seemed to defer to Iaghi as their senior. That night Iaghi told them that he would take her and Anthony to the village of Lovencraft. He said that the people there were friends and relatives of their father and that the mayor of the town was their great uncle and that they would willingly take them in. However, he also said that the rest of the children would be taken to an old converted Catholic monastery where the Fengani ran an orphanage and used it as their headquarters for proselytizing.

Katrina didn't like the idea of being separated from the rest of the children, especially Jan who she had become attached to, but Iaghi said that they would be well cared for.

She asked why she and Anthony weren't going to the monastery too. Iaghi just gave her a funny stare. "That would be too dangerous, for the monastery receives too many outside visitors who might notice your unusual abilities and mention you to the wrong people. Not everyone in the universe will be excited to learn of your rebirth. The Eye of God has shown us that it is safest for you to live somewhere out of the way and off the beaten path, and the Eye of God believes Lovencraft is perfect."

Katrina frowned. "what's the Eye of God?"

Iaghi said, "You'll learn about it in time when you are older." After that, he became silent again.

Two weeks later, she and Anthony stood just outside the village of Lovencraft, alone. Just before Iaghi had abandoned them he said, "Learn to open up your mind and become one with the locket and learn its secrets. It is a very powerful ally. Don't forget to tell the Pickfords who you are. How good is your Universal? No one speaks English or any other language on Earth anymore. Mega-Corp has seen to that."

"They teach it at school and My father and mother wanted us to be fluent in it, so we spoke it at home on occasion. I can understand better than I speak, but I can get by I am sure," Katrina said.

They glanced sideways at the wooden and brick saltbox houses of the small town as they walked down the main thoroughfare. They hoped that Iaghi had been right, and these people would take them in.

EIGHT

Some years later…

Anthony crept forward through the woods as the sun peaked over the distant treetops along the horizon. He yawned from lack of sleep. When he came upon a large clearing, he gestured to the soldiers behind him to halt. Inside the clearing stood six large concrete block buildings surrounded by a ten-foot-high chain link fence and several rows of barbed wire like a moat around an ancient castle. The only way into or out of the compound was a narrow stone road that cut straight through the maze of wire and ended at a gate. Guards watched from four towers that stood at each corner of the rectangular compound.

Anthony felt pity for the humans held inside. The people in slave factories generally worked sixteen-hour days seven days a week with little food and none of the amenities of life. Many of those they had rescued in the past had suffered from constant beatings, torture, and rape. He pushed sympathetic thoughts from his consciousness. There would be time for being sympathetic later. This morning, He had a tough job to do.

His sister and her squad were roughly a hundred yards to his right. He waited for her signal. When it came, a bright blue beam of light shot high into the air, Anthony and his men jumped up from their positions and ran forward, firing their weapons.

The guards in the camp towers returned fire with their rapid-fire cannons into the surrounding woods at random blasting one-hundred-year-old trees down like matchsticks. The surprised guards on the ground joined in the fight firing automatic rifles.

Something's wrong, Anthony thought. There were far too many guards for a simple slave factory. It looked like an entire platoon inside. *A trap?*

The guards' heavy resistance caused them to seek cover and their advancement soon stopped. Their liberation and rescue mission had turned into a desperate firefight for survival. Anthony was about to give the signal to retreat when he saw his sister standing up holding the glowing blue crystal of her locket over her head. A shimmering, semitransparent, blue-tinged shield surrounded and engulfed her. The entire garrison's firepower now concentrated on her, but none of the enemy's weapons could penetrate her shield.

Katrina raised her other hand and pointed her open palm towards the camp guards emitting balls of blue light that flew towards the guards' positions on the ground exploding on impact.

Seeing the opportunity, Anthony and his men advanced; with little resistance, they surged ahead. After a well-placed explosive along the chain link fence, they ventured inside the camp.

When Anthony rounded the first building, he surprised two heavily armed Soldiers. They reached for their weapons, but Anthony was faster. He raised and emptied his pistol into the chest of the closest guard who fell backward and into his companion.

Before the second guard could fire, Anthony's men who were just behind him, fired their weapons, and he went down.

They moved quickly to open the locked door of the first containment building. To their surprise, it was empty. It contained no slaves or machinery, and they quickly discovered that so were all the other buildings.

When they heard a noise that sounded like a convoy of trucks approaching, Anthony peeked out past the chain link fence and saw a full division of Mega-Corp and possessed troops moving fast to surround the complex. Some were on horses, and others were riding four-wheeled all-terrain vehicles. *So, this was a trap.*

Someone on a bullhorn said," Drop your weapons. All who surrender will not be harmed. If you insist on fighting no quarter will be given."

His team began to panic but then Katrina called out, "Everyone, get behind me."

As soon as both teams were behind her, she recreated the shield she had used earlier. This time though, it was much larger and shielded everyone. Anthony wondered how long she could keep it up. She looked like she was in great pain. Using the locket this way was taking a huge toll on her.

She created more balls of blue flame and fired them into the enemy positions outside the compound with the same devastating effect. After several volleys of exploding balls, the enemy that had surrounded them began to pull back. Katrina then gave the signal to make their escape.

Soon they were back in the forest outside the compound. The portal that Katrina had created wasn't far ahead, and they reached it without further incident. Katrina ordered everyone through single file while she maintained guard. When the last soldier had stepped through, Anthony was about to do the same when he saw a black object floating just above the treetops and moving fast towards them.

The object grew quickly in size and he did a double take when his eyes told him that flying towards them was a hundred-foot-long, ebony-black, dog-faced monster, looking everything like the Egyptian god Anubis.

Katrina saw it too and they both just stood dumbfounded and watched its flight approach. It landed less than twenty yards in front of them where it shrank, solidified and morphed into a bipedal creature slightly taller than a man covered with black fur and creepy, black-leathery wings. Its ugly face sported a doglike snout full of sharp looking teeth, out of which flicked a snakelike forked tongue. The strong stench of sulfur loomed in the air.

It wore a glowing red pendant on a heavy silver chain that dangled loosely about its neck. When Anthony looked into the creature's burning red eyes, an overwhelming sense of impending doom and hopelessness struck him like a giant tsunami racing over a flat shoreline covering and destroying everything in its path. His thoughts instantly became dark, and he found his lips voicing, "It's hopeless." He desired more than anything to just surrender, to lie down and let this creature have its way with him.

Fortunately for Anthony, the foul creature took no more interest in him. Instead, it fired a red ball of light at Katrina.

Her blue shield instantly surrounded her and intercepted the red ball and it exploded harmlessly in front of her. Katrina and the mysterious creature then exchanged volley after volley of explosive balls.

Concerned for the safety of his sister, Anthony stood his ground oblivious to his danger just a few feet away for he had no defense if one of those balls of light were aimed at him. *Just what was this thing attacking her and what kind of a threat did it propose?*

Finally, a huge ball of blue light exploded disintegrating the mysterious creature's shield and throwing the creature back over twenty feet. But the creature quickly recovered and was back on its feet before his sister could follow through with another volley, and it managed to return fire.

With its face contorted with utter hatred, it then counter-attacked like an enraged and cornered animal. It fired red flaming bolt after red flaming bolt with ever growing intensity in rapid succession.

But Katrina remained protected behind her blue shield and she countered and threw the most powerful ball of light he had ever seen her conjure. The blast when it struck the mysterious creature's red shield was so intense the very ground shook, and the shock wave knocked him down. For several seconds he was unable to see, blinded from the explosion.

When his vision returned, he saw the mysterious creature lying on its back, but still alive as it moved and tried to get up on wobbly legs.

Before it succeeded, however, Katrina knocked it down again and shoved the silver-plated heal of her black leather riding boots into its chest and with her staff raised above her head yelled," Yield! Or die!"

However, the creature simply transformed into wispy black-smoke and her boot heal passed through it and touched the ground.

She stepped away quickly, but too late. An amorphous smoke drifted up from the ground, and before Katrina could take two steps back, a solid black hand with long dagger-like talons for fingers shot out of the smoke and grabbed her by the neck.

Katrina struggled but to no avail. Those hands had her locked in a steel grip. Red streaks of power erupted from the iron hand like red bolts of lightning shocking her. Her body went rigid then, and she fell to the ground.

Anthony upon witnessing his sister's demise ran towards them firing his pistol, oblivious that he had no suitable weapon or defense. But his bullets had no effect and before he could reach the creature, it morphed back into its giant form, picked up his sister in one of its man-sized talons and rose into the air. It quickly flew up over the tops of trees and out of sight.

Anthony stepped into the still open portal looking lost and forlorn; trying to make sense of what he had just witnessed. Just what the hell was that creepy thing?

So, there were more pendants. As it was the source of his sister's power, a similar pendant was obviously the source of that creature's. He forced his overstimulated mind to focus by recalling all that he knew about her pendant. *Where did it come from? Who made it?*

He remembered that during their desperate escape from Sanctuary, Iaghi had said that the locket was more powerful than anything they could possibly imagine. Soon after they settled in with the Pickford's in Lovencraft, Katrina announced to him in secret, "This is the key to finding and rescuing our parents." She began to work with the pendant whenever she could, desperately hoping to unlock its powers. But after several months of no results, she grew frustrated and she told him she was about to give up when she had her first breakthrough. She managed to make it light up just as it did that night in the tunnel when the power had gone off and they were stranded in the dark.

"How did you manage it?" A surprised Anthony had asked.

Katrina looked at him with her eyes glowing from excitement. "Until just now, I kept trying to command it like it was something external that I could command with my mind. When nothing happened, I rationalized that I needed to concentrate harder... but that's not how it works at all." She paused for a moment to organize her thoughts. "Think of your arm. If you want a glass of water and if you verbally command your arm to reach out and grab that glass nothing happens. Right?"

"Of course not," Anthony said beginning to understand. "You simply want it and your body responds by reaching for it."

"Exactly! It's more like having a third arm, only we're not physically connected."

51

After that marvelous breakthrough Katrina spent all her time experimenting. She quickly learned how to make harmless orbs of light that could float aimlessly inside her room and it was nothing for Anthony to see dozens of orbs in the air around her at a time.

The next breakthrough came some weeks later. That's when they discovered that those harmless balls of light could be transformed into powerful weapons. She and Anthony just had an argument over something he couldn't even remember what about. When he left her room, she fumed and sent several of her harmless orbs flying at him. He ducked behind her bedroom door and the door disintegrated upon impact. "Hey, you could have hurt me," he remembered saying.

His thoughts returned to the present. Why did Katrina always have to be so bold? Now things were worse. He had no idea how, but he swore to himself he was going to muster a strike team and rescue her.

When Anthony exited the portal, he stepped into the ruined streets of Sanctuary. He and Katrina had first returned here a little over a year ago, just after she had learned how to create inter-dimensional portals of her own.

To their wonderful surprise, they discovered that the Ophidians and Mega-Corp had abandoned this world and hadn't even left as much as a garrison. And despite the heavy bombing, many of the downtown buildings, and even whole suburbs had been left unscathed. They quickly formulated a plan. Why not bring people to live here again? So, they began a single-handed crusade of rescuing and liberating humanity from the slaver factories that were run more like concentration camps, and search for their parents at the same time. From the people they rescued, they formulated a rag-tag and growing clandestine liberation army using the ruins of Sanctuary as its headquarters.

He walked towards the library building; it was one of the many buildings left standing and they had adopted their mother's old office as their headquarters. The survivors of tonight's debacle would be assembled there waiting for him and Katrina. However, when he rounded a corner he came face to face with Iaghi.

Since the day of their rescue from the mountain pass, he hadn't seen him at all, and now here he was again showing up in the middle of another crisis. He had to be here because of what had just happened to Katrina. How did he always seem to know what was going on?

"Anthony," he said, and it seemed like he heard his voice directly in his mind. "Follow me. We need to leave at once."

"But I need to debrief my troops and prepare a plan to rescue my sister."

"But that's where we're going, to rescue her, and we'll need every bit of your reckless luck and hope that fate is with us if we are to succeed." He motioned for Anthony to turn around. "Let's go. We're leaving now."

What could just the two of them accomplish? "Just us? What about a strike team?"

Iaghi's reptilian pupils stared at him. "None of them have the skills we would need. You would just be sending them to their deaths. Your sister can't be rescued from what just captured her with a team of men rushing in with guns blazing."

Frankly, he was surprised and relieved for his offer of help. A few minutes ago he had been on the verge of despair but now he dared to hope, at least a little. And Iaghi had been right. His basic strategy would be to charge in with guns blazing and hope for the best.

He turned around and caught up to Iaghi. A short time later, they met a stable hand, a young man who Katrina and Anthony had liberated and brought to Sanctuary a few months ago named Edward. He stood in their path holding the bridles of four horses. Two of the horses were saddled and ready to ride and the other two were loaded up with supplies.

"We'll need these horses. I dare not teleport us too close to where Draka's holding Katrina lest he detect my presence, and loud motorized vehicles would attract unwanted attention."

Anthony had to agree. They had found a few abandoned motorized vehicles in the city that worked, but they rarely used them. If a vehicle broke down there was no one around who could fix it. Motorized vehicles demanded a populated infrastructure and a skilled labor force for maintenance, neither of these now existed. Someday maybe, when the population was larger things might be different. But for now everyone walked or they rode on horseback.

After transporting to Earth, they rode together for half an hour until they came to a fork in the road. Anthony knew exactly where they were. One fork led to Lovencraft and the other lead to the old monastery where a band of Fengani lived and maintained the orphanage.

Iaghi pointed towards the road that led to the old monastery and said he had urgent matters to attend to and that he must consult with the eye of God, and would catch up with him after he had passed through Lovencraft. They said their goodbyes and then Anthony continued his journey.

While riding, his mind mulled over Katrina's capture by that strange creature and how Iaghi fit into all that had just happened. That Iaghi was holding back information was almost certain. But of course, he knew that if it wasn't for Iaghi that fateful day years ago he'd either now be dead, or putting in sixteen-hour days in a slave factory.

When Lovencraft was less than a dozen miles ahead, Anthony quickened his horse's pace. He looked forward to seeing his uncle Myles and aunt Margaret Pickford. They had gladly taken him and Katrina in after the fall of Sanctuary, and they had become good second parents.

They understood and supported Katrina and Anthony 's quest to find their parents. They provided supplies to their growing army and even occasionally helped hide the many slaves they rescued until they could be transported to Sanctuary.

The Ophidians and Mega-Corp seldom came around here. The tough locals were good at keeping them out. With much of the Earth returned to wilderness, Mega-Corp didn't have the resources to control everyone. Small pockets of free people existed all over the planet.

The gently rolling land was cleared and planted with fields of golden winter wheat almost ready for harvest or young corn not yet in tassel.

Riding in familiar territory to Lovencraft his spirits lifted a little, and he began to whistle a tune until he saw smoke up ahead. After that, his mood soured, and he became quiet and returned to being a soldier at war.

He stopped his horse to check the loads in his pistols and rifle. He then picked up his pace bringing his horse into a steady canter.

He monitored his surroundings with watchful eyes, wary of any sign of movement or anything out of the ordinary. The smoke clouds grew with his approach and soon filled up half of the sky. He could now make out the faint sounds of distant gunfire.

When Anthony came to the crest of the hill, he looked down onto the burning town of Lovencraft nested inside the valley below. Slavers, he spat. The town's people were putting up a terrific fight, but they were hopelessly outnumbered.

He spurred his gelding in the ribs and began a hell ride to the town below. Several slavers on horseback saw him riding in and rode to cut him off. They rode at him from eleven o'clock riding hard and fast with their pistols already firing. He sunk forward in the saddle, let go of the reins and grabbed his horse's mane with his left hand. Making himself as small a target as possible, he spurred his horse forward and he launched into a full gallop. He fired with his right hand while the air around him crackled with the sound of bullets barely missing him and his horse. As they galloped past each other, he managed to gun down two. He came around hard and fast taking out the third and then continued his desperate gallop towards Lovencraft.

When he was almost to the town, several more slavers popped up from hiding in a thicket that ran along the trail and spooked his horse. It reared throwing him backward. He fell and lost his pistol as he tried to break his fall. He rolled to a crouch and pulled out a backup revolver inside his boot. But before he could aim it at his assailants, the closest man swung a Billy club and struck his hand, throwing the pistol into some bushes. The three men then threw themselves on top of him, hoping to overpower him through sheer numbers. They wanted him alive if possible. Anthony wasn't a big guy, but he was athletic and wiry. He rolled and fought like a maniac, throwing them off and he bounced to his feet. He backed away from them where they still lay.

When they got up they all held Billy clubs and by the sadistic looks on their dirty faces, they fully intended to make full use of them.

He prepared to defend himself with his bare knuckles. They kept their distance as they circled like vultures around a wounded and dying animal waiting for it to die. They began to cuss and launch curses at him, hoping to rile him up causing him to lose his cool and make a mistake.

He glanced at each of the three thugs, looking for any kind of weakness, hoping to find an edge. There! The man on his right had a slight limp and favored his left leg. He lunged towards the man's left side, hoping to get past and away without suffering a major blow from his club. But the man shifted as quickly—a feint!--And closed the opening. But as he brought up his club to swing, from out of the bushes, a wild looking woman jumped up, dressed in black combat fatigues and

56

armed with only a staff. She struck the man in the Adam's apple hard with the end of her staff, crushing his windpipe. She moved incredibly fast. Quick as a demon running from an exorcism, she pranced around the other two with her wooden staff, reminding him of a cat toying with a mouse. They lunged at her, but she easily slipped past them and before they could turn around, she hammered several blows with that hard staff of hers into them.

Within seconds, Anthony's assailants were now all lying on the ground, either dead or unconscious. He didn't bother to check. He whistled to his horse while he retrieved his sidearm and boot gun. The whole time the strange woman stood by and seemed to be waiting. "Thank you, maim, you saved my life," he said, but she just stood there staring. When he mounted his stead, he let out his hand and offered her to ride up in the saddle with him, but she merely gestured for him to move. He took off and she followed behind on foot.

When he reached the town barricade, the town's people moved an overturned wagon and he rode past. As soon as the strange woman who still followed behind was inside they quickly closed the barricade.

He dismounted and took his rifle from its saddle case. He spotted Myles at once and after a hearty reunion, Myles said, "This is weird; I've never seen slavers involved in so organized an attack before. They usually only go after easy targets such as small caravans or stragglers."

"War is coming. The Ophidians have discovered another young civilization in the multiverse to conquer. Mega-Corp needs more humans to man their factories for munitions and the Ophidians need more possessed humans for cannon fodder. They've offered a huge bounty."

"Well, then we'll make sure these bastards earn their pay today! Every last damn penny!"

Anthony quickly told Myles what had happened to Katrina and what he was attempting to do.

"Good luck with that. I hope that Iaghi can help you," Myles said as they walked over to the barricade. The grim-faced Myles looked out and watched as the enemy prepared to make another attack. "When they Attack, this time they'll try to finish us off. They prize the children most. They adapt better and bring a higher price. If you get on your horse now, you and your new friend there…" he said pointing to the strange woman who had begun tending to the injured "…you just may slip away. Go and rescue your sister. No one here will think any less of you."

Anthony shook his head. "It's not in me to run from family in need. I'll stay." He took up position behind an overturned wagon.

"Have it your way."

Anthony glanced over at the strange woman. She had an athletic build, and she had long black hair that she wore in a single thick braid down her back. She was very pretty in an exotic way. Around her neck hung a conspicuous silver amulet shaped like a unicorn.

"Do you know who she is?" Anthony asked Myles?

"She comes here sometimes with several older women from the old monastery up in the hills to buy supplies. They're a strange bunch those raised by the Fengani."

"She certainly knows how to fight."

"Yes, that's all part of their education. Every one of them is taught from the time they're very little, the martial arts. It's mixed in with their religion, *The Way*."

Anthony walked over to the strange woman. She was putting a poultice on an older man's wounded arm.

"Keep this on overnight. It'll protect against infection." He heard her say.

It was refreshing to see a stranger caring about the wellbeing of another. The woman certainly had a caring and motherly way about her. "My name's Anthony. I'd like to thank you again for saving my life back there." He offered his hand. "What's your name?"

The woman looked up from her patient. She had dark, almost black eyes that hinted Asian ancestry mixed with Caucasian. It made a nice match with her black hair. She grasped his hand firmly. "My name's Jan. You've no need to thank me. I was sent here to protect you."

Anthony wanted to question her more. But there was no time for the next attack could start in any moment and he wanted to give her the opportunity to get away, so he said, "You know, as good as you are at hiding you might be able to slip out of here before the attack."

"Are you leaving?" she asked.

No, these people are my friends and the Pickfords are family.

She stared at him with those exotic, black eyes of hers. "Then I'm staying too. I'm not going anywhere without you. You might need me again."

"Maim, no offense, but I can take care of myself."

She snickered. "Not from what I just witnessed."

"Touché," Anthony said blushing.

Jan looked up from her patient. "Ok, it's settled then we're both staying."

Anthony walked back to Myles who watched the slavers as they prepared for another attack.

Then from somewhere a horn blew and the attack began…

NINE

The attack commenced with the enemy opening fire and pouring a barrage of bullets into the town. After several minutes of this continuous fire, the rate of fire abruptly slackened and Anthony did a quick glimpse out through a four-inch space separating two overturned wagons. Slavers were now up and advancing rapidly towards the town. He heard his great uncle yell, "Hold your fire." When the slavers were fifty yards out a bugle rang out and they charged, making a mad rush towards the town.

Myles screamed, "Fire." Anthony and the town's people fired as fast as they could but to little effect because the slavers were wearing protective armament that protected most of their bodies. Soon enemy combatants began climbing over their makeshift defense barrier of overturned wagons and barrels.

Anthony and Jan rushed into a group that had just crossed over an overturned wagon; Jan hammered into them with her staff aiming for either their groin or Adam's apple. She never missed with her crushing blows.

The battle quickly turned into a seething mass of close quarter hand to hand combat. Anthony still had his pistol in his belt but their protective armor made it almost useless. Instead, he used a hatchet that he had borrowed from his uncle.

The slavers carried stunners similar to a large cattle prod. Whenever a slaver managed to prod someone with it, they would immediately go down and the slavers were quick to rush in to bind their hands and legs. The townspeople were dropping like flies. As more slavers pushed through the town barrier, the remaining townspeople fell back. Defeat seemed certain. Despair began to sink into Anthony's heart, but he fought even harder refusing to surrender.

When Anthony, Jan, and uncle Myles were the last remaining fighters standing back-to-back and fighting hard, a bright blue light appeared in the sky above them. Dim at first, it grew quickly in intensity as it descended to the ground and then a brilliant burst of light occurred. The fighting stopped with everyone blinded.

Several seconds later, when he could see again, in place of the light, there stood a very determined Iaghi. He raised an open Hand above his head and a ball of light appeared in it. It detached from his hand and shot upwards and stopped at a point hundreds of feet above his head where it grew even brighter and became a giant blue-white ball of lightning arcing and shedding sparks.

When it became so bright that it rivaled the sun, it descended upon the slaver army. With a seeming intelligence of its own, it hunted them down with impunity and vaporized the first dozen or so men that it touched. After that, dozens more fell to the ground, their bodies smoking and ruined. By the time the ball of light had dissipated, those few still standing unharmed lost all will to fight and fled. Then Iaghi disappeared again.

So, Iaghi also had the same powers as his sister and the evil creature who had bested her. He remembered his history, and nowhere did it mention power such as that except in make-believe literature. But this was real. Even the Ophidians had not shown such ability. Except for their intellect and exceptional telepathic powers they were rather ordinary overgrown snakes. They didn't even possess any technology of their own.

Anthony spent the rest of the day assisting the residents of Lovencraft in fortifying their position in the unlikely event of another attack and digging graves for the many dead. At least half of the town needed burying. All the while, he kept reminding himself he needed to move on. He must not delay. Katrina needs me. But he just couldn't leave. He knew every survivor by name.

Towards evening, when he was just about finished with the last grave for a poor woman whose husband was also killed and left three young children in the world without either parent, his friend Myles stopped by. "Why don't you come home for supper when you're done? It's too late to travel anymore tonight. You can spend the night, get a good night's rest and start out fresh in the morning."

Anthony, who was completely exhausted and very hungry, gladly accepted the offer. He learned that the offer had been extended to Jan as well. She had turned out to be quite the nurse; her hands-on knowledge of medicine proved very useful, and she had doctored the wounded most of the day.

That evening, Anthony and his new friend Jan sat beside each other on the familiar stout, rustic wooden table in the country kitchen of the Pickfords.

While Myles sliced up a large head of cheese, Margaret came in and sat down at the table. Anthony introduced the gentle-faced, gray-haired woman to Jan while she explained that she had been hiding in the hills with most of the children.

While Myles sliced up bread, Anthony told the story of Katrina's capture. He started with their attack on the empty compound and left nothing out. As he told the story, Jan attentively listened without saying a word.

"So, you plan on marching into Draka's compound, do you?" Miles said. "I wish you luck in your adventure, but only bad news reaches us about that place."

"I know, but Iaghi says he'll be with me. With him along, I've allowed myself to have a glimmer of hope."

Anthony was about to ask Jan for her story, when she asked, "What will happen to the orphaned children? Our monastery will gladly take in any children you can't find a home for."

This was a valid question Anthony realized as many children of the village probably now had no living parents.

Myles smiled warmly. "We're all friends and relatives here. The surviving families will take them in." He paused in his slicing to look at Margaret. Their eyes met, and she gave him a nod. "We should be able to find a home for everyone. We'll be taking in a couple ourselves. We're not so old that we can't raise a couple more. But it's nice of you to offer and think of them."

"Well, anything you need, just ask. The monastery will gladly assist you in any way they can."

"Why don't you all move to Sanctuary?" Anthony said.

"It's a whole world almost exactly like Earth except it's largely uninhabited and there is no Mega-Corp or Ophidians to contend with."

"We'll have to think about it. It's a nice offer, but this is our home. Our families have lived in this land for a long, long time."

"You could also move to the monastery." Jan offered. "It's safer there. They'd gladly take all of you in and being in the hills it's much more defensible."

Myles scratched his head, thinking. "That is all very nice of both of you. But our people will have to take a vote on it. I'll present both of your propositions at tomorrow's town hall meeting."

While Myles sat a large platter of bread and cheese on the table, Margaret got up and placed plates and knives and forks and a pitcher of fresh milk next to the platter of bread and cheese.

Anthony, who was famished, grabbed a plate and a fork and started to fill up his plate but stopped curious while Jan sat in repose with her hands folded and her eyes closed. She mumbled something he couldn't make out then opened her eyes smiling.

"What did you just do?" He asked.

"I said grace. I thanked the eternal one for this fine food among friends."

"I've read about it in ancient literature, but until now I've never actually seen it done."

She smiled. "I'll teach you sometime."

The food was delicious, and he washed it down with several stout glasses of delicious milk.

"Now Anthony," Myles said after dinner while cleaning his teeth with a toothpick. "You need rest. I'll have supplies laid out for you in the morning. Jan, you can sleep in Katrina's old room. It's the other bedroom upstairs."

Anthony climbed the stairs dead tired. He ate too much he decided, and the food was having a narcotic effect. Each foot felt like it had a twenty-pound weight attached. After pointing a just as groggy Jan the direction of the other bedroom, He undressed, and he fell asleep at once.

The next morning, Anthony woke up to the delicious odor of frying bacon and toast. Refreshed from a good night's sleep, he felt ravenous and dressed quickly.

At the table downstairs, Jan was already up and eating breakfast looking well rested and even more beautiful. He had a hard time keeping his eyes off her.

After a huge delightful breakfast of bacon, eggs, home fries, and more of that delicious fresh milk, he left with Myles to head for the stables and Jan followed. As Anthony saddled his gray gelding, Jan began saddling a white mare. "I hope you don't mind, but since she insists on going with you, I gave her that mare. I figured you'd make better time if you were both on horseback."

"Can you ride?" Anthony asked.

She smiled. "Better than you, I saw how you ride yesterday, remember?"

Anthony blushed. "They spooked my horse."

After a warm goodbye, Myles and Margaret wished them well. Anthony departed with Jan following closely behind with the pack horses. His head filled with anxious thoughts while they rode on the south road out of the city.

TEN

Alert for any sign of an ambush, Anthony's eyes methodically scanned the countryside. Some of the slavers could still be about, and two strangers traveling alone might be too inviting a target to pass up. Jan rode beside him and neither of them spoke. He needed to think, and she seemed to sense that.

They rode along an old ancient highway that was a simple path barely wide enough for single file wagons. Occasionally, they passed small groups of strangers, some walking and some on horseback, traveling in the opposite direction. Everyone they passed seemed apprehensive and carried their weapons out in the open announcing to all passersby that they were well armed and prepared to defend themselves.

For a brief while, the road turned from dirt into a wider stretch of decaying concrete. It was rumored that long ago this old highway had been completely paved. However, time and neglect had allowed most of it to rot away.

Anthony's thoughts returned to rescuing his sister. He reviewed everything he knew about Draka, which wasn't much, rumors mostly. He'd heard that the Ophidians considered Draka to be some sort of a god and that the Ophidians allegedly fed him the souls of humans. Just how does a being eat another's soul? He shrugged. It just didn't make sense.

He sorely needed Iaghi and wanted to hear his rescue plan. Where was he? He caught himself absently looking back over his shoulder hoping to see Iaghi trailing behind like a lost puppy after its mother.

He realized then that he wasn't accomplishing anything except to feed his fears and doubts. Sometimes the best way to solve a problem was to think about something else. So, he put the plight of his sister out of his mind for now and turned his thoughts to Jan.

He remembered she had said something yesterday after she had rescued him. He had been meaning to ask her, but he didn't want to ask her in front of Myles or Margaret. The less they knew about what was going on the safer they would be. He trusted Myles and Margaret with his life, but there were spies, traitors everywhere. He didn't want any harm to come to them on his account. You just didn't know who to trust these days and they might slip up and say something to the wrong person. If a desperate person determined that you knew something that they could sell to the slavers, then for a few coins they might do it. He laughed; he realized that he was becoming secretive just like Iaghi.

"So, Jan, yesterday you told me you'd been sent to be my protector. Did Iaghi send you?"

She glanced at him and turned away as if considering her words. "No, Iaghi didn't send me.... She paused. "The voice did."

"The voice?"

"Yes, that's the name I've given it. It speaks to me. There's no mental image of it, just an auditory voice. It tells me what I must do and then it shows me a vision of what will happen."

Anthony had a sudden insight. "Did this voice show you where to hide before I fell off my horse?"

"Yes."

Another prescient being. This alarmed Anthony. How many different powers were at work? First, there was Iaghi, a being who can inter-dimensionally shift between alternate worlds as easy as going out for a Sunday walk. Next, Katrina learns how to unleash the powers of her locket first as a formidable weapon, and then she too learns how to shift inter-dimensionally as well. Then this mythical soul-eating creature called Draka suddenly becomes the real deal and bests his sister and takes her prisoner. And now, this new player, who Jan has aptly named the voice.

His head was beginning to spin. The big question that remained unanswered was just whose side is this voice on? He needed to learn more. "This voice, your narrator and the events it shows you, you say they come to pass?"

"Yes, always."

She turned and gave Anthony a look that said please don't think I'm crazy. But of course, he didn't. Much stranger things had happened to him since the destruction of Sanctuary. He lived in a city that existed on an alternate-dimensional plane that that common sense told him couldn't exist, yet, it did. "How long have you heard this voice?" He asked with a serious face.

She hesitated and seemed vulnerable suddenly. "My first night at Sanctuary just after you, Katrina and Iaghi split with the rest of us." She glanced at him and smiled.

Anthony whistled, and his eyes lit up. "Now wait a minute. You were one of the children that Katrina and I escorted out of the tunnels of Sanctuary."

"Yes, Katrina even carried me.

"I remember! That cute pigtailed little girl was you?

Jan smiled. "Yes."

This was incredible. Finally, after years of searching, he finally ran into someone from his distant past. Never mind that he had hardly known her.

"You know, you and your sister could have come and visited us. We were less than a day's walk away."

Anthony blushed she was right. Neither he nor Katrina ever did. "I do apologize for that. There is no excuse, we should have."

He cleared his throat. "If it's any consolation Katrina and I are trying to locate and rescue as many enslaved survivors of Sanctuary as we can, especially our parents. For Katrina, it is an obsession with finding and rescuing them. It's all she thinks about. I want to too. I mean it would be awesome to have our family back. It's just, maybe it's because I was a few years younger, and I don't remember them quite as well. But I do think I have a more practical understanding of it. I mean they could be anywhere in the universe in any of several dozen different realities. And we have no leads." He paused and turned his head to look at her. "Do you hope to see your parents again someday?"

"I barely remember the faces of my parents. I was younger than you, remember? Sure, that would be nice, but I hardly ever think about them."

At that moment he felt a connection to Jan. They were both refugees from the same home town. She like him had found herself uprooted in childhood from a home where she had loving and caring parents until a really bad day came along and made her a homeless refugee. Suddenly, she was the most interesting person he'd ever met. "So, what was it like growing up in the monastery?"

"I was frightened at first. Here I was, plucked from a loving world where I was the center of the universe, thanks to my doting and loving parents, and suddenly plunged into this great big, cold, alien world where everyone in my life was a total stranger. But it was that first night as I slept, frightened and lonely; quietly crying myself to sleep in the community barracks, surrounded with dozens of other small orphaned children, just like me, that the voice first spoke. It reassured me that everything would be alright and that I was safe now.

"Every night after that while I lay down to sleep it would come to me and keep me company. I soon began to think of it as my best friend and I looked forward to our nightly chats. Gradually, it revealed to me that it had chosen me for a purpose, that someday I would be part of a very important mission that would decide the future fate of the universe."

Jan turned, and he stared into those beautiful dark eyes of hers and began again to lose himself.

"And it told me for this mission to succeed, I would need to become an expert at every form of hand to hand combat known, and to become familiar with every weapon I came in contact with."

She's beautiful. "That's a pretty tall order."

Her eyes smiled at him. "I know."

Just then, a blackbird took off as if something had startled it from a top branch as they passed an old, large, twisted oak along the narrow road. Anthony and Jan both lightning fast drew their side arms. Jan had her pistol out of the holster and aimed before he had his pistol even halfway out. *Damn, she's fast no one had ever beaten him at a quick draw before.*

They both scanned the side of the road, alert for even the slightest incongruent movement. After several long vexing seconds, convinced that all was well, they began to move again.

"To become proficient at the martial arts you certainly grew up in the right place. I've heard that the monastery trains everyone that grows up there to be proficient in all methods of hand to hand combat."

"Yes. It's part of our religion. We don't prescribe to violence, but we know that there are many hostile elements in the universe, and we do have the moral right to defend ourselves and we do need to be prepared. We start training as soon as we can walk. I am an expert with any weapon, be it a knife, sword, longbow, crossbow, handgun, or rifle."

Anthony remembered how well she fought yesterday. He believed her. "Are they all as good as you?"

She blushed. "No, my teachers have told me that I'm the best student they've ever had."

When Anthony glanced over at Jan, his eye caught sight of the thin silver chain and that trinket around her neck. "That silver unicorn pendant that you wear, what exactly does it mean?"

"It means I've taken the oath, but not yet become a full priestess." Jan toyed with it. "If I choose to become a missionary and take my final vows, I'll wear a golden unicorn."

"You mean the oath to live permanently celibate?"

"Yes, but also to always live a life in poverty fully committed and devoted to helping all and any who are in need and as a teacher proselytizing to everyone who will listen of the peace of soul and the liberating happiness that comes from living according to *The Way*."

"*The Way*, that's the name of your religion isn't it?"

"Yes. You could call it that, but we don't have a formal creed or definitive set of doctrinal beliefs."

"But you do believe in something?"

"Yes, we believe in a higher power which we call the divine intelligence. We believe that the cosmos is composed of three things, matter, energy, and *sentience*.

How interesting, thought Anthony. "When you say sentience, do you mean awareness?"

"Yes, but more so. All things are aware it's a property of being."

"But a rock doesn't know that I just picked it up does it?"

"No, of course not. The rock is not conscious which is a state of awareness, but it does have a *latent* sense of self, it merely lacks the ability to interact with its environment. It just isn't aware you've picked it up."

Anthony had never thought of objects quite that way. This was going to take some time to consider, so, he decided to move on. "What other things do you believe?"

"We believe that everything in the universe has meaning. There is no such thing as coincidence. Every life, from the smallest insect to you has a definite purpose and a meaning for being. If your life seems to lack meaning, then it's because somewhere along the way you lost focus of your true path."

They continued riding in silence for a time. About midday, they passed a large caravan of peddlers traveling in small, canopied wagons.

He was grateful for Jan's presence. He was enjoying her company and for a short while as they had talked he had forgotten about his problems. Against his better judgment, he found himself uniquely attracted to her. Suddenly, he feared for her safety and he didn't like the idea of her accompanying him into harm's way, and he couldn't see how she could help him against a creature that ate souls. As if reading his thoughts, she said, "Do not underestimate my abilities. You cannot succeed on your mission without me. The voice has told me. Our fates are locked together."

"You would willingly accept your destiny even if it meant following me to your death?"

"Yes."

They stopped as evening approached to make a hasty camp, a hundred yards off the road under some bushes where they wouldn't be seen. They had cold rations for supper with no fire.

"You go get some sleep. I'll take the first watch," Jan said to him after they finished eating.

As he lay in his sleeping bag, he went back to working on a plan to rescue Katrina.

According to the map Myles had given him, Draka's compound was almost three hundred miles due south. He needed a plan in case Iaghi didn't return, and he estimated he had two to three weeks to come up with it.

Even if he had a large assault team, Draka would simply escape and take her with him. Or worse, kill her outright rather than see her free. A small strike team of just two dedicated expert fighters just might have a small, slim chance to stealthily sneak in and get her out. Yes, it might just work he muttered just before he fell a Sleep.

ELEVEN

Anthony pointed to the large pyramid in the valley below. "That white pyramid is their snake temple. Rumors say that the center room inside is a very special portal and is the same room in all of their pyramids everywhere in the universe."

"What do you mean?"

He shrugged. "It's a room that's independent of space as we know it. Anyway, the center room is where they conduct their religious ceremonies and perform secret rituals that turn slaves into possessed souls." Anthony turned to Jan and grimaced. "I've also heard that not everyone who goes in there comes out again."

"What happens to those who don't come out?" asked Jan. They stood side by side looking down into the tree covered valley holding hands. The initial connection had grown strong between them. During the three weeks journey, they had talked about their pasts, their hopes, and desires for the end of the Ophidian rule and liberty for all of humanity. They delightfully discovered they instinctively knew what the other person was feeling, and sometimes what the other person was about to say before they said it.

Anthony had fallen hopelessly in love with her. He had suggested that if they survived their quest that she reconsider her rescinding on her plan to complete her vows and make her oath of chastity permanent, but she remained steadfast in her commitment. She believed there was just too much need in the world, and she could do the most with her life by living it devoted unconditionally to helping others.

"The rumors say that the Ophidians feed their souls to Draka, and then they feed on the body," Anthony said. "But it's just a rumor. No one knows for sure." He adjusted the focus of his binoculars and began to inspect the perimeter's defenses.

His heart sank when his eyes fell upon the four strategically placed guard-towers on each corner of a tall chain-link fence topped with high voltage wire that surrounded the entire compound thus making it nearly impossible to approach from any angle unseen.

He wished once again that Iaghi was here. Where is he? Maybe something had happened to him. He knew he was reclusive, but he didn't impress him as the unreliable type. He was on the verge of despair and Jan, picking up his dark mood, suggested that attempting a stealthy rescue at night would give them the best chance of success. He listened and agreed with her.

He studied the surrounding heavy forest terrain with his binoculars hoping to map out a decent approach route that they could follow in the dark. A broad winding river made its way up to and alongside the compound on the eastern side emptying into a large lake. On the left side of their ledge was a small rocky path wide enough to traverse in a single file that wound down along the vertical cliff face into the fertile valley below.

Jan tapped him on the shoulder and pointed back to the trail behind them. He turned to see Iaghi hurriedly walking to catch up with them. A small glimmer of hope returned to him. He smiled and breathed a sigh of relief. "It's about time. We were just about to march in there without you. Where have you been?"

"I had to take care of some very urgent matters. For that, I apologize. Fortunately, I arrived in the nick of time. I read your minds. Marching down there at night without me would have been suicide."

"What's your plan?"

"It'll be getting dark soon. We wait until morning."

But, in the daylight we'll be seen," Anthony said.

"The forces of evil aren't as strong in the daylight. And trust me, Draka is down there and he is strongest at night. I can feel his foul presence even here. He's become very powerful." We'll need every edge we can if we're going to rescue your sister."

"How do you suggest we get inside? The whole place is unapproachable."

Iaghi made that toothy grin of his exposing his razor teeth. "Why.... We will walk up to the front door and knock."

"But they'll arrest us," Anthony said, shocked.

"No, they won't. They'll see us as three Mega-Corp senior officials wanting in. You forget, I'm a telepath and we Fengani are powerful telepaths, much more powerful than our Ophidian friends." He pointed at the compound. "Those guards are all possessed, people with no telepathic ability or thoughts of their own; they'll simply see us as whatever I want them to see."

"And then what?" This was all too much for Anthony. He'd spent the last several weeks on the journey here with Jan worrying the whole time barely able to sleep and now Iaghi says they're just going to walk up and knock on the front door.

"Once we're inside, we must move fast. Draka's liable to detect our presence at any time. We must grab her and get out."

The next morning, after Jan and Anthony had cold and tasteless beans and hard tack for breakfast, Iaghi pulled out a map. "If we encounter Draka, let me handle him. He's beyond your abilities. If anything happens to me or we become separated make your way there." He pointed to an x on the map. "I created a hidden portal there that's about three days travel by horse from here. It leads back to Sanctuary."

Anthony took the map from Iaghi, glanced at it, and then stuffed it in his shirt pocket.

Iaghi frowned. "I don't know if I have the strength to defeat Draka in combat. Whatever happens, I want you both to promise me that you'll stay out of the way. Just get your sister out. She's all that matters."

"Absolutely!"

"See that you do."

* * *

They walked up to the front door and knocked. As Iaghi had promised, no one questioned them or tried to stop them. The guards opened it for them suspecting nothing. They headed directly for the pyramid and simply walked in. Once inside Iaghi created an orb of light much like the ones Anthony had seen Katrina often do. It hovered in the air above them and illuminated the way.

They entered a large amphitheater. The room contained two burning black candles on each end of a black altar. The candles' candlesticks were each carved in the image of a coiled cobra. The weak light showed Katrina spread out and tied on top of the altar. They raced over to her. Her blue pendant lay exposed on her chest and pulsed emitting a weak blue light like a heartbeat. Jan began to cut her bonds while Anthony checked her pulse. He breathed a sigh of relief when he touched her warm hand and he felt a week pulse. *She's alive.*

Anthony tried to wake her. She stirred to his urgent prompting and then suddenly her feverish eyes popped open. Her face filled with fear and terror and she seemed delirious. He shook her again more forcibly. "Katrina, it's me, Anthony."

But she recoiled from him as if he was a stranger, and with her freed hands she seized her pendant and it burst into life. Her entire body glowed bright blue and he had to shield his eyes from its intensity. She chanted something in a foreign language he'd never heard before and then...she disappeared...

Anthony ran his fingers over empty black stone. At that moment a horrifying, eardrum-breaking roar erupted from something less than twenty feet from them. When the roaring ceased, a furious Draka appeared out of the shadows and a cold chill raced up his spine.

Iaghi's orb of blue light struck Draka full in the face and exploded. The shock wave from the blast almost knocked Anthony over. "Run! Run for your lives!" Iaghi shouted.

The orb seemed to have had no effect and Draka lunged at Jan. Without a thought for himself and acting instinctively, Anthony jumped in between, and Draka slammed into him. They struggled. Draka bit and clawed at him. Anthony shrieked in pain as Draka's snakelike fangs sank deep into his shoulder all the while his dagger-like claws ripped and tore at his heavy leather clothing. "Go! Go, I don't know how long I can hold it." Anthony bellowed.

An instant later and Draka broke free of Anthony's hold casting him hard away like a rag doll. He landed on his back some thirty feet away and had the wind knocked out of him.

As Draka turned to resume his attack, an intense beam of light many times brighter than the previous orb erupted from Iaghi's hands.

This time, when it struck Draka tentacles of light, like the arms of a luminescent octopus, wrapped around him pinning him in place. The beam intensified until it was as if a blue sun had descended into the amphitheater and Anthony had to shield his eyes from the intensity of the light.

Draka began to smoke and screamed in a bone-chilling roar. Iaghi began chanting, "Die, die you, wicked creature!" Dark, black sulfur smelling smoke began to emit from the ruby pendant around Draka's neck and quickly filled the room. Draka's scream of agony changed into a long drawn out Nooooo...., and his own pendent brightened and began to pulse a bright a ruby red light that formed a bright red shield of light around Draka. The tentacles of blue light lost their hold on him. He turned and ran away.

Anthony managed to stand up with assistance from Jan who had rushed to him. What a mess, he thought looking over his shredded and bloodstained clothing. The room began spinning and he could feel his strength leaving him.

Iaghi turned towards them looking haggard and worn. He gasped, "Come to me quickly before Draka returns."

Iaghi then teleported them all back to the ledge where they had spent the night.

With worry written on her face, Jan said, "Let me look at you."

Anthony showed Jan his shredded shirt and two deep wounds on his shoulder. "I'm ok, except for my shoulder where Draka bit me." Jan looked at the punctures and paled. "Iaghi, can you look at this, please?"

A very old and spent looking Iaghi made his way over. He seemed to have aged many years in just minutes. This morning he had seemed strong and in his prime. But now he seemed more stooped and his reptilian skin had lost its sheen. When his tired eyes inspected Anthony's wounds his face became stone.

Anthony asked, "What is it?"

Iaghi stared at him. "He's injected you with his venom."

"Venom? Is there an antidote?"

"I don't know. We need to leave and get far away before he recovers and tracks us up here. I don't have the strength to transport us far. I need time to regenerate. We were lucky."

"What about Katrina? What happened back there? Where is she?"

"She's certainly someplace safe. When Jan cut her bonds and she touched the locket, she willed it to protect her. The locket, sensing that she was delirious and where she was at responded to her need and transported her somewhere where it knew she would be safe.

"But where's that?" Jan asked.

"I don't know, but I'm sure she's out of immediate danger. I wish I could say the same for us. We need to get going."

"What about Anthony? Is there anything you can do for him?"

With concern etched in his face, Iaghi glanced at Anthony's shoulder. "There's a healer, who lives in the hills not too far from here. Perhaps she would know of an antidote."

"Are you sure she is still there? Slavers have been very active in these hills and valleys the last several weeks," Anthony asked with a dry raspy voice. His tongue and mouth tasted dry and he discovered he was very thirsty.

Iaghi laughed. "I'm sure she is. Slavers don't frighten her. Trust me, she's still there," Iaghi said with a twinkle in his eye.

They teleported again. They stood in a meadow surrounded by rolling hills covered with grass and trees. Up the hill stood an old, weather-beaten, log cabin with a thatch roof.

Anthony gestured he needed to rest. Jan stooped over him and touched his forehead. He felt hot. Deep lines of worry cropped up on her forehead.

"That old cabin up the hill is where she lives. Please rest here and lie down while I fetch her," Iaghi said.

Anthony complied, and he fell asleep.

When he woke, he looked up to see an old lady, with long white hair, dressed partly in clothes and partly in animal skins hovering above him. She looked very frail and thin almost like an old piece of thin china that is all chipped and cracked and covered with stains from long constant use. But the eyes were different. There was a bright intelligence behind them, and they seemed to stare through him. He blushed, feeling naked and exposed.

"Young man, how are you feeling?" the old lady asked him in a crackly voice.

"I've felt better," he answered.

"Well, you have a sense of humor. That is a good sign. Now tell me, how do you really feel?"

"I feel like my skin is on fire and where that thing bit me, it feels like someone is sticking a red-hot poker into me."

The old lady looked up to Jan who was standing nearby watching. "Help me get him into the house. We don't have much time. Draka's poison works fast."

"Where's Iaghi?" Jan asked.

"He's gone. He and I don't enjoy each other's company." The old woman saw that Jan didn't quite understand. "Don't worry honey; he knows that if anyone can help your friend, it's me."

The old woman and Jan picked Anthony up. He had to clench his teeth from the waves of pain.

❄ ❄ ❄

Inside, the house was an old simple one-room log cabin with a loft for sleeping. It was rustic, but it was clean and neat. A large, stout hand-hewn wooden table occupied the center of the kitchen.

Much of the table was filled with jars full of seeds and herbs. Every jar had a label and date on it. Jan worked quickly at cleaning the table of all items.

When they laid Anthony onto the cleaned table, the old woman said, "Tie him down in case he wakes up. I don't want him to start squirming around when I start to sew."

Jan watched as the old woman fired up the wood burning stove and set a small pan of water on top. She then went through the jars on the floor that had been on the table. After selecting several, she returned to the stove. "We'll make a potion and salve from these," she said.

When the water began to boil, she added the contents of the jars into the water. After the mixture boiled for several minutes, she poured part of the potion into a small pan that contained several large spoonfuls of melted lard. "This will make a salve for his wounds." She set it aside to cool and then put on a large pot of water to boil. Into the pot, she added a sewing needle, thread, a small knife and strips of cloth. "Everything needs to be sterile," she said.

Using the boiled strips of cloth, the old woman meticulously cleaned his wounds. Anthony moaned with each touch, but he didn't wake up. She then applied large amounts of her freshly brewed salve into the wounds.

Jan didn't turn away but watched in interest when the old woman began sewing on the deep gashes in Anthony's chest." She held Anthony's hand in a firm grip desperately hoping this old woman could

82

save him. Strange, a few weeks ago she hadn't even known him and now she couldn't bear the thought living without him.

Anthony certainly had courage, and he didn't walk away from a fight. He could have ridden away in Lovencraft, but he chose to stay help people even when the odds had been stacked against him. And he had just saved her life. That should have been her lying there on the table. If he hadn't jumped in front of Draka when he did, she was sure Draka would have had her despite her training.

"I'm glad that you're strong," the old woman said while she continued to sew. "You're going to need it. You're all lucky you weren't all killed going into Draka's temple like that. Iaghi never did have much sense."

Jan remembered an old woman at the monastery telling her of a great healer that once lived apart in these hills and that she used to visit when she was a child. Could it be this same woman? She appeared to be in her late sixties or early seventies. On a whim, Jan asked, "Are you really human?"

"Yes and no child," the old woman paused. She glanced up at Jan to whisper," I was a watcher once, but not one of the inner council members. When Draka appeared some of us lesser beings decided it was time to leave. I did, and I wandered the multiverse until I discovered, and I fell in love with these hills. Life's simpler here. When the first humans started coming here, I took on the form of this kindly old woman. I've been in this form for so long now, it's who I am."

"Wow," Jan thought. This kindly old woman healer had just given her a massive amount of information. What was a watcher and what council was she talking about? She had a million questions rushing through her head. But she knew she'd better start at the beginning and keeping with her manners, she said, "Thank you so much for helping us. I hope we didn't put you in any kind of danger. What is your name?"

"The name's Hannah and you're welcome. But don't be thanking me just yet."

Jan managed a weak smile. "It's nice to meet you, Hannah." After shaking hands, a tired looking Hannah turned back to the patient and said. "If he makes it through the night, he might just have a chance. I've done all I can. The rest is up to him. He needs plenty of rest, and so do I." Hannah reached out and clasped her hand. "I can see your mind is filled with questions. That's right. I'm telepathic. I'll try to answer some of your questions tomorrow, but you have enough to worry about tonight." Then she climbed up the ladder to the loft and to bed.

TWELVE

Anthony's fever remained high throughout the night. Jan stayed up and followed Hannah's instructions. She gave him sponge baths to cool him down, and every few hours, she fed him a teaspoon of a tonic Hannah had brewed earlier. She assured Jan the sponge bathing would ease his fever and the tonic would help him to ward off infection.

His fever finally broke about an hour after sunrise and Jan breathed a sigh of relief as she watched the color return to his face. Hanna, who was now up, tried to coax her into going to sleep, but she refused to leave Anthony's side.

By early afternoon, Anthony started to wake up, and he even managed to squeeze her hand. Hannah on seeing this patted her shoulder. "Don't worry; He's passed the danger. Dear, there's an old cot in the back of my loft upstairs, you go bring it down and get some rest. He'll still be here when you wake up."

Jan still didn't want to leave, but Hannah kept insisting. She acquiesced and retrieved the cot from the loft. However, sleep eluded her. Her mind refused to shut down. She kept wondering about what had happened to Katrina. Once Anthony was well she was sure they would continue searching for her. *Where could she be?* Hannah gave her an herbal tonic to drink. The alluded sleep finally came.

✳ ✳ ✳

Jan spent the next couple of days inside the cabin tending to a fast-improving Anthony. When Anthony began to hobble around in the cabin on crutches, Hannah said, "His wounds are healing up nicely, you need to get out and get some exercise and fresh air. Why don't you cut and chop me some firewood?"

While carrying an armload of firewood towards the cabin, she was surprised to see Anthony standing in the doorway without crutches.

"Thought I'd get out of that claustrophobic cabin and get some fresh air."

Jan smiled, dropped her load of wood, and rushed over to him and doted on him and insisted that she help him to a log-hewn deacon's bench along the outside wall of the cabin.

They sat together without speaking, just holding hands. At that moment she felt so alive and in love. The rich smell of new fall was in the air and occasional splotches of red and yellows could be seen in the surrounding tree-covered hills beginning to break up summer's hold of ubiquitous green, a foreshadowing of the dazzling beauty about to come.

She'd never been in love before and was caught unprepared for the intensity of her feelings. Why hadn't the voice or the Fengani warned her about this? She felt her desires had betrayed her and might compromise her ability to complete her mission. Why had she allowed herself to fall totally and hopelessly in love?

Every instructor she had ever known at the monastery since the time she was a little girl had stressed the importance of self-reliance, but she knew that she couldn't be self-reliant while in love. You were totally vulnerable.

Dark thoughts crept into the awareness of her mind. If Anthony rejected her in any way she'd be devastated. Or even worse, what if she survived whatever she was meant to do, but he didn't? Imagining life without Anthony would be a life not worth living. She wished she could tone down her feelings just a little--*but how?*

"What's the matter? You seem distant all of a sudden." Anthony asked.

"It's nothing," she lied not wanting to hurt him. "I'll be fine. Let's just enjoy the moment."

The next morning, Jan and Anthony were both sharing a breakfast of biscuits and honey from a honey tree that Jan had raided the day before when they heard a knocking on the cabin door. A displeased Hannah opened the door and said, "About time you returned. What was the point of taking these two children into Draka's temple like that? You could have gotten them both killed."

"Look, there was no other way. I needed Anthony's assistance. Their sibling bond binds them. I thought I might need that," Iaghi said sheepishly.

Hannah shook her finger at Iaghi. "But she didn't, and now we have no idea where she is."

"That's not exactly true. There may be a way to find out. But I need to borrow Anthony again."

"If it involves marching back into Draka's temple, then I'm not going to allow it," Hannah said with a stony face and started to close the door.

Iaghi put his hand out and caught the door before it shut. He shuffled past the threshold taking a firm position inside the cabin. "Relax. There's no danger. Trust me," Iaghi said, in a voice that hinted he wasn't accustomed to having to explain his actions.

Hannah furrowed her white eyebrows. "Tell me what you're planning, or it's no deal unless you want to take me on too."

Iaghi threw his hands in the air. "All right then." Can you at least invite me in, and I'll explain."

"Appears to me, you've already invited yourself in. But alright, come in take a seat. I'll make you some tea."

"Thank you," Iaghi said coolly.

Iaghi sat down at the head of the kitchen table. After several long sips of steaming hot tea, he set his cup down and grinned exposing his long teeth. "I wish to perform the Vanwanung with Anthony."

"No, it's too dangerous. His mind isn't trained for it. Besides, he's no telepath," Hannah snapped. "I don't see how that will help you to find Katrina?"

Iaghi smiled, "You're right Anthony is no telepath, but Katrina is a powerful telepath and he is Katrina's sister and they both love each other very much; their sibling minds are linked because of this.

"Now...she's obviously delirious we all saw that. But she had enough sense to call upon the spirit of the pendant for protection. It read her subconscious mind and has sent her somewhere where she believed she would be safe. Hopefully, her subconscious mind still thinks of him. It may even be projecting thoughts to him now. If I perform the Vanwanung with Anthony, I may be able to tap into these thought waves and by eavesdropping discover where she is."

Hannah rubbed her chin in thought. "You're right. It might just work."

"Just what is a Vanwanung?" Anthony asked.

"It's a joining of two or more telepathic minds into one. It has the memories of each of its component minds, but a consciousness of its own. While the joining lasts, the individuality of the component minds is lost. It's like they no longer exist."

"I see. But as soon as the joining ends they return, right?"

"Yes, but…"

"So what's the danger?" asked Anthony.

"The danger is that for the joining to cease the Vanwanung consciousness has to die," said a grim-faced Hannah. "It may refuse to terminate itself and choose to live on instead."

Iaghi placed a small clear crystal the size of an egg in the center of the table. Anthony sat across from him, "Anthony, grab my hands." Anthony complied.

"Now concentrate on the clear crystal."

Anthony stared for several minutes. Nothing. He was just about to give up when the crystal began to emit a dull red color. It was as if a small match burned inside it.

"Good. Keep concentrating. Don't stop now," he heard Iaghi say in his mind.

The colors slowly changed from red to orange, to yellow. When the stone turned a deep blue, it began to brighten. Anthony could feel the world spinning around the stone. He felt his consciousness moving towards the crystal. When his mind entered the crystal he lost consciousness.

✳ ✳ ✳

Visions of a strange world popped into the Vanwanung mind as it became aware of telepathic images emanating from Katrina's mind into the telepathic realm, a place independent of time or space. It saw strangely dressed people and exotic buildings. But there was one dominating prevalent thought, a time before the Ophidians.

The creature understood at once. Katrina had wanted to escape, and she had wished for a time free of the Ophidians. The faint images forming in its mind came from mid-21st-century Earth.

"I know where Katrina is," it said to itself. "She's sent herself back in time on Earth to just before the invasion…"

✷ ✷ ✷

Anthony regained consciousness and glanced over at Iaghi. He remembered the experience and thoughts of being the Vanwanung as if he had just watched a movie or read a book about someone. In a detached manner, he remembered discovering that Katrina was in the ancient past. "But how? How did she accomplish it?" Anthony asked aloud.

"I don't know how, no one has ever done that, but don't underestimate the power of her pendant," Iaghi answered.

"How can I return my sister to our time?" Anthony asked.

"I do not know."

THIRTEEN

Katrina screamed. Fearing another touch from those dagger-length talons of her monstrous captor, her freed-hands instinctively reached for her pendant. The moment her fingers contacted it, it flashed in her hand, and its power flowed through her.

She dared then to open her eyes, but the creature was nowhere about. Instead, she found herself lying on hot blacktop. The blinding sun stood directly overhead. Feverish, she managed to stand up on wobbly legs. Through squinting eyes, she glanced around at the tall concrete and brick buildings surrounding her. She didn't recognize anything except for the familiar Mega-Corp logo, a black capital M superimposed with a capital red C stamped on a large building in the distance, but the building itself was all wrong; it was too tall, too square. Several of the buildings were many, many stories high. And the ubiquitous blacktop left no room for grass or trees.

Katrina hobbled onto a busy concrete sidewalk filled with people wearing odd style clothes. Foreign, unmoving vehicles sat bumper to bumper with their engines running producing an obnoxious smelling gas. They're using antique combustion engines she realized.

The people she passed ignored her, but a few were downright rude when she asked them for food or water. What was wrong with these people? They only seemed to care about themselves.

Finally, a pleasant looking middle-aged woman with dark skin and the most disarming smile came over and said in archaic English, "Child are you hungry?"

"Yes, very much so," she said trying to mimic the dialect.

"Follow me. I own a soup kitchen not far from here," the woman said, smiling.

While they walked, the woman glanced her way and said, "Have you been living on the streets long dear?"

Katrina had no idea where she was. Could she trust this strange woman? She desperately needed to trust someone. She chose to move cautiously until she learned more. "No, I just arrived here, today, actually."

"Goodness, by the looks of you, you've had a rough time. Can you tell me where you're from?

Katrina thought for a moment and didn't think the truth would hurt. "It's a place called Sanctuary," she said watching the woman to see if the name elicited any kind of response.

"Is that in South America? Your accent is unique. I've never heard anything quite like it."

Katrina, who desperately wanted answers waved her hand in the air said, "What city is this?"

The woman looked surprised. "Honey, this is Chicago."

Katrina took that in. This looked nothing like the Chicago she remembered. "Where are the Ophidians?"

Linda looked at Katrina like she had no idea what she was talking about and asked, "What's an Ophidian, honey?"

"They're the aliens that rule here."

"There are plenty of aliens here but none of them are in charge. They're mostly illegal."

When they arrived at the soup kitchen, Linda had Katrina sit down at a table. She brought her out a bowl of soup, a platter of vegetables, milk, and several slices of bread from the kitchen. Katrina consumed everything.

"Land sakes child, you were hungry."

Katrina said she was tired, and Linda showed her to a room with a single bed where she could lay down and take a nap.

Katrina slept until it was late in the afternoon and when she woke, Linda came in and asked, "Do you have a place to spend the night?"

"No," Katrina said with worry etched into her face.

"Let me make a phone call. I'll be back shortly."

Several minutes later Linda returned and said, "I've good news. This room is still available. You can spend the night here." There'll be several other people staying in other rooms, so you'll have company if you want it. I'll be back tomorrow."

Before Linda left, Linda handed Katrina an old-style newspaper, printed on paper, and said, "Can you read?"

"Yes, I can."

" There's a TV in the corner if you want to watch anything. There's no computer or internet though, I'm sorry." Katrina had no idea what a TV or the Internet was, but she was thankful for the paper.

After Linda left, Katrina sat down in her room and began to read. The paper was written in archaic English, but she could read it. She had taken an Archaic English class once as an elective. She glanced at the date on the newspaper. No, that can't be, she thought. The date said that she had gone back in time almost two thousand years. But that was impossible. Wasn't it? But then she saw the headlines and almost screamed aloud. The Headlines said in big, bold, dark lettering **WE ARE NOT ALONE**.

This was like 9/11 all over again. Linda remembered those events watching it on TV from when she had been a little girl, only much bigger, and this time it affected everyone. First physical Contact with an alien species was happening. Everyone in the whole world now watched the news nonstop. After several pictures leaked to the press showing the aliens looking everything like giant boa constrictors, the entire world had gone crazy. Some Headlines read *Quetzalcoatl Returns*.

Empty churches began to fill up again; some feared it was the beginning of the end. If this was the end, then so be it, thought Linda. If not, well, there were still desperate people to feed and shelter her no-nonsense practical Midwestern mindset observed.

Linda left the house early and drove through the back streets of the city towards the soup kitchen. Today wasn't her day to work at the shelter, but the Sparks would be dropping off Lisa in the afternoon and she couldn't get the strange young woman she had left at the shelter out of her mind. She had promised to be there, and she always kept her promises.

Rescuing the downtrodden was Linda's obsession. It was what made her go to the soup kitchen even when she was dead tired. This strangely dressed woman with the exotic accent was about to become her latest adopted stray, Linda decided during her first cup of coffee.

That poor young woman almost had to be an illegal alien. She had no papers or identification, and she spoke in the strangest dialect. She hadn't even known she was in Chicago until Linda told her. And that talk on alien rulers. Where did she get that idea? She must be letting her imagination run wild after watching too many of those old late-night cheap Sci-Fi's they'd played nonstop on TV the last few nights.

When Linda reached the shelter, she invited Katrina to sit at a table and share a cup of coffee with her. Katrina seemed very agitated and full of nervous energy. "Is everything OK?" Did anyone bother you?" she said looking around.

Katrina looked at her for a moment, unsure of what she was asking. Finally, she said, "Oh this place is fine, everyone here is *so* nice." She pulled out the paper, spread it out on the table and said, "This is what has me upset."

Linda looked at the headlines Katrina pointed to. "Well, yes, the whole world is concerned. You're not alone, child."

Katrina frowned. "You don't understand." Katrina glanced furtively around. The kitchen was half full of hungry patrons. "Is there someplace we can go and talk in private?"

"There's a park a few blocks away. We could go there."

They left the shelter, walked the few blocks to the park and sat down on a park bench beside a large pond with a fountain of water in the center. There were many ducks by the water and they made much noise as they waddled among children, looking for handouts.

Katrina looked at Linda like she was about to step out into a busy street full of heavy traffic. "We must get out of the city right away. Have everyone you know to leave at once for the country. Tell them to get far away from here. These aliens will soon attack and destroy every major city on the planet."

Linda listened. "Katrina, how can you know all of this? Yesterday, you didn't even know what city this is."

Katrina gulped. "I know this because I'm from the future. These aliens with the help of people working for Mega-Corp will destroy everything and make the survivors slaves and soldiers for their empire.

"Why would these creatures come halfway across the universe to make us slaves?"

"They didn't have to come halfway across the universe; they come from an alternate-earth on an alternate timeline, think multi-verse. They plan to make us slaves because it's part of their religion. They worship a terrible being who has commanded them to destroy and control the entire cosmos."

"I'm sorry Katrina, but I find all of this hard to accept."

Katrina looked at her as if questioning something. Finally, she sighed and said, "I can prove it; all of it."

"How?"

"I can temporarily merge our minds into a single consciousness. It's called a Vanwanung. Your mind will instantly absorb all of my life's memories as will I also absorb yours. When I end the Vanwanung, we will permanently retain each other's memories."

Linda considered this. She decided to play along. "You won't hurt me in any way, will you?"

"No."

Katrina placed her hand over the locket around her neck. "Please relax." The locket began to pulse a soft, bluish glow.

Linda became alarmed. *How is she doing that?* She wondered.

"Please place your hand over mine," Katrina told her. Linda was no longer confident in her skepticism. She hesitated. But finally, Linda reached out and placed her hands over the locket as well.

Blue. Everything became blue. There was no sky, nor horizon. Linda could feel the pulse of her rhythmic thoughts, not unlike the heartbeat of a living organism.

When their minds touched, their minds merged and became one. In a heartbeat, they exchanged a lifetime of memories with each other.

Linda could feel Katrina examining her personal memories. Especially, the ones that created her incessant care for the downtrodden and the reason she bought the soup kitchen, and why she insisted on personally managing it.

Linda shared her deep regret that someone hadn't helped her family forty years ago. She shared her memory of her father losing his factory job because of Globalization. Within two years, their family went from living in a safe suburban neighborhood to living on the streets. She watched her father turn almost overnight from a positive hard-working family man with a prospering job, into a broken man who died a few years later from a bad liver brought on by heavy drinking and drugs.

But Linda showed Katrina that despite her world falling apart she managed to stay in school and keep excellent grades. She studied hard and made it into college with scholarships. She had graduated at the top of her class and she had a photogenic memory. She earned a law degree and became a successful lawyer championing the little people. She quickly became one of the most successful lawyers in Chicago and it made her very rich.

Instead of spending all that money on herself and having a family of her own, she used it to start a charity and a homeless shelter for families in desperate need.

Linda then quickly relived Katrina's life. All her memories were now hers, growing up in Sanctuary always fearful of becoming discovered. She remembered Katrina's parents. She relived their last days before the attack. And she relived the attack and capture by the dark creature Draka, the Ophidian's god.

Good heavens. This young woman is telling the truth. We are in great danger. I must warn everyone.

As much as the joining felt pleasurable, the process of separation felt painful, like a tearing.

Linda opened her eyes and discovered she was sitting on the park bench again.

Katrina looked at her and said in perfect English, her thick accent gone now that she had absorbed Linda's memories and made them part of her own, "Do you believe me now?"

Linda looked at her with rock hard conviction and said, "We must stop them."

"I agree."

FOURTEEN

L ater that same day, Katrina woke up after a nap. She had slept miserably; her mind had refused to shut down. As she lay there, the reality of being stuck in the past hit her. She sorely missed Anthony. He had always been her one constant in her troubled life. After their parents had been captured, a special bond, far beyond what normal siblings shared, had formed between them, and they had learned to always be there for each other. For the first time in her life, she found herself completely alone.

Despair and hopelessness overwhelmed her. She buried her face in her pillow and let her emotions go. She cried to herself for a long time. But then, the tiny voice of a little girl asked, "What's the matter?" She opened her eyes, and before her bed stood a very cute little eight or nine-year-old girl in pigtails. She had a thin face with wispy-brown hair, but it was the little girl's bright eyes that caught her attention. They were youthful and bright but had a deep sadness that marked her as being someone who had already weathered tragedy in her life.

Katrina managed a weak smile while she wiped her eyes with a tissue from a box next to the bed. "Hello. What's your name?"

"My name's Lisa."

"Well, Lisa, I just felt lonely with no one to talk to. I'm far away from my home and my family, and I miss them."

Lisa smiled. "When I feel that way I talk to my friend Missy." She held up an old naked and worn-out Barbie doll with half of its stringy hair missing. "She's my best friend, besides Linda. Would you like to talk to her?" Lisa said, holding out her doll. She always listens."

Katrina took an instant liking to Lisa and forgot about her own problems. With her young maternal-instincts aroused, she said, "That's OK. I have you. Where do you live?"

"Sometimes I live with Linda, and sometimes I live with the Sparks." Lisa bent closer and whispered, "They can't have any children of their own. They're thinking of adopting me."

Katrina smiled too. What a sweet young girl. "Adopt? Where are your real parents?"

Lisa shrugged. "I don't have any. They died in the war."

Katrina's face filled with pity. The little girl's situation sounded strikingly like her own childhood. "Oh, I'm so sorry to hear that."

"It's OK. I hardly remember them. Hey, do you like games?"

"Sure. Do you have something in mind?"

Katrina watched Lisa happily race out of the room. She returned a few minutes later carrying a bundle of games. The boxes all looked worn and used. "Miss Linda and I play these sometimes. They were hers when she was little. Would you like to play Trouble, Parcheesi, Sorry, checkers or chess?"

"I've never played any of them."

Lisa pulled a worn and frayed deck of cards out of her pocket. "Do you know how to play Go Fish?"

Katrina looked over her choices. "I'm afraid I never played Go Fish either." She smiled. "Which one is your favorite?"

Lisa picked up the game of Trouble. "This one is because you never know what's going to happen. You can be losing really badly and suddenly if you get lucky you can still win."

Katrina spent the next hour playing with Lisa and forgot about her own problems while she got to know her new best friend.

✳ ✳ ✳

When Katrina worked with Linda later that afternoon while they prepared dinner for the hordes of homeless families who would soon come into the shelter looking for a filling hot meal and a warm place to hang out, she asked Linda about Lisa.

Linda looked up from the large kettle of instant mashed potatoes she was mixing with a spoon almost as large as a small shovel. "Such a sweet little thing. Her parents were in the military. They were both killed in the line of duty when she was little fighting in another stupid war. Heck, I don't even remember what it was about anymore. I found her a few months ago living on the streets after her grandmother, who was raising her alone, died suddenly. Imagine that, a nine-year-old girl trying to make it on her own. I took her in and got legal temporary custody until a more permanent home can be found."

"She said that the Sparks family is thinking of adopting her," Katrina said.

"I sure hope so. He's my younger partner. They are so nice. You know, they're young, but they can't have any children of their own. I love Lisa dearly, but I'm too old and too busy to be raising a child. She needs parents who can devote most of their time and energy to her."

They didn't talk about it anymore after that. They were both too busy serving dinner to the hordes of rag-tag homeless families who began coming in droves. Katrina's heart filled with pity for the desperate people who came into the shelter every day. They came in for food, but their eyes were hungry for a better way of life. They wore worn-out, patchwork clothing, and many had health problems but said they couldn't afford to see a doctor. Sadly, she realized these people were even worse off than the poorest people, the slaves who worked sixteen-hour days in the slaver's factories from her own timeline. They at least were given proper healthcare, food, and basic housing.

Yes, the families she met that morning lived a rough life with little hope for a better future. Yet everyone she met seemed like good, honest people who, if just given half a chance, would gladly put in a full day's work. But the only kind of work left in this country these people called America was working for the military.

So much for the idyllic past. She once believed that before the Ophidians invaded and destroyed Earth's prospering civilization that humanity lived in a utopian society, where each person was free to grow, and develop according to their personal ambitions and abilities. But she now knew that such a belief was just a delusional fantasy.

While Katrina cooked hamburgers, an odd thought formed in her mind. *Perhaps living in the past is a golden opportunity, and I can change our destiny.* If the teleporter were sabotaged before it became operational, then everything would change. Just maybe the coming invasion and destruction could be prevented altogether. *Why not?*

Later, when Linda and Katrina finally sat down for a break and a bite to eat, Katrina shared her idea.

"You know if the teleporter were destroyed, then the invasion will never occur."

"You want to sabotage the teleporter, so you can change the future! Honey, I'd bet that teleporter thing has more guards than Fort Knox. Besides, how are you going to get into space to accomplish it?"

"We just ride up on the space elevator." She showed Linda an ad she had found in the newspaper.

Linda began reading. Deep furrows formed on her forehead. "As a tourist? Do you have any idea how much those tickets cost? I could feed thousands of people for a year on those prices."

"But you do have the money?"

" Honey, I'm on your side. But I don't think my credit goes that high."

"We have to destroy the teleporter before it becomes operational," Katrina said. "I can't do this on my own. I need your help."

Linda became secretive and whispered, "OK, I have some friends in low places; let me make some inquiries. Maybe there's someone who can help us."

Two days later, Linda announced to Katrina that they were going for a ride. "I want you to meet someone who I'm told might be able to help you."

Katrina was elated. They hadn't talked any more about her idea of sabotaging the space teleporter, and Katrina was beginning to suspect Linda had forgotten about it.

When they went outside, she followed Linda to a very shiny, black sedan. "This is my pride and joy," Linda said as if she was in love.

Katrina hadn't ridden in a motorized vehicle for many years, and the car seemed to go incredibly fast. Katrina passed the time looking out of her car-seat window trying not to get car-sick from Linda's constant swerving to avoid potholes along a dilapidated road that Linda called the freeway. Just beyond the road, endless rows and rows of makeshift cardboard and shack houses stretched as far as her eyes could see.

"Sad isn't it. This used to be the suburbs," Linda said as she drove. "Look at it now. It's been reduced to one big area of broken-down shanty housing where only the poorest of the poor live. It's hard to believe that this was once an upper-middle-class neighborhood."

Katrina couldn't imagine living in such squalor. *No one should have to live like this.*

After a twenty-minute ride, Linda pulled onto an exit ramp and parked the car along the curb in front of a rundown brick building with an old neon sign in the window that only half worked, flashing the name, ..irsty Inn.

"Be careful, honey, this is a rough neighborhood. There be some inside that'd slit your throat for a few pennies," Linda said just before they stepped inside. "But the man you need for this heroic mission of yours is in there. My sources tell me he's the best." She paused. "That is when he's sober."

It was so dark inside that at first Katrina could barely see. The interior lighting was feeble, and she had just come in out of the bright, early-morning sunlight. The bar reminded her of a dingy, run-down stable. The stench of stale beer and excrement wafted her nose. Inside, the place was sparsely populated with lost souls for only the hard-core drunks and addicts occupied it at this time of day.

An old man, with long unkempt gray hair, a shaggy beard, and a dishonest face stood behind a scratched-up bar polishing its worn surface with a dirty rag. He turned towards them and said, "What can I do for you, strangers?"

Katrina took an immediate dislike to the man. The pervert had very hungry, x-ray eyes. "We're looking for Jeb Payne," Linda said.

The old man stopped cleaning the bar and shook his head. "He's not in much shape to talk to anyone today, but he's sitting in that corner over there."

Katrina and Linda walked over to a single table in the corner of the room. A man whose face was hidden in the shadows was seated at a table with his back to the wall and a half-empty whiskey bottle sitting on the table before him.

Linda spoke up and said, "Are you, Jeb Payne?"

The man said, "What do you folks want?"

"My name is Linda, and I need you to listen to my friend, Katrina. She needs to do something, and it's vitally important that she succeeds." She hesitated to see if he was listening. "And to do that, she desperately needs someone with your background and experience."

"Go away. You don't need my kind of experience. I'm not interested. I don't kill anymore," the man said shooing them away with his arm.

"We are not interested in killing anyone. In fact, we want to save lives --a lot of lives."

The man staggered up to his feet. He was thin and wiry, and he smelled strongly of whiskey. He gave Katrina and Linda both a cursory glance and said, "I don't like sex-slave runners or drug dealers."

"We're none of those nasty things. I assure you," Katrina said, stepping forward.

Jeb made brief eye contact with Katrina, and she saw in his eyes something that captured her interest. Sure, the man was dirty and drunk, but his eyes were honest and intelligent. It also didn't hurt that his weather-beaten face was handsome. And just from that brief glimpse, Katrina was able to use the powers of her locket to glimpse into his soul. She saw an honest soul being haunted with overwhelming guilt causing deep, deep inner pain.

"Well, then. I'm still not interested," Jeb said, sitting back down breaking eye contact.

Katrina reached down, picked up the half-empty whiskey bottle, and studied its blue label. "What happened to you, Mr. Payne, to want to throw your life away like this?" She asked, waving her hand in the air.

"That's not your business?" Jeb answered gruffly.

She put the bottle back on the table. "No, you're right, it's not. I do apologize for being so forward, but there's not much time if we're going to save lives. We just don't have time to get to know each other in the usual way. But I'm willing to hear your story. That is if you're willing to talk about it."

Jeb screwed up his face with confusion. "Whose lives do you want to save?"

"The lives of almost everyone on this planet. A near extinction level event is about to occur."

Jeb considered this while he grabbed the whiskey bottle and refilled his empty shot glass, "Save them from what?"

Katrina grimaced. *Will he believe me?* "From the alien invasion that's about to occur."

Jeb chuckled and shook his head. "Apparently, I'm not the only one that's drunk." He became serious again and said, "Are you two members of one of those crazy religious end-times' cults?"

Katrina sat down next to Jeb. "No, but I can prove what I'm telling you is true." She paused. "Would you be willing to let our minds flow together?"

Jeb furrowed his eyebrows in thought. "You mean like in those old science-fiction shows from the last century?" Jeb asked just before he the tossed the entire contents of his shot glass down his throat.

Katrina thought about this as she assessed the memories she had absorbed from Linda about science-fiction shows. When she found the memories, she smiled and said, "Yes, exactly."

"Is someone putting you up to this?" Jeb asked as he began to look around the room for anyone taking an exceptional interest in their conversation.

"No, we're alone and this is not a practical joke. Would you care to try? You don't have to be afraid. It won't hurt, I assure you."

"Don't worry ma'am, pain or death doesn't scare me."

"Really? Everyone's afraid of something. There has to be something that frightens you."

"Living," Jeb said with finality. "It's having to live with my past that frightens me." Jeb checked again to see if anyone was interested in their conversation, but nobody was around. Even the pervert bartender with x-ray eyes had stepped away and disappeared into a door that led into the back several minutes ago. "Ok, do we do this here?"

Katrina sat down next to Jeb. "Here is just fine. It'll only take a minute or two, I assure you." She had him place his hands around her locket and…. Contact, their minds came together in a rush. Pain and pleasure at the same time threatened to overwhelm her. This was much different than her Vanwanung with Linda. Her mind was calm and disciplined. She knew exactly who she was and what she was about. Jeb's mind, however, was a raging torrent of conflicting emotions. Accusing faces of enemy combatants all killed by Jeb from his many tours of duty lurked hauntingly just below his level of consciousness. They paraded around as a constant reminder of who he was, a poor soldier who had been in far too many battles. No wonder the man drank. Unending guilt and remorse for taking their lives were feeding on the essence of his soul.

As Katrina lingered at the edge of Jeb's subliminal mind, she saw that after his initial shock that the mind meld was real, he was trying frantically to hide a particular memory from her. But his efforts were futile, this memory had become dominant, malignant and malformed from its never-ending feeding on Jeb's guilt. When she focused on it, Jeb's mind reacted with horror and he pleaded, *No!*

"Let me help you."

Terror and guilt flowed out of Jeb's mind, but she continued, "Please, let me help."

Finally, a defeated Jeb said, *Fine...*

✳ ✳ ✳

Sand! Jeb woke up and rubbed his eye. Damn, he hated this crap. It blew into your hair. You ate it in your food, and it made taking showers to feel like scrubbing with steel wool.

A woman screamed. Jeb looked down from his lookout perch at the tight rows of bivouacked camouflage tents below. A local civilian had a young woman tightly pinned in his arms.

Through his riflescope, Jeb could see the man held the muzzle of a short-barreled revolver pushed tight against her temple. She squirmed to get away while he shouted in Arabic.

This didn't make any sense, Jeb's tired mind thought. Why would someone burst in with a hostage? No one is even supposed to know we're even in this damn country. His Special Forces squad began piling out of their tents.

Jeb sighted on the man's head. Their lieutenant came out of his tent and walked towards the man, unarmed, with his hands in the air. They began speaking to each other in English, but Jeb couldn't make out any of the words.

One false move and I'll plug you, he thought. The lieutenant moved closer. The man's prisoner continued to struggle like she was possessed.

And then... suddenly, she was free and began to run. The man brought his pistol up and pointed it at her back. My God, the man was going to shoot her! Jeb squeezed the trigger.

The man dropped. The woman turned around, and ran back to the dead man and pulled what looked like a cell phone out of his pocket. She laughed, but it quickly changed into a blood-curdling scream. His lieutenant made for her on a dead run, but he was too late. An explosion blinded him...

And then a translucent image of his long-dead lieutenant appeared before him and said "Jeb you let your unit down. We died that day... because you fell asleep while on guard duty and then failed to understand the ensuing situation...!

Tears streamed down Jeb's face. "I'm so sorry, sir, for you and the others. There's not a day goes by I don't ask God's forgiveness."

✳ ✳ ✳

So, everyone in Jeb's unit died in that explosion, and he blames himself for their untimely deaths.

Katrina's mind spoke to Jeb. "You know it wasn't your fault. How could you have known?"

"But that's it! I fell asleep on duty in hostile territory. And we're trained to read hostage situations, and I read it all wrong."

"I also saw that you had been awake without sleep for over thirty-six hours...You were exhausted. I can erase this memory from your consciousness. It'll be like it never happened...If you wish."

Jeb considered this, but then he said, "No, it's part of who I am now. Besides, I'm not sure if I want to forget. It feels like that would be dishonoring those that died."

"Then, you must learn to forgive yourself."

"How? How do I forgive myself?"

"By finding purpose in their sacrifice."

"But that's it; I came to realize shortly after their deaths that we were all fighting for a lie. We naively believed we were working towards liberating the common people in that country from tyranny. But in reality, we simply deposed a cruel tyrant only to be replaced by an even more callous tyrant who simply was more amenable to having Mega-

Corp setup up shop and illicitly acquire their natural resources for next to nothing."

"I have a mission for you where your training and experience would be invaluable. It would restore meaning and purpose to your life. May I share my memories with you?"

Jeb hesitated for a moment, but then said, "Sure."

Katrina opened her mind and graphic memories flowed through Jeb's consciousness showing Jeb the future of what was to come. He learned about the alien invasion that would soon happen in this timeline. And how the Ophidians had made a secret agreement with Mega-Corp to build the teleporter and how they would then use it to send a battlecruiser through and proceed to destroy every major city on the planet.

Katrina shared with him, what her life was like growing up in the future hidden city, Sanctuary, the last remnant of free humanity, and how it too would be destroyed by these same aliens. She showed him the survivors of this coming destruction would soon become the chosen cannon fodder and soldiers of these aliens in their lust to conquer or destroy every free civilization in the universe.

And then Katrina shared with him her idea of sabotaging the teleporter, now under construction, in space so none of this ever happens.

"Will you help me stop this madness?" Katrina asked, practically begging.

A very dumbstruck and now sober Jeb said, "Yes."

FIFTEEN

The next morning, before sunrise, a clean-shaven and well-dressed Jeb Payne walked into the kitchen of the homeless center and sat down at a table.

Katrina took a break from beating eggs and walked over to him, smiling, and said, "There's fresh coffee. Would you like some?"

Jeb's sober eyes stared at her. He smiled. "Coffee would be great."

"How do you like it?"

"Just some cream, please. Make it the color of cardboard."

When Katrina returned, she carried two cups and sat down across from him. Gone was the three-day beard that hid a boyish face, and he smelled clean and looked good in new clothes. Yesterday, when she first met him, she guessed his age at fortyish. But now, being sober and cleaned up, she could see that he could pass for under thirty. She blushed unexpectantly at discovering she was attracted to this strikingly handsome man and his big green sober eyes.

He pulled out a list from his pocket and handed it to Katrina. "Here's a list of the people we'll need. A pilot who can fly shuttles, one expert computer hacker capable of hacking into any system, two expert commandos proficient with any weapon and experts in the martial arts, and any other form of hand to hand combat."

"You have names to these people in mind?" Katrina asked.

"Yes, and I believe a very small strike team consisting of the people unmentioned on that list has the most chances of success. I've worked with each of them before and they're all pros and best in world class."

This was wonderful. So, he would help. "Great, when can I meet them?"

"How about tomorrow? I'll be back, say this time again?"

"Sounds good. I'll get Linda to find someone who can fill in for me." For the first time since waking up in the past, she felt happy.

The next morning Jeb walked into the soup kitchen at six o'clock sharp. Right on schedule, Katrina observed.

Jeb hustled Katrina outside into an old rusty minivan after she said goodbye to Linda and Lisa, who was waiting outside for the school bus.

Inside in the van were three men and a woman. They all wore faded fatigues that marked them as ex-military.

Jeb escorted Katrina to the right front passenger seat. Jeb pointed to the seat behind her and said, "Katrina this is Maureen O'Toole. She served two tours in South America before quitting the army."

Katrina studied her. She looked to be in her mid-twenties, and in excellent shape. If it weren't for her hard face, she would be considered pretty.

Maureen looked at her and said, "I quit the army because "I came to see what we're doing to the rest of the world as wrong. We kill and blow up innocent people. For what? So, Mega-Corp can run everything…everywhere? I got up one morning from another sleepless night disgusted at myself and tired of being one of their lackeys."

"So, what is your expertise?" Katrina asked.

"I can hack into any security system…"

Jeb interrupted, "She's the best hacker I've ever seen. No computer system is safe once she decides to infiltrate it."

"I'm Bob Jordan," a balding medium-sized man sitting next to Maureen said. "I'm a pilot. If it has wings I can fly it."

"The two men in the back row seats are Bernie Paxton and Ed Bruce. Two of the toughest men I've ever met. They have extensive training in hand-to-hand combat, explosives, demolitions, and can shoot every small arms weapon ever invented. Either of them can shoot the wings off a buzzing fly."

Both men in the back seat waved at her. They reminded her of cats. They both had lean wiry builds, and their movements seemed fluid and quick. Later, she found out that they all belonged to a secret group they called the movement.

While Jeb drove out into the country, they traveled in silence. Katrina passed the time looking out her window; she enjoyed the beauty of the gently rolling hills of planted corn and soybeans.

After more than an hour of driving, they finally arrived at their destination. Jeb pulled off the main road and turned onto a stone drive that wound around through a field of green corn taller than the van. The plants were just starting to go into tassel. Finally, the driveway ended and at an old two-story, brick farmhouse sitting on a half-acre of recently mowed grass surrounded by a sea of corn. "This is it," Jeb announced.

"Where are we?" Katrina asked.

"That's my house and this is my home. I grew up here right in the middle of nowhere. This land has been in my family for generations," Jeb said. The others piled out of the van and began unloading suitcases and duffel bags from the back. "This is where we train." Jeb picked up a large, black suitcase and opened it. Ed and Bernie opened the door to a shed and began removing silhouettes.

The suitcase Jeb opened contained two black identical pistols. "Ed and Bernie show her what you guys can do with these Glocks," Jeb said.

"Four pop-up silhouette targets will pop up in rapid succession," Jeb said explaining. "I can set the speed," he said pulling a small black box out of his pocket. What setting do you guys want?"

"Give us the fastest setting," They both said in unison.

A target popped up ten yards out. They both fired, and then the next target popped up a microsecond later. They both fired again, and again and again. Double holes in the heart area could be seen in each target.

Katrina whistled. "They can shoot. No problem there."

Katrina, I think it's time you showed them what you can do," Jeb said.

"Pop the targets back down, keep the speed setting as it is," she said holding her right hand above her head. They all gasped when several softball-sized blue orbs appeared above her hand."

"Tell me when you're ready," Jeb said, holding the control box.

With the blue orbs hovering above her upraised hand, she gave a nod, and this time when each target popped up, an orb flew from its stationary position above her hand with great speed colliding into each silhouette. A flash of intense blue flame popped briefly into being and the silhouette was gone, vaporized, with only a black stain on the ground where it had once stood.

Turning back to her audience of open-mouthed, staring faces she thought, *Oh boy, They're never going to believe this one.* "My name's Katrina and I'm from two thousand years in the future. I need each of you to help me to sabotage the space teleporter before it becomes operational. Otherwise, the alien race you've just made first-contact with will destroy every major city on the planet. They will then round up the survivors and

Prop up key leaders of Mega-Corp to rule over the rest of us as their slaves."

Her audience was continued to stare at her without making a sound. "So, are you guys prepared to follow me into space and blow up the teleporter?"

"Oh man, this sure beats the shit out the wimpy street demonstrations we've been organizing," Maureen chimed looking like she had just opened a great Christmas gift. "It's being built by fricking Mega-Corp isn't it? You can count me in."

SIXTEEN

Jeb stared at the maps and their layout that filled the living room wall of the old farmhouse. Weeks of planning were now pinned there, creating a road map into an unknown future. His forehead creased. "You know, we have planned for everything except the most likely."

Katrina studied the wall, trying to discern what he was thinking, but she drew a blank. The wall contained notes on every detail and every possible scenario that they could imagine. And now Jeb just told her that they were missing the obvious. "What could that be?" Katrina asked.

Jeb smiled. "The most likely scenario is that we fail."

"You're right," Katrina said.

"And if we fail, then everyone we love dies." He paused for emphasis. "But not the ones that make it to Sanctuary."

"What are you suggesting?"

"I know how much you have grown to care about Linda and Lisa. I have to admit that I have a brother, Neal that I would wish to save as well. What if we have our loved ones go to Sanctuary before the invasion?"

"What about the timeline? Dare we risk changing the future? What happens if they weren't part of the original group of settlers?" Katrina said.

"By you entering the past you may already have changed it. And besides, isn't that exactly what we are trying to do by sabotaging the portal? I cannot morally justify sentencing our friends and loved ones to a horrible death because it might hypothetically change a timeline that didn't work out so well in the long run anyway. I suggest we take a break from planning and take a trip to Colorado to check out the portal."

* * *

Katrina, Jeb, Jeb's brother Neal, and Linda, left the Denver airport in a rented a car. A bright-blue, sunny sky made for a delightful drive through the Colorado countryside.

While Linda drove, Neal sat in the front passenger seat. Jeb and Katrina, who were becoming fond of each other, were thrilled to sit in the back seat. Their hands met and Katrina relaxed onto Jeb's shoulder and soon fell asleep.

When they turned on to Interstate 70, Linda turned to Neal and asked, "Neal, do you know why Jeb asked you to accompany us on this trip?"

"Jeb told me that you have your eye on a commercial property that you are interested in buying and developing and would like to hire me as a consultant and project manager."

"That's right. Jeb explained that you have experience designing commercial buildings and project scheduling."

"Yes. I started out in my career doing design work, but for the past five years I have specialized in Project Management overseeing commercial building construction."

"We want to build where there exists no infrastructure. We will need buildings able to operate independently off the grid. Do you have any experience with that?"

"I have developed buildings that utilize solar power, but never exclusively."

"Have you ever worked with wind?

"No, but I know of an electrical engineer who has the background and expertise you would need."

"Good. Is he available?"

"He'll be expensive. He is considered one of the best in his field."

"Money is no problem. I have deep pockets and some very rich friends."

After driving for an hour and a half west on interstate 70 they turned off an exit and headed north. After another hour and several turns later onto ever smaller and smaller roads, they arrived close to the cave that contained the portal.

Linda parked the car along the side of a stone road and they got out. They wore hiking clothes and began to hike up the side of a mountain along a well-worn hiker's path.

Finally, after an hour of hiking they left the hikers trail and twenty minutes later, they arrived at a vertical wall of rock that contained the mouth of the cave opening, a vertical slit in the rock wide enough to drive a pickup through. After taking out flashlights, they moved to pass the slit and walked less than thirty yards in the narrow tunnel when it abruptly ended. There was no portal.

"I don't understand it. I know this is the right place. But the portal is not here," Katrina said.

"Maybe it will open when it's needed," Linda said.

Jeb looked around, went outside and came back in. I have your memories from our mind sharing experience, and I agree it should be here. Jeb scratched his head. "It's late afternoon, let's stop and have lunch and think this out."

They found some large rocks to sit on and shared a lunch of sandwiches, granola bars, chips, and water that they took out of their backpacks.

Neal sat on a large rock across from Jeb and pulled out a sandwich from his backpack. "What is it exactly that you are looking for? I am confused."

Jeb and Linda both glanced at Katrina. She nodded in agreement. "Neal, I believe it's time we told you what we are about. She held out her locket and it began to pulse. The easiest way to explain this is to show you. Please open your mind…."

After their brief lunch, Katrina got up and stood before the wall of rock in front of them. "If I had to guess, the Fengani have a meddling hand in this and they are planning to open the tunnel just before, during, or after the invasion.

Katrina raised her hand and a blue light enveloped it. "Well, we came to see Sanctuary. We don't have to wait for them. I can open it now. Let's change the future and see what fate has in store for us."

The blue light shot from her arm and bore into the end wall of the cave. It increased in intensity and the wall disappeared and a tunnel began to form in its place. When she stopped the tunnel now continued on into the mountain. They all got up and walked into the new addition. Hours later they stepped out of the cave and into an open grassy area.

"Welcome to Sanctuary," Katrina said.

"So this is where we will build the city?" Neal asked.

"Yes," Katrina said.

"If you want to build a civilization from scratch, my brother's the man you need," Jeb said.

Linda looked at Neal. "Neal, my pocketbook will be funding this operation. What will you need?"

"We're going to need teachers to educate the future generations, farmers, especially ones that know how to farm without modern equipment, carpenters, stone masons, machinery and fuel, computers, books, enough spare parts to last a lifetime, and a lot of SHTF preppers."

"I know some Amish families. I may be able to convince a few to come this way," Linda said.

"You will also need a fair amount of soldiers and hunters with weapons designed to kill really big game. There is no advanced civilization here, but there are some very large dangerous animals. This planet was never hit by a meteor that wiped out the dinosaurs. They still exist on this world," Katrina said.

* * *

Neal took a break from studying the architectural layout of the library to look out through the open flap in his tent to watch the semi-trucks roll by. They came through the portal about one every minute. They already had enough supplies to last 10,000 people for years. They also had drilling teams and enough equipment to build a refinery, along with the people with the know-how to do it.

Linda wasn't kidding when she said she knew people with deep pockets. She even managed to get the Earth-side area around the cave purchased and privatized so there would be no questions asked.

Neal returned to studying the plans for the library. Since the Vanwanung with Katrina, he knew exactly how it should look and he already had it sketched out.

SEVENTEEN

The hemline of Katrina's embroidered satin-blue dress stopped at her mid-calves -- rather short for her tastes. Taken with the plundering neckline, it left her feeling half naked.

When she walked into the lobby terminal for the space elevator she had to walk carefully because she wore highly impractical black shoes that Linda had picked and referred to as stiletto pumps. She hadn't wanted to wear them, but Linda had insisted. She couldn't imagine why such shoes ever became popular; wearing them was torture. Women in her timeline didn't wear ridiculous dresses or awkward high-heels; they wore practical pants and shoes.

In the center of the lobby, there stood a bar with teakwood siding and a mahogany top. The left side of the bar perched an antique brass-cannon. Large, aged pictures of ancient sailing vessels from when wind was the only navigational power source adorned the dark-wood paneled walls.

Several waiters dressed in vintage blue sailor outfits with matching Dixie-cup hats scurried around on the oak-hardwood floors of the nautical-themed lobby. They worked their way through the crowded room in their efforts to keep everyone satisfied with beverages.

As Katrina studied a canvas of two mast ships battling at sea, a young handsome male waiter approached her and asked if she cared for a drink.

She ordered bottled water and made sure to tip him as Linda had told her.

To blend in without having to engage anyone in conversation, she picked up a newspaper-sized sheet of clear plastic off the coffee table. The people of this time-period called these smart newspapers. As soon as she touched it, the sheet turned white and populated with black lettered words. There was a menu with a dozen or so options in the upper left corner underneath the Mega-Corp logo on the first page. She could change newspapers by simply running her finger over the menu. She sat down on a sofa and pretended to read. She observed coyly that her fellow conspirators were all in their respective places.

When the docking doors opened, a line formed, and they began to load into the space elevator. She looked up through the glass ceiling of the Terminal at the cylindrical object above her. It looked more like a small skyscraper than traveling vessel. It seemed hard to believe that that giant cylinder could be lifted into space by shimming up on a Nano-carbon tether no thicker than her body.

"Every time I see it, it reminds me of a flying saucer," A middle-aged woman next to her said.

While everyone waited to be shown to his or her rooms, Katrina flagged down the same handsome waiter and ordered another drink. This time she had coffee.

Her first-class room had a large king-sized bed with soft Egyptian cotton sheets.

As she lay on the bed and breathed a sigh of relief at their successful boarding of the elevator ship, she considered the next phase of their operation.

Maureen's expertise as a hacker had already proved useful. She had managed to forge a manifest and documents that enabled them to smuggle their weapons inside a standard shipping container, innocently marked as janitorial supplies, into the cargo hold without requiring inspection, and since the cargo hold was un-pressurized, there were no guards to contend with.

At a specified time, Maureen would once again apply her hacker expertise to disable the alarms on the docking bay to the cargo hold, thus allowing Jeb, who had a stolen spacesuit in his luggage, time to slip in and retrieve their gear.

On the third night out (right on schedule) there was a knock on her door. She waited ten seconds then opened it and retrieved a large duffel bag. She pulled it into her room.

Once inside, she opened it and retrieved a 9mm pistol with three extra clips of ammo, and several packages of tightly wrapped plastic explosives. Everything appeared in order. She hid the contents in her room.

* * *

So that's the space-teleporter, Katrina thought, as she looked out her room window at a large ring-shaped object the color of silver. She could almost imagine that it was a giant wedding ring if she didn't know it was more than two kilometers in diameter and floating in space. She watched a small shuttlecraft fly to and fro around it.

She heard a knock on her door and watched Maureen take awkward steps into her room. "I just can't get used to these Velcro shoes on a Velcro floor," Maureen said.

"It does take some getting used to. Fortunately, we won't need them for much longer. Since the teleporter spins, we will soon be back in 1 g of gravity," Katrina said. She picked up her duffel bag and they left together.

They approached the docking bay to the teleporter and saw that their fellow conspirators were already waiting for them. They entered the docking bay and crossed over to the teleporter.

When they stepped out on the other side and into the teleporter's main visitor lobby, a young pretty woman, hired for her patronizing voice and eye candy, smiled and said, "Welcome to Mega-Corp. If you're here for the evening tour, you're two hours early."

Jeb walked up to her looking friendly and unfolded a map. "Maim, I believe we're lost. Can you help us?" While she focused her attention on his map, Ed walked behind her and shot her in the back with a Taser. He then gave her an injection and they placed her in the lobby's closet.

"She'll be fine in a couple of hours," Ed said aloud.

Katrina hated having to do this to innocent people, but she saw no way around it.

Maureen took her place at the desk. "I should be able to hack into their system from here," she said while she played with the receptionist's terminal.

Katrina said, "Good. Keep watch and alert us at the first sign of danger."

A few minutes later, while Katrina had everyone going over their checklists, Maureen slapped her hands over her head. "I'm already inside their security system. This is all too easy."

Katrina said, "That's what worries me. Look around and let us know if you see anything strange."

"What the hell is this," Maureen said aloud just seconds later. They all walked over to the terminal to see what she was looking at.

The Receptionist's computer screen displayed a giant snake slithering through a hallway.

Katrina paled. "It's an Ophidian. Quickly, everyone put on your thought-bands." They all obeyed and put on the thought bands she had made for them.

"Do you think it read any of our minds?" Jeb asked?

"I doubt it. They don't have any reason to be searching for us, and they have to focus on you to single out your thoughts."

But we mustn't take any chances." Don't take off your thought-band for any reason. Ophidians can completely control the minds of unprotected individuals. Bob, the shuttle bay, is down that hall. Steal us a shuttle so we can get the hell out of here, and don't forget to take the unconscious receptionist with you."

When they were halfway to the control room, Katrina used a cell phone and called Maureen. "What's the situation?"

"I've deactivated the alarm system. I'm looking through the camera in front of the control room. There are no guards but there are several more of those giant snakes inside overseeing some humans working at a workstation. There are also several small gray creatures that look like those aliens from old movies."

"Those are grays. Their race is dying out, and that's why the Ophidians, who have no hands or arms, now want humans, to replace them. Ophidians don't like or trust artificials. They can't read or control their thoughts."

"I've tapped into what they're doing. They're preparing to charge up the teleporter. And get this; the ship they intend to bring through is unbelievably big."

Katrina pulled out a small pocket screen, "Show me."

When the picture on the screen appeared Katrina said, "It's the battlecruiser I told you about. It has enough onboard firepower to destroy every city on Earth. I guess the invasion starts tonight."

Katrina sent a coded text-message to Linda. It was the signal to begin the full evacuation to the cave with the portal in Colorado that led to Sanctuary.

Jeb tapped Katrina's shoulder. "What do you want us to do?"

"The rest of you can go and find Bob, but I'm going ahead, and I'm going to try to accomplish what we started out to do."

"I'm in; this was a suicide mission anyway." Everyone else agreed.

"Let's go."

✳ ✳ ✳

The Ophidian named Caluja had just toured the command center for the finished ring-shaped teleporter. It was fine workmanship. These humans did outstanding work. Their ability with technological gadgets was unmatched, even better than the grays. They will make a great asset to the empire as techno slaves and warriors. Good thing these humans made what they call first-contact when they did. Ever since one of the renegade grays had intentionally poisoned their species with an incurable laboratory plague they had almost become extinct, and without a suitable replacement, their ability to use technology and travel inter-dimensionally and through the multiverse would have come to a halt.

Too bad that these poor humans had such limited telepathic skills; they will be such an easy race to conquer. If he hadn't known better, it was almost as if they had been bred to specifically to become their servants. He almost had a moment of pity for them, but then he began to wonder how they would taste.

So far, only a handful of humans, mostly members of the ruling elite, and key members of an organization they called Mega-Corp knew of their true purpose. And they had welcomed them with open arms. The leaders of this Mega-Corp had even struck a deal with them. They would gladly sell out their own species if they could maintain their position of power. *Incredible.*

Caluja looked down at their chief scientist who was monitoring the vortex control unit to the teleporter. "How long before our ship comes through?" He said telepathically but also projecting the false image that they were speaking in words." They didn't want the humans to know of their telepathic powers, just yet. Most of their scientific caste didn't believe any kind of telepathy was even possible. Why ruin their day and shatter their illusion of reality?

The bright, young scientist named Brian smiled excitedly. "Within the hour. The vortex is already forming."

At that moment, they were interrupted by his second in command, Comradon. *"Sir, I'm picking up strange thoughts."*

Caluja responded telepathically in kind, *"There are several thousand humans in this vicinity. All of them are wild. Of course, you're picking up strange thoughts."*

"But sir, do you remember the receptionist I pointed out to you the other day? The one that was always so happy."

"Yes, the one we marked as potential good breeding stock for her temperament?"

"Yes, please get to the point. We're rather busy right now," Caluja said.

"Well sir, I found her mind pleasantly unique. So, I've been continuously monitoring her thoughts and… something's happened."

Caluja now angry said, *"Please Comradon, get to the point."*

" Well sir, I was in her head, earlier today, when several people came in to see her, and then her mind blanked. I'm only picking up random thoughts now and it's like she's asleep having a nightmare."

"So, who's on duty now?"

"The roster says she is, but there's someone whom I've never seen before sitting at her desk."

"So, maybe she was ill, why don't you just tap into the new receptionist's thoughts and find out?"

"That's it, sir, I can't read her mind."

"That's impossible. None of these humans have shown the slightest telepathic ability. Her mind should be as transparent as a piece of glass. Show her to me."

The receptionist's desk appeared on the screen before them, and he saw a young woman sitting there typing very quickly, seemingly very focused at whatever she was working on.

"Wait!" Caluja cursed under his breath. *"She's wearing a thought-band. But how could these humans know about that?"*

"I've also tried to access her terminal, but I'm locked out. I don't know what she's doing."

"Brian, we believe that there may be intruders on the teleporter."

"How? That's impossible. Mega-Corp's best security team is guarding this entire operation."

"Didn't you tell me that not all humans were excited about our coming?"

"Only a few religious fanatics that see your coming as some sort of doomsday scenario."

"Well some of them must be on board."

"Yes, we'll take corrective action immediately."

"Thank you," Caluja told him.

✳ ✳ ✳

When Katrina opened the door to the airlock, a sixth sense told her to duck. She did, and several bullets zinged by where her head had just been. As she hopped to the floor, she returned fire and shot a man dressed in a military uniform. There were several more soldiers a few paces behind him and instead of returning fire they chose to duck for cover.

With her pistol ready, she kept her eye on the passageway that the other soldiers had ducked into. She tried to listen to their voices, but the high pitch sound of air hissing out of the hull behind her foiled her efforts.

Without warning, dozens of small insectoid repair bots came scurrying down the hallway towards her. At first, she thought they were cockroaches, because of their similar size and appearance. She watched them as they raced like angry little bees up the wall to the hissing holes.

The first repair bots that reached the holes placed their Bodies over the holes. Then others began climbing over them while their plastic abdomens exuded a fine filament much like a spider does spinning a web. Within seconds, the hissing stopped completely.

As she continued playing cat and mouse with the soldiers down the hallway, she glimpsed many enemy reinforcements filling the hallway and moving towards her. She knew that it was hopeless without the element of surprise. "Jeb, we're getting the hell out of here." They backed out of the hallway and took off for the airlock with the shuttles.

Katrina pulled out her phone. "Maureen, we're abandoning plan A. We won't be able to blow up the teleporter control room. It's too heavily defended, and we've lost the element of surprise. How are you coming with plan B, operation virus?"

"I'm almost done. Another two minutes tops and our surprise package will be delivered."

"As soon as it's delivered make it to the shuttle bay."

"Trust me. I have no intention on being on this flying ring once the package is activated."

Katrina put her phone away. "Let's go."

Five minutes later, they arrived at the shuttle bay and climbed aboard a shuttle that Bob had commandeered. When she saw the unconscious receptionist strapped in a shuttle chair, she breathed a sigh of relief. *Thanks, Bob.*

No sooner had she secured the buckle on her own seat, when Maureen came running in and said, while shutting the shuttle door, "Let's go, Bob. The posse's right behind me."

Maureen took the seat beside Katrina and gave her thumbs up. "At least the package is delivered. We may still accomplish our mission."

The shuttle shook violently as the engines roared to life. Katrina hoped Bob really knew what he was doing, or this was going to be a very hot ride when they hit the atmosphere at 22,000 miles an hour.

When they pulled away from the docking bay Katrina said, "Bob, fly through the teleporter ring, close to the forming vortex. They won't dare fire at us lest they strike the vortex."

"Isn't that a little dangerous?"

"So is getting shot at."

"OK."

✻ ✻ ✻

Brian tried to power down the teleporter but discovered his controls wouldn't respond. "Damn! All of the controls are locked." He began running through his diagnostics. "I can't shut down the vortex. There's a virus in the system. It's causing a feedback loop. If I can't shut it off soon, the teleporter will explode. Everything within several thousand miles will be vaporized. And that ship they've stolen, it's flying too close to where the vortex will open up any second."

Caluja looked out the window. *Those fools. Serves them right. They'll be destroyed for sure.* "Brian do you have any ideas?"

"If we're lucky, they'll hit the vortex before it fully forms. It should cause it to implode and harmlessly disintegrate. It's our only hope."

Caluja looked at him. Brian, can you tap into the camera on the bridge of that shuttle."

"Yes of course."

The bridge of the shuttle appeared on a large viewing screen above them. Caluja reached out telepathically and contacted every Ophidian on the teleporter. Dozens of minds responded at once. "Yes," they asked.

Concentrate with me on that pilot. We must get him to remove his thought-band. *What will work? Perhaps, if they combined their thoughts as one they could amplify their suggestion enough to break through the dampening field of his thought band.* They all joined minds and together they sent the suggestion that the pilot's head itched with the simple suggestion to remove his headband just long enough to itch his head. The man began itching around the headband. Caluja smiled. It was working. And then…

Katrina looked out the window as they flew through the teleporter, and then she felt a gentle tug to the right. But that would take them directly into the vortex. She looked up at Bob and saw that his thought-band was off. "Bob put your headband back on. That's an order."

"No, I don't want to."

"My God, she realized, the Ophidians have him under their control. She reached down frantically to unbuckle her seat belt, but before she could get out of her chair, the engine thrusters came on full thrust. She was thrown back into her chair; the forming vortex was directly in front of them. She grabbed her Locket and it flared into life just as their shuttle hit the vortex and…

✳ ✳ ✳

"I've lost them. They went into the vortex, and now they're gone." Brian breathed a sigh of relief. "And so is the vortex."

"Good. Can you isolate that virus they planted?"

"We'll just purge the entire system and reboot from our back up files. We'll be back online in a few hours."

"I'm curious though. That shuttle completely disappeared. Where did it go?"

"Hopefully, someplace where its occupants can't cause any more mischief."

EIGHTEEN

S o, she's in the past? What does this mean? Is she a part of history? Did she try to change the future, somehow? You bet she would. These were some of the many questions that nagged Anthony.

The first place they visited when they returned to Sanctuary was the main library where they searched online through old newspaper articles written in archaic English, which thanks to his earlier education, Anthony could read. Knowing his sister, Anthony knew she wouldn't have just stood by and let the Ophidians annihilate Earth's civilization and kill ninety percent of the world's population without putting up a fight.

Luck was with them for within an hour of searching they came across an article about a failed sabotage attempt on the new teleporter that had been published just a day before the Ophidians had begun their attack on Earth. The saboteurs had been led by a woman that fit Katrina's description perfectly.

The article continued to say that after the failed sabotage attempt the conspirators had escaped in a shuttle that had flown into the teleporter and disappeared. So, where did it go? He printed the article and planned to show it to Iaghi who was presently off consulting with a group of Fengani priests who had been waiting for them when they arrived in Sanctuary. Just before he left them he told Anthony he would meet up with them at his home tonight.

Anthony walked out of Sanctuary's library into the bright afternoon sunlight with Jan at his side. They held hands and he basked in her calming presence. He was glad she was here.

As they strolled, neither of them spoke. Both of them were still too deep in thought trying to grasp what traveling into the past meant. When Anthony came within sight of his address, he saw Iaghi sitting in a wicker rocker chair on the wooden wrap-around porch rocking away as if he lived there.

Upon return to Sanctuary, he and Katrina had moved into a modest empty home in the suburbs that had an old for sale sign in the overgrown front yard. The house was unscathed and suffered no damage from the war.

When they came close, Iaghi's face erupted into that infamous reptilian grin of his.

"Back so soon? I thought you had important business."

"Yes, I did, and I have something that we've decided is time to share with you," He said.

"Well, what is it?"

"It may take a while. Can we go inside?"

"Sure." Anthony opened the front door. "Please come in and make yourself comfortable."

Before entering the home, Iaghi and Jan both waved their hands in the air and said the word "Noyami." And at prompting from Jan, Anthony did the same. He shuffled them both into the kitchen. While Jan and Iaghi sat and talked small talk, Anthony made fresh coffee and relished the idea of a fresh hot cup. It was a weakness he had inherited from his mom.

Finally, after serving his guests and finishing two, hot, invigorating cups, he interrupted their small talk and asked, "So what's this important news?"

Iaghi turned and smiled. "We've decided it's time to tell you where your parents are."

Anthony choked spewing coffee everywhere. "Where? What How?" he stammered. Could this be true? He and Katrina had spent the better part of the last several years looking everywhere for any sign of what had become of them. He had given up hope of ever seeing either of them. And now Iaghi says it time to tell you like he's known for a long time. Why didn't he tell them earlier, and just how long had he known? Anger brewed in his heart, and he screwed up his face with confusion. "Please explain yourself."

Iaghi reached into his pocket and pulled out a small transparent sphere the size of a fist. He smiled and said, "This is no ordinary stone. It's a memory crystal and it contains the complete mental recording of every thought and image of your father's mind from the last several weeks up until his arrest two days ago on the planet Toyama."

Anthony, accustomed to the paranormal, accepted without a second thought that if Iaghi said he had a record of his father's memories then it was so. After all, telepaths *were real* and as such, they could already read another's mind. It only took a small leap of faith to realize if someone could access your thoughts that someone with techno-savvy would eventually figure out a way to record them as easily as recording sound waves. However, his instincts said it was wrong. Peeking inside someone's head just seemed like an invasion of a person's right to privacy. "Arrest?" Anthony said.

"Yes, he's been arrested."

What for? And just how long did you know where he is?" Anthony asked, rubbing his chin.

"We discovered his whereabouts by accident about a year ago. Your father who is now a general in the Ophidian army…"

"Wait, my father is a general in the Ophidian army?" Anthony's head began to swim. Even the coffee was proving ineffective. Today was turning out to be a day full of new surprises. First, he discovers that Katrina has transported herself into the past, where he just learned she apparently disappeared a second time, and now Iaghi tells him his father is working for the enemy.

"Yes, the Ophidian high command sent him to our home world to oversee its integration into the empire using the strong arm of military coercion."

"But my father fought the Ophidians here on Earth and Sanctuary. I just find this very hard to accept…"

Iaghi reached over and gently grasped Anthony's hand. "Please allow me to explain, it'll all come clear to you then."

"Sorry, please go on with your story."

Iaghi took a sip from his own coffee and said, "Let me backtrack a little. As you know, we Fengani, like the Ophidians, are telepaths. But what no one knows is just how powerful. We hide the scope of our mental abilities even from the psychic Ophidians. Anyway, when your father first came to our planet, we immediately noticed that something had been done to your father's mind. We began working on undoing it.

Iaghi paused while Anthony filled his cup. When Anthony returned to the table, Iaghi resumed with the story. "He was already having nightmares; pieces of his past were trying desperately to resurface. Your father's mind is quite strong, and he shows signs of having some small, latent telepathic abilities of his own, as does your mother."

On mention of his mother, Anthony's face lit up. "Wait! You know where my mother is too?"

The Fengani smiled. "Yes indeed. In fact, she's the one who had him arrested." Iaghi raised his leathery hand. "Please allow me to continue uninterrupted; most of your questions will answer themselves in just a few moments."

After taking another long sip, Iaghi resumed. "Anyway, we began eavesdropping on these nightmares and we amplified their magnitude until they were very vivid. This had the effect of making your father even more restless. Next, we implanted the suggestion that he needed to seek out help about these vivid nightmares from one of our local shaman doctors, a Dr. Humli.

Under hypnosis, Dr. Humli was slowly able to undo most of the damage to your father's memories. You see, Mega-Corp thought that they had successfully erased his entire memory and implanted into his mind a false past. But his true self was still intact, just deeply submerged, not really erased at all. Given the right nudge, it was just a matter of time before his real memories returned and he remembered who he was on his own. We gave him that nudge and when his full memory finally did return during a hypnotic session, his first desire was to find you and Katrina and then seek out the whereabouts of his wife.

It was then that we the Fengani approached him and convinced him that in time you would all come together again.

So, he agreed to wait and to become a mole for us, which he did. He fed us much needed intelligence on troop movements and strategic planning from the high command. He began working subversively to undo and hold back the Ophidian efforts to subjugate our planet." Iaghi picked up the memory crystal and played with it. "Anyway, would you care to relive the last few weeks' of your father's life before you go with me to rescue him?"

"But I don't have a few weeks, and what about Katrina? She needs me."

"We have foreseen that Katrina will make it back to us on her own without your help. However, we've also foreseen that your father will be executed unless you come with me now. The process of absorbing your father's memories will only take a few moments; the memories will simply become a part of you. You'll just absorb them."

Did he really have time for all this? Anthony thought. He so wanted to find his sister and he still believed she needed him. He could feel it. But, now after all these years, finally, the first real lead to his parent's whereabouts, and Iaghi did say that his father needed him more. How is it that these Fengani also talk about knowing the outcome of future events? What sort of technology are they using to accomplish that? He bit his lip and said. "OK, why not, how do we do this?"

Iaghi smiled. He placed the memory crystal in the center of the table and hovered his knobby, three-fingered hands over it. He closed his bulbous black eyes and began chanting in Fengani.

Jan looked over at Anthony. "You need to concentrate on the crystal and try to see it using your mind's eye." She then held out her hands with open palms pointing towards the crystal and closed her eyes. Her lips silently moved in sync with the Iaghi's.

He hesitated. He wasn't a follower of their religion and what they were doing appeared foreign to him. But Iaghi said that the crystal contained his father's memories and that his father desperately needed him. Finally, feeling a bit awkward he decided to go along. He closed his eyes and held out his hands.

All he saw was darkness, nothing. He was about to give up when he heard a voice in his head. It was Iaghi speaking to him telepathically. *Imagine how the room looks using your mind with the crystal on the table as the focal point. I'll help you.* He tried again… Something… He did see the crystal and when he focused on it, it began to glow. Then he saw the crystal turn into a small fire, and then his consciousness moved and suddenly the fire was at the very center of his existence. The fire roared up when this happened almost as if someone had just thrown an accelerant onto the small fire and...

NINETEEN

"If an enemy laser blast or bullet had his name on it, then so be it," Kyle thought. Passing through the destroyed and burned-out Fengani village of Carpaq on his way to the Airfield had soured his mood. His men had been through here and had given the all clear, but one never knew. An aide walked on each side of him brandishing assault weapons alert for any sign of hostility. He also carried his sidearm ready for quick action.

Stacks of blown up and shot up bodies of the reptilian Fengani of all ages accusingly reminded Kyle that until this morning they had happily lived here and had called this once-peaceful village their home.

Two days ago, in this same village, the foolish Fengani rebels had managed to assassinate a senior officer in the Ophidian high command. His Ophidian superiors had immediately ordered him to destroy this village and make an example of it. He had been given no choice. If he had refused, they would have just had him executed and had someone else do it. The best he could do was to secretly send his Fengani servant Bukatan, who also happened to be a member of the Fengani resistance, to warn of the coming attack.

So, why hadn't they left? No one should be dead. Most of the dead were most likely innocent bystanders whose only imperial crime was being in the wrong place at the wrong time.

Why did the Ophidian Empire want to make war with the peace-loving Fengani, anyway? The Fengani were powerful telepaths, therefore they couldn't be turned into simple mind-controlled slaves or become possessed like humans. They'd always gotten along and until last year had managed to peaceably coexist. As far as he could see, they posed no threat to the Ophidians.

This war wasn't making much sense to his men either. Desertion had become like a pestilent plague. In the year he'd been here, nearly a quarter of them had simply abandoned their posts and run away into the jungle.

Kyle arrived at hanger deck twelve, on time, and his mind focused on the present situation. Thanks to the assassination, Internal Affairs was sending some top-notch officers to investigate and determine the root cause.

This was just great, Kyle thought. It's probably a smart young mind reading Ophidian, hoping to make a name for himself in the empire. Hopefully, they wouldn't be looking to read Kyle's mind and discover that he was feeding information to the Fengani rebels.

When the transport's door opened, an austere medium-sized human male of about fifty but who walked with the athletic spring of a man half his age stepped out followed closely by an attentive female human officer not quite forty. Her uniform insignia said she had the rank of a captain. He outranked her, but only in theory, as she worked for Internal Affairs.

However, when Kyle caught a glimpse of her face he had to work very hard to maintain his composure. *She's here.*

The man stopped in front of Kyle, and they saluted in unison. Then the woman saluted and held out her hand,

Kyle blurted out in a crackly voice, "Emily?"

"Why, yes. Good." She smiled thinly. "I'm glad to see you took time to read my itinerary. Most field officers don't. Impressive."

He hadn't, but he nodded his head anyway. Someone from internal affairs was the last person you admit to experiencing memory recall, former lover and soul mate or not. Seeing her took his breath away and he was having difficulty focusing on the problem at hand, which was the real reason she was here.

After several minutes of general amenities, the older man identified himself as special agent Faraday who would be conducting an independent investigation of the terrorist threat on Toyama. "I'll leave you in the hands of my very talented assistant. Please show her around the planet. Good day," he said and stiffly walked away, followed by a half dozen muscle-bound goons of various races and a young Ophidian whom Kyle pegged immediately as a mind rapist. Kyle could feel his psyche playing touchy-feely with his mind as he walked past. He shivered from the thought of that icky parasite's mind inside his head.

Now alone, Emily turned towards Kyle and said, "You're not properly dressed general. Your uniform lacks your insignia and rank."

So, Emily was just as intelligent and observant as he remembered her. Does she remember anything? Kyle had to be very cautious. Her presence here now could cause him a lot of pain. Despite his feelings for her, for now, he had to consider her a loose-cannon, very dangerous.

"Welcome to the planet, Toyama." Kyle shook hands with her. "We've just been through a serious battle, and we've discovered that the Fengani snipers like to target our officers." *She doesn't remember me.* "Allow me to escort you to our commons. Have you eaten?"

"No, and I am hungry."

Do you eat meat?"

"Sometimes."

"Good. Have you ever tasted Orshank?"

"I can't say that I have. Is it a local cuisine? I've never been to this planet before."

"Yes, it's a local animal similar to a cross between a goat and a pig, but it's quite tasty. The purplish meat is marinated in a local fermented fruity beverage, cooked on barbeque bricks made from an indigenous plant that imbibes a garlic tanginess to it. But it tastes like chicken with the texture of steak; it's deliciously exotic, I assure you."

The mess hall was a large semi-circle rapid deploy military structure within five minutes walking distance of the landing hanger. Inside were rows of folding tables and chairs set up for feeding several hundred soldiers at a time.

Kyle walked over to the coffee machine and poured two cups. When he returned, he handed her a cup. "Let me guess. You like two creams and one teaspoon of sugar."

Emily sipped and smiled. "Why yes. How did you know?"

Kyle returned her smile. "Just a lucky guess."

After going through the serving line and finding an empty table, Kyle said, "Surely internal affairs didn't send you all the way here because of one assassination."

Emily sipped on her coffee and gazed at him as if she was deciding how much to divulge. "You're right," she said setting her coffee cup on the table. "The situation on this planet has become much more difficult than our supervisors first imagined. We believe that there's a mole, and someone is feeding the Fengani information."

"Kyle didn't blink. *What would she do if she knew she was talking to the informant, now?*

"Also, I'm here to reassess this entire project. The high command no longer believes this planet carries any strategic importance."

Kyle swung his arms and knocked over Emily's coffee. *No strategic importance!* Half of the men who had landed on this planet with him had died for their empire and now this woman with the name and

144

face of somebody from his distant past says that their deaths had no meaning? "I apologize, but I hope you understand why I seem upset. My men have paid for this world with their lives," he said, as he wiped up the spill.

Emily patted Kyle's arm. "I do. But, even the more reason the sooner this madness stops the better. True?"

✳ ✳ ✳

The next day Kyle paid a visit to his good friend Dr. Humli seeking advice on how to proceed around Emily. He put faith in Dr. Humli, for he had given Kyle back his former life and restored his identity.

Dr. Humli's Spartan office was small, just large enough for a couch and a large desk that was filled with old books and parchment scrolls. For being so technically advanced, the Fengani at times seemed to almost have a certain disdain for technology. They preferred to read from books and scrolls. A scroll lay open upon the desk. And Kyle glanced at it. The pages were filled with undecipherable picture grams. That scroll, he guessed, most likely belonged to another race that they may have met in their voluminous travels. The lighting in the office, emanated from the ceiling, Fengani didn't use lamps, and the entire ceilings in their buildings emanated a soft light that could be controlled by their voice. The lighting reminded him of the fluorescent ceilings that humans employed except there were no bulbs and the entire ceiling emanated light producing a soft light that left nothing in shadow.

It was shortly after arriving on this poor planet Toyama that the awful nightmares had started. They had ended every morning with him waking up in a cold sweat crying out the name Emily.

Desperate for help, Kyle had not known where to turn. If he had gone to someone on the base, he risked being relieved of command. After hearing from several of his men who were having similar problems with nightmares about a Dr. Humli, a local Fengani witch doctor who they all claimed had done wonders, he had decided to see for himself, and he had begun seeing him discreetly.

This witch doctor had suggested that Kyle's memories may have been tampered with and that the real memories of his true past were slowly beginning to emerge and that was causing the nightmares. To speed things up he had suggested hypnosis.

It had worked. He soon remembered everything.

"Do you think that Emily remembers anything about your past together?" Doctor Humli asked, sitting at his desk.

Kyle's eyes rested on the soft reptilian face of the witch doctor, and he stared into those bulbous unblinking black eyes. He allowed himself the luxury of sinking into the padded sofa of the witch doctor's small office. "If she did, I didn't sense it." Kyle sipped from a glass of ice water.

The alien witch doctor contorted his face in a gross attempt to make a human grin. "The last time you were together you said she was depressed."

"Yes, she had given up on everyone and everything."

"She may not want to remember. That may explain why she no longer remembers and hasn't started having memory recall like you. The block in her brain may be reinforced by her own psyche. In fact, until she learns that her children are still alive and well, she may never *allow herself* to remember."

"If that's the case how do I get her to remember?"

I don't know....

TWENTY

Over the next several days, Kyle gave Emily the full tour, and they inspected all the military bases on Toyama. The way she walked, her love of coffee, and the way she puckered her lips when she laughed all reminded him of the Emily he had once known. He found himself falling in love with this new Emily. He so desperately wanted to ask if she had any memory of her former self, but he knew he must be discrete. Emily now worked for internal affairs, a very selective organization that only took in the brightest and most capable. She was certainly all of that. False memories or not, she was just as driven as when they had first met. He had to give the Ophidians credit. What better way to win a war if you could capture the best and brightest of your enemy then reprogram their minds so they now worked for you as diligently as when they were your enemy.

She wouldn't believe him if he suddenly just told her that her past was a lie and that they were really husband and wife. She smiled at him often, and he took that as a good sign. Thank the eternal one, the mutual physical attraction at least was still there.

After they finished the inspection of the fourth and final military base, Emily mentioned that she'd like to see something of the Fengani people as part of her investigation.

When they arrived in the bustling city of Hoshama, the congested streets were filled with the short, bipedal, and brown or green reptilian-skinned Fengani moving to and fro going about their business. They didn't use motorized vehicles; instead, most walked or rode short, squat bicycles. Massive lumbering crocodilian beasts pulled freight-filled wagons through the cobblestone streets.

"Are you hungry?" Kyle asked Emily when they reached the crowded Fengani market place some forty minutes later.

Emily smiled at him. "Yes, I'm starving."

"Follow me I know the perfect place."

Five minutes later, they stood before the doorway to the Yingzutan restaurant. A ceramic bust of a very large Orshank was raised above the doorway. Kyle and Emily dipped their fingers into the bowl of ashes beside the doorway and whispered, "Noyami."

Once inside, Kyle asked the young Fengani waiter for a table on the terrace. "You'll love the view. It's fantastic," Kyle said as they elbowed their way through the patron filled establishment.

The open terrace to the restaurant protruded out from the main building and seemed to hang suspended in mid-air. The waiter seated them at a table that provided a picturesque view of the lush cultivated rolling green hills. "The Fengani take great care of their city. Every plant, every bush is planted only after careful thought," Kyle said smiling.

While eating Orshank sub sandwiches, stuffed and dripping a piping hot purple meat, Emily became misty-eyed and said, "Sometimes, I like to imagine that if I ever married that I might experience times such as these past few days. I have to admit, I've enjoyed the time I've spent with you."

Kyle had to bite his tongue from saying, but we are married. Instead, he said, "You've never been married?"

148

Emily focused on the distant hills. "No, I've had a few relationships but I always ended them when they began to get intimate." She paused as if struggling within herself. She turned her head and their eyes met. "For some reason, none of them ever felt quite right." She shrugged. "I always had the strange feeling that I already belonged to someone else."

Kyle remembered that even before he had begun to regain his real memories, he had always felt the same way and consequently he had never formed any lasting relationships either.

Without thinking, his hand slid across the table and her hand met his halfway. She smiled and they both just stared at each other without speaking. Finally, Kyle became self-conscious of their adolescent behavior and let go of her hand. "So, did you grow up on Earth?"

"Yes, my parents died on Earth, killed by the human resistance there because they were executives in Mega-Corp."

Of course, Kyle knew that to be a lie. Her parents, both Sanctuary scientists, had died during a slaver raid on Earth where she had been captured just before they had met those many years ago.

For the next five minutes, she raved about the good of Mega-Corp. He sat and listened without comment, merely nodding his head. He surmised that her speech was really a pep talk for herself because she was beginning to have doubts. Perhaps her conditioning was finally wearing off. That's how it had started with him.

He had to compliment Mega-Corp on the effectiveness of their mind control abilities. For years he had fully embraced everything about Mega-Corp and the Ophidians that in his former life he had hated. Truth had been successfully turned upside down.

The strong urge to pull Emily into his arms, embrace her and reveal the truth of who she really was almost overpowering, but Kyle knew he *must not.* She wouldn't believe him. She would most certainly turn him in. She was, after all, looking for a mole and he was it.

But how was he going to help her to discover her true past? Why had recall happened to him, but not to her? Perhaps the Fengani witch doctor was right. She truly believed that Katrina and Anthony were dead and her unconscious mind had lost hope. He remembered how dark and lost she had become during their forced march to New San Diego. Filled with utter despair and emptiness she had lost all reason to live.

When they went back out into the market place, they came upon an old and weather-beaten Fengani who stood in the center of the market square. A large audience of Fengani and a small group of many different alien races had seated themselves around him and was listening attentively to his speech. He wore a long black robe and he seemed familiar. Kyle gave him a closer look. It was the same priest that had given them the locket so long ago.

Kyle and Emily stopped and listened to him preach about living according to *the Way.*

"Our souls are like matter and energy in that they cannot be created or destroyed only transformed. Have you ever met someone that you instantly felt that you already knew? Sometimes you felt an instant attraction like meeting an old friend or lover. Other times you felt instant dislike as if you are encountering an old enemy. Consider this: That maybe it's because you knew each other before in a previous life. Our souls lovingly bond and cling to each other and the eternal one arranges it so that they can be together lifetime after lifetime and share in the reality of the world. Sometimes they are our parents, siblings, or children. They can take turns sharing these roles. Sometimes they become lovers and friends…"

They listened to the priest preach for almost a half hour before they decided to move on. Once they were out of earshot of the crowd,

Emily said, "You know this religion of theirs, *The Way*, is now spreading throughout the empire thanks to the slave trade."

"They believe that all souls in the universe are on a mystical journey to rediscover and reunite with the soul of the eternal one. It does have a universal appeal."

"Well, I'd like to learn more and include a report on their beliefs in my investigation. Some of my superiors are of the mind that proselytizing *The Way* is not in the long-term best interest of the Empire."

Emily and Kyle spent the rest of the afternoon walking through the busy market streets of Hoshama, holding hands and having Kyle recite to her practically everything he knew of their culture. When it started getting late, they decided to spend the evening downtown and booked two adjoining rooms in the Rasmutan hotel, a popular establishment that catered especially to the exotic needs of off-worlders.

Emily had dinner for them both delivered to her room. Dinner consisted of Orshank roast and white baked potatoes, imported from earth, served with a large bottle of red wine.

Kyle attacked his dinner. All that walking about had made him famished. However, after only a few bites, his fork stopped in midair when Emily said, "Kyle, what do you think the empire should do about the Fengani problem?"

Kyle felt a cold chill race down his spine. His hunger died, and he dropped his fork back onto his plate. "What problem is that?"

"The fact that they don't fit in, and they are unable or perhaps refuse to assimilate into the empire." She paused to see his reaction. "My superiors have asked me to come up with a final solution."

Kyle sighed. He didn't like where this was going. He loved and admired the Fengani. "I thought the plan was to force them to accept assimilation. I mean that's why I'm here with an army."

151

"And you're failing miserably. Look around you. We just had another senior officer assassinated, yesterday."

"OK, so what is your final solution?"

"We pull out all of our forces, and we advise all aliens to leave within three days."

"And then what?"

"We blow this planet up."

Kyle took a big drink of wine. "But you're talking about the annihilation of an entire race." Kyle didn't know how, but he had to talk Emily out of this. "Why now? I mean the Ophidians have always tolerated the Fengani as long as they stayed out of the way."

He sensed that the person he once loved was somewhere deep inside her and it had just become imperative he must reach that hidden part of her real self soon. That empathetic person would never consider such a mad scheme. How could she have the same looks, tastes, and intelligence of the Emily he had known but not the same level of compassion? How had she become so cold? And how had her moral compass deviated so much from the person she had been? Even with false memories, his basic personality hadn't changed that much. He suspected something had been done to her that hadn't been done to him.

Emily picked up her fork. "Let's discuss this in the morning. I'm tired and hungry."

Kyle complied and took another long sip from his wine. He refilled his cup and decided that they would soon need another bottle. Why did he still love her? A minute ago, she was talking to him about exterminating a sentient race much older and possessing a technology many times more advanced than man's like she was planning the eradication of an ant hill that was homesteading in her garden.

After dinner, they played music through the sound system and both drank too much. Later they tried dancing and between the alcohol and the physical closeness to Emily, against his better judgment, he found himself sleeping in her bed that night. They spent the entire night making love. Their lustful desire for each other proved insatiable.

Every time Emily looked at him with those deep chocolate eyes of hers, he found it difficult to breathe. He desperately wanted to tell her the truth that they were married, that they still belonged to each other that their children were alive, and they were now the two most wanted people back on Earth. But he knew he couldn't. She wasn't ready for that kind of announcement. Hopefully, someday soon.

The next morning when Kyle came out of the shower he overheard Emily say, "Meet me in the lobby of the Rasmutan hotel within the hour." *Who was she talking to and who was she meeting?* He walked out of the bathroom wearing only a towel and a large grin with the events of last night still fresh in his mind.

Emily was already dressed and sitting in a chair by the window. "Were you talking to someone, dear?" Kyle stooped and Kissed Emily on the forehead.

She looked up and smiled. "I just scheduled an impromptu meeting with some local authorities. Get dressed. We need to leave."

✳ ✳ ✳

As Kyle manhandled Emily's heavy luggage through the hotel lobby more than a dozen heavily armed soldiers jumped from out of nowhere and yelled freeze. Kyle stopped in his tracks and knew better than to so much as twitch a leg. They both stood immobile for several minutes until agent Faraday entered the lobby.

Faraday walked up and gave Emily a very warm handshake. "Good work Emily, I'll see that breaking this case gets you that big promotion." Faraday gave Kyle a cold stare. "HQ has been wanting the identity of this mole for a long time."

Emily turned toward Kyle, screwed up her face like she was looking at a creepy crawly slug and spat, "That's him. Get this scum out of my site."

A very confused Kyle looked at Emily for an explanation. But Emily said nothing. Instead, she marched over to Kyle and slapped him on the side of the head so hard he saw stars. "Traitor!"

TWENTY-ONE

What just happened? Anthony focused on the memory crystal which sat in the center of the kitchen table. It no longer glowed and now looked like an ordinary piece of quartz.

Wow, in just a few short minutes, he'd just relived the highlights of the last several weeks of his father's past. Even now, his subconscious mind continued to collate, process and make sense of his new memories.

His poor dad betrayed by Mom like that and by someone, he loved *that* much. Anthony was just beginning to feel those same deep feelings towards Jan and he could only guess how devastated he'd be if she ever rejected or betrayed him. "When is the execution of my father to take place?"

Iaghi stared at him with those bulbous unblinking eyes of his. "He is to be executed in thirty days."

Anthony cursed. "Thirty days!" Then perhaps there was time to execute a rescue. "Why the wait? Wouldn't they just turn him over to one of their mind rapists and squeeze out everything he knew?"

"Mega-Corp's military high command has successfully blocked internal affairs request to do just that. They are in full damage control. They're already embarrassed, and afraid any new information learned would ruin what little prestige they have left. It's now to be a public execution on the anniversary of the day Mega-Corp first landed on Toyama."

Katrina was lost somewhere in the unattainable past, a place that he couldn't possibly go to, whereas his father was in the same timeline just in an alternate universe and his father's needs were immediate. This did change everything.

"Can you create a portal and take us there now?"

"No, but we can go in my ship."

"I thought you could teleport to any reality?"

"Yes, of course. However, not very far through space. Remember, Earth is not my home planet, and in my universe, this planet is totally uninhabitable. My home planet is the planet you call Venus."

"But Venus is an uninhabitable oven of a planet?"

Iaghi made a lipless grin. "In this reality, yes, but not in mine."

In my reality, a moon orbits Venus, and the Earth is moonless and sterile.

Anthony rubbed his chin. "You said you have a ship?"

"Yes, my ship's in Earth orbit waiting for me even as we speak."

"But how do we get to it?"

"We ride the space elevator like everyone else."

"In case you haven't heard, I'm one of the most wanted humans on the planet. The local authorities will arrest me the moment I try to board."

Iaghi smiled exposing those sharp jagged teeth of his. "Trust me. They'll let us through."

"I'm going too," Jan said placing her hand on Anthony's.

Filled with concern, Anthony said, "This'll be dangerous. You don't have to go."

Jan huffed. "All the more reason for me to go. Someone must look out for you. Don't forget, I've already saved your butt."

Anthony frowned. "No, I haven't forgotten."

"Good," Jan said. She turned to Iaghi and said, "When do we leave?"

"It's getting late. How about first thing in the morning. Your friend here looks like he could use a good night's rest."

Anthony yawned. He couldn't agree more. A good night's sleep in his own bed for the first time in weeks sounded just too good to pass up. After showing Jan and the priest where the spare bedrooms were located, he went straight to bed and he fell fast asleep.

The next morning, everyone got up early. Anthony fixed everyone a quick breakfast, and a large pot of fresh, hot coffee. Family troubles or not, nothing dimmed his appetite.

Anthony discovered to his surprise that Iaghi had an appetite for eggs that rivaled his. He had to fry over three-dozen eggs before Iaghi said he was full. And he'd always thought reptiles were cold-blooded and didn't need to eat often. So much for hearsay.

As they prepared to leave, Iaghi came into their room with his arms full of uniforms, and they looked terribly familiar. "Here," Iaghi said. "Put these on."

Anthony stared at him. "You can't seriously want us to dress as slavers!"

"But my ship is a slaver vessel."

"You're a slave hauler?" Anthony spat. He detested everyone and anything to do with the slave trade. "How can you justify hauling sentient beings around like they're dumb animals?"

Iaghi shrugged. His unblinking eyes shimmered.

"Trust me. If I had another way, I'd do it. But before you pass judgment; please consider that as a slave trader it allows me to travel anywhere I want to with no questions asked." Iaghi reached out and gently patted Anthony's arm. "In many situations, life forces us to decide between the lesser of two evils."

Anthony didn't like it, but he decided that for now at least, he had no choice. As they walked out the door that morning, he hoped no one saw them in these outfits. Someone just might take a shot at them before asking questions.

"Please follow me, this way," he said walking at a brisk pace out the front door and quickly down the road.

Anthony glanced at Jan who seemed just as confused. They clasped hands and began to follow. The familiar vortex of a portal opened in front of them. *Just who are these Fengani anyway?* They claimed to have even more telepathic powers than the Ophidians, yet their world was under control of the Ophidian Empire that maintained a sizable occupation force on their home world. And Iaghi just admitted that he engaged in the slave trade.

They stepped into the portal and the tunnel vortex seemed to go on for about fifty feet. When they stepped out, the landscape had completely changed. Off in the distance, Anthony could make out the familiar black Nano-carbon walls of the slaver city of New San Diego. "Please follow me and let me do all of the talking. Please stay out of trouble while I purchase us a cargo."

"I can't believe you're going to buy humans," Anthony said.

"As I said, I need a cargo. How do you expect me to stay incognito if I transport around without a purpose? The Ophidians are lazy, but they're not stupid. Trust me. This is the best way." Iaghi paused to grin. "Think of it as a catch and release."

He and Jan followed close behind Iaghi past the outer walls and towards the bustling slave market in the center of the city.

That afternoon, they boarded a convoy of transport copters with a cargo of several hundred new slaves, made up of mostly women and children. Iaghi purchased mainly those who looked dejected and had given up all hope, mostly a sorry lot. Even Anthony, who wasn't a businessman, could see that Iaghi would be hard placed to make any kind of profit on this venture.

After the sale, Iaghi convinced Anthony to oversee his new slaves. While he was escorting them to the cargo hold of the plane that would fly them to the space elevator, Anthony made the mistake of passing too close to a pretty, young woman. She lunged at him quicker than he had thought possible, and almost succeeded in getting one of her wrist chains around his neck, but he pulled his head back at the last second. She stood before him at the end of her chains and launched a wave of profanities at his face. Anthony was unnerved. He had never experienced such outward hatred. He decided his best course of action was to ignore her and simply walk away.

However, a slaver guard who stood nearby saw this as a cruel opportunity. Before Anthony had taken three steps, he began to use his whip without mercy on the young woman.

He turned and wanted to slay the guard on the spot. Instead, he moved between the guard and the poor woman, so he couldn't whip her anymore. "Hey, be careful with that whip. Can't you see that she is exceptionally pretty? She'll bring a nice price in the sex market. If you damage it, you buy it," he said, confident that the guard didn't have that kind of money. Anthony tried to fondle the woman's hair, but she pulled away and spit again into his face.

The guard grew sullen and threw his whip down, not pleased that his fun was over. Anthony wiped his face and resumed walking away.

After they landed on the airstrip of the island where the space elevator was located, Anthony marched their human cargo into the loading terminal. No one cared or bothered to ask them their business.

Once aboard the elevator, Anthony watched as Iaghi paid the Ophidian guards for their cargo and dismissed them. To his amazement,

Iaghi pretended to hand them money, but there was nothing in his hands. After they left he turned and said, "How'd you do that?"

Iaghi smiled coyly. "The power of illusion can be a powerful weapon, especially on the most arrogant who think that they can't be fooled."

"How long until we reach Toyama?"

"A day's travel at most, but first we must drop off our cargo."

"Where's that?"

"There's an uncharted reality that the Ophidians are unaware of. It's mostly uninhabited Earth that's very similar to yours. We'll drop off our cargo there. It has a small but flourishing settlement of humans and several other sentient races that we've already rescued from slavery. It's a place where they can start their lives over in complete freedom and be safe."

TWENTY-TWO

"Let me introduce you to the crew," Iaghi said to Anthony who had followed him onto the bridge.

As they moved around the instrument filled bridge, Anthony counted twelve Fengani. All of them wore the familiar robes of priest and priestess orders of *The Way*. Most of them wore the simple gray robes of an initiate; however, a few wore the familiar blue robe identifying them as masters. Iaghi asked the crew to speak in universal instead of another language or telepathically.

Iaghi Introduced Anthony to his second in command, communications officer, Xelana. When Iaghi introduced him, Xelana stood up and reached out with his three-fingered hand making that familiar and unsettling grin. He wore the blue robe of master and he stood a head taller than Anthony. His body was stout and more rounded than any Fengani he had met before.

"Prepare to leave orbit," Iaghi said when the familiar vortex began to form.

"Sir, a ship just flew out of the forming vortex and appeared in our space," Xelana announced.

"Can you get a visual?"

"Yes sir, it's within a thousand meters off our bow."

"Great, Put it on the main screen," Iaghi said.

The image of a small ship appeared on the main viewing screen. Even Anthony who knew almost nothing about space flight could see that the ship looked odd. It had a streamlined fuselage and wings that served no useful purpose in the vacuum of space.

"Does anyone aboard recognize that insignia blazoned on its fuselage?" Iaghi asked.

Xelana played with his console quickly flipping switches and turning dials. "Sir I'm picking up a signal, and get this, they're broadcasting in primitive analog-RF instead of tachyons."

Iaghi's face lit up. "Can you lock onto it?"

Xelana played some more with his console. "Sir, I've got it!" he announced in an agitated voice.

Anthony again studied the five-pointed white star displayed on the vessel's fuselage. It was on a blue background with left and right red and white armbands. "Wait! I know that insignia," Anthony said aloud remembering his history lessons.

Everyone on the bridge focused on him. "Yes?" Iaghi asked.

Anthony's mind raced. It must be Katrina. Who else would suddenly appear in this timeline on an ancient vessel that predated the Ophidian invasion? "It's an ancient Earth symbol, that once belonged to a country called the United States which was considered the world power until the Ophidians showed up and destroyed their civilization two thousand years ago."

Iaghi began pacing with his arms behind his back. "Can anyone get any readings that confirm this?"

"Sir," the navigations officer said, cutting into the conversation. "Several fighters just launched from that battlecruiser parked beside the docking bay to the space elevator. They're moving at top speed in this direction."

"How long before they reach us?" Iaghi asked.

"They'll be here in less than ten minutes."

"Can you establish communication with the strange ship using RF?" Iaghi asked Xelana.

Xelana worked very fast now, typing at his console and flipping switches. "I'm trying sir, but we're not designed to broadcast using such primitive technology. However, I think I can do it after a few more adjustments." He reached down below his console and pulled the panel cover off. Then he reached inside with a device that appeared to Anthony to be a simple screwdriver.

Xelana sat back up flipped a switch and said in perfect archaic English, "Aircraft please identify yourself and state your purpose."

When Xelana reached below his console again, Anthony reached over, flipped the same switch, and said, "Katrina, it's Anthony, can you hear me?"

Xelana popped back up and said, "Hey, don't touch anything!" His bulbous eyes became even larger. "None of us have any idea who is on that ship. But if the crew were human we'd know, we'd already been reading their thoughts."

"Not if they were wearing thought..."

"Anthony is that you?" said a familiar voice through the intercom speaker.

Anthony desperately wanted to say yes, but Xelana maintained his three-fingered hand over the switch. He shifted his gaze to Iaghi. Neither spoke. Anthony guessed they were communicating telepathically and having a private conversation.

"Anthony? Is that you?" That familiar voice resounded again through the intercom cutting through the icy atmosphere of the bridge.

This time the Xelana moved out of the way and said, "OK."

"Katrina, hang on! We're about to rescue you," Anthony said. He flipped the intercom switch off and said to Iaghi, "Right?"

Iaghi nodded an affirmative and then turned to the crew and said, "Get a tractor beam on that vessel as we come alongside. We'll carry it into the vortex with us."

As they approached the vortex, Xelana announced that he was receiving a signal from one of the fighters.

"Put it on the main screen," the priest said.

"Slaver vessel, release that ship or we'll be forced to fire. That vessel is the property of Mega-Corp."

Iaghi turned towards the helmsman and said, "How long before we enter the vortex?"

"Less than tens second, Sir."

Iaghi smiled and looked hard at Anthony. "They won't dare fire. If a stray shot from a laser cannon were to accidentally hit the vortex now, all space and anything occupying it in an area of over several thousand miles would be completely obliterated which includes that battlecruiser."

When the jump occurred, Anthony experienced a sudden painful jolt like an electric shock that seemed to last for almost a minute. When it was over Iaghi slapped him hard on his back and said, "Congratulations, you've just made your first space jump." He smiled then, exposing his jagged teeth. " It's not as nice as traveling through a portal."

The view screen showed a blue and white planet. "This is an alternate Earth that has evolved in a slightly different manner. It will become the new home to the slaves I purchased yesterday." He pointed to an area on the largest continent that looked vaguely like a stretched out North America. "There's a small but growing city along the coast there. They'll soon come to call it home."

"But they'll never again see the loved ones they left behind," Anthony added.

"True, but they'll be masters of their own destiny, no longer slaves."

An hour later, Anthony and Jan were reunited in the main cargo hold. Jan had spent the entire trip so far with the passengers helping them and seeing to their needs. After the Fengani pulled the shuttleship inside the main hanger bay, they waited expectantly for the ship's airlock to open.

Anthony couldn't wait to tell Katrina the news about their parents and he anticipated the jubilant expression on her face when she heard. She had spent years following dead lead after lead, frantically searching as if she had been possessed. That she'd want to come along to Toyama, he had no doubt.

When the main door of the shuttle finally opened, Katrina walked out smiling and holding the hand of a handsome young stranger. This stranger walked like a coiled spring and his wandering eyes clearly missed nothing.

"Katrina!" Anthony said. They both ran to greet each other. "I see you have a new friend," he said pointing to the man beside her.

"Oh, this is Jeb," she said smiling. "He's from twenty-first-century Earth. And who's your new friend? Don't think I wouldn't notice that you two were holding hands?"

"This is Jan," he said letting go of Katrina.

Two females, one of whom seemed frightened to death, and two dangerous men with cold predatory eyes next emerged out of the shuttle.

Everyone spent the next ten minutes getting acquainted and providing a brief account of who they were.

Anthony discovered that he liked Jeb. He had warm eyes and a disarming smile. He seemed happy to be here and asked about life in this time period.

When Katrina learned that Jan was the same little-pigtailed girl she had carried during their escape from Sanctuary they became quickly engaged in nonstop catch-up conversation.

Finally, Iaghi cut in and he broke everyone into small groups for a tour of the ship. The two dangerous men went off with Xelana. The two women went with another Fengani. It was someone Anthony hadn't met before but he also wore a blue robe. Iaghi escorted the rest of them And afterward everyone convened in his private quarters.

When everyone seemed comfortable around a conference table, Katrina turned to Anthony and asked, "So what's this news you're dying to tell me? I can read you like a book. It must be pretty important."

Anthony looked over at Iaghi and nodded. Iaghi got up from the table, reached into a small drawer of his desk and pulled out the memory crystal. Anthony's face lit up. He fidgeted with his fingers and his palms were sweating in anticipation. Only after Iaghi put the memory crystal in the center of the table, did he continue with, "I know where our parents are and…"

TWENTY-THREE

While waiting for Mr. and Mrs. Sparks to get in the car, Lisa sat in the back seat with Missy propped beside her while she wrote in her new pink diary. It was her going away present from Katrina just before she had left for her secret mission. She loved it, and she couldn't wait to fill its pages with all the wonderful things happening in her life. She wouldn't write anything about Katrina's secret mission or reveal that Katrina was from the future. *What if the aliens got hold of it?* Maybe they could use what she wrote here against her friend.

Katrina had said she was going to save the world from imminent destruction. She must have failed because cities were being destroyed everywhere. Maybe she died. She didn't like secret missions. Her real parents had gone on a secret mission, too, and never returned.

She felt for her headband that Katrina had made for her, making sure it was still on. Katrina had given it to her with the instructions that if aliens started attacking, then she must always wear it. "This will protect you from them taking over your mind."

She stopped writing when Mrs. Sparks opened her door, gasped and then closed the door hard. "Saaaam?" Why is there a gun on your front seat?"

Mr. Sparks came out of the garage carrying a large cardboard box that seemed heavy by the way he carried it. "That's my old shotgun honey. It's the one my parents got me for my thirteenth birthday. Can you hit the button on the dash and pop the trunk, please?"

Lisa put her diary in a plastic box next to her for safekeeping and picked up Missy stroking her stringy hair. She didn't like how her new parents were acting. She was young, but she was street smart. She recognized fear. She wished Linda or Katrina were here. They were both brave and she always felt safe around them. Hopefully, soon she would see Linda. Anyway, that's where they were headed. To someplace Linda called Sanctuary. They got the message yesterday from Linda to leave at once, but Mr. and Mrs. Sparks didn't take her warning seriously until they woke up this morning and turned on the news.

Mrs. Sparks opened the door again and reached for the button. She made a face when she looked down at the shotgun.

After popping back out of the car, she said, "I thought I told you to get rid of it when we got married."

"I know but I just could never get myself to part with it. Every time I look at it, it reminds me of growing up on the farm. Sorry, I had it hidden in the garage."

"Ok, so you hid it from me. But that's not the first thing I asked. I first asked… why is it in the front seat of our car, now?" She slammed the car door shut. "You know how I feel about guns."

Mr. Sparks placed the box in the trunk. "You saw the news. There's rioting everywhere. We may need some protection."

"What about the National Guard and the police?"

"In case you haven't noticed, they're busy fighting aliens right now. There won't be any police or guardsman to protect us."

Lisa watched Mrs. Sparks just stand there rubbing her hands together for several seconds. Finally, she nodded her head. "Ok, you can have the gun." She pointed at the trunk. "But can you please put it in the trunk along with those canned goods?

"But how can I wield it to defend us, if it's not beside me?"

Mrs. Sparks put her hand on his shoulder. "Sam, please, I told you that you can take it with us. Can you please give me time to adjust? Please?"

An hour later while sitting on Interstate 88 in a traffic jam where they hadn't moved ten feet in the last ten minutes, Mrs. Sparks turned on the radio and they listened to a newscaster say that Washington D.C., New York, and Philadelphia were totally gone, destroyed by a powerful death ray that emanated from the giant alien ship. Then the station began broadcasting live interviews of survivors that were coming out of what was left of Philadelphia.

They talked about seeing giant snakes and about seeing a giant floating pyramid, like the ones in Egypt, float down from the giant ship in the sky and land where these short, mostly naked gray aliens with bulbous eyes and slits for mouths, forced thousands of rounded up refugees to enter the pyramid, and where only a few came out the other side and those that did, walked zombie-like and took up weapons that the grays handed them and then began assisting the grays in herding more refugees into the pyramid. One squeaky-voiced teenage girl said, "I saw tens of thousands of people of all ages walk into that alien pyramid-shaped building that should have been full after a few thousand, but only a few hundred ever came out on the other side."

"Can you speculate for the audience what may have happened to them?" the interviewer asked.

"Well, I don't know. Maybe, the pyramid is a teleporter and they're no longer in our dimension. Where else could they be?"

* * *

Inside a military-style commando tent staked out on a grass-covered mountain plateau in the middle of an alternate world's Rockies, a walkie-talkie came to life on a makeshift desk of extra supply crates and a piece of plywood. "We just finished installing the false dead end to the portal cave," the weary voice of Neal Parsons announced.

Linda stopped fidgeting with her laptop and picked up the walkie-talkie. "Thanks, Neal. You come to see me when you get back to Sanctuary, you hear? I'm going over your list now and I agree we need to get the water purification system online, ASAP. We don't want five thousand people coming down with dysentery."

"Be there in an hour."

Thank God for Neal, she thought. He had proved invaluable these last few weeks. What an organizer. When Jeb first introduced his brother to her she took an immediate like to him. He had a determined face and intelligent eyes that showed he was the kind of man you could rely on to get things done. She returned to studying his report. She planned to tell him that she wanted him to personally take over the construction of the proposed sanitation facility. He might balk at the added responsibility, but there wasn't a more able-bodied man available.

At that moment the door to her tent flew open, and a soldier stepped in. She took off her reading glasses to see who would be so bold as to enter unannounced.

Before she could scold him for his rudeness, the man's appearance shifted from that of a common private into a being wearing a black robe with a hood that covered the face.

"What's the meaning of this?" she said to the stranger. She gasped when the intruder pulled back the hood to reveal a leathery, brown, reptilian face with a lipless grin. Linda became frightened. Another creature from her Vanwanung with Katrina just walked into reality. "Iaghi, is that you?" she said.

The Fengani priest grinned, exposing rows of sharp teeth. "No, I'm not Iaghi. Although our life span is several times longer than a human's, not even we Fengani can live that long. My name is Tau."

"I'm sure this isn't a social visit. Tau, what brings you to see me?"

"May I sit?" he asked ignoring her question.

"Absolutely."

As he sat down he pulled a softball-sized object out of his pocket and placed it on the desk beside her laptop.

"Do you know what this is?

She glanced at a round crystal-ball that looked like an ordinary piece of violet-tinted glass except it glowed with a soft sheen that seemed to emanate from the glass itself creating a soft violet aura around it. "No," she said after quickly rifling through her shared memories with Katrina.

"This is a type of memory crystal. Believe it or not, we possess the technology to record a person's memories and store them inside quartz crystals such as these. However, this memory crystal is very special, because it contains the living memories of the eternal one." He paused. "Think of it this way. It's tapped into the mind of universal consciousness. Using it, we can gain access to the memories of anyone, no matter whether they live in the past, or present just by thinking about them while attuned to it. Sometimes we can even catch visions of possible futures and tap into someone who may live in the future if the current timeline is continued unaltered. This is the only one of its kind. We call it the Eye of God."

This interested her. "Just how does it work?"

"Once we connect to it telepathically, I can access the memories of any individual as if they're my own, simply by thinking of that individual by name and visualizing them in my mind. At that moment, all the memories of their future life become mine."

Linda frowned. "So, you're saying the future is set? That our actions are scripted and free will is a myth?"

Tau grinned. "On the contrary, only the past is fixed. Seeing into the future is tricky. The farther into the future the murkier it becomes. Seeing into the far future is like trying to forecast the weather. The farther you project, the less certain the future you see becomes."

"This is all interesting, but what has this to do with me and why are you here? You're not here to harm me, are you?"

"No, since you do share Katrina's memories, you should know we would never intentionally harm an innocent soul, but… we do wish to tweak your memories so that you forget about the impending destruction of Sanctuary 2000 years from now. You realize, only with your permission, of course."

Tampering with people's memories, mind melds, aliens, she was getting very sick and tired of feeling like a helpless victim. *And now this?* Yeah right, go ahead and play with my mind? The idea of giving this overgrown lizard access to her head and her memories like she was a lab rat infuriated her. She gritted her teeth. "Won't that damage me?"

"No, because I will only extract your memory of the destruction of Sanctuary, and Katrina's teenage years of growing up on Earth without her parents, and lastly of my visit today. I will replace them with harmless fake memories."

She sighed. "What if I said no?"

"Then all will be in vain. The Ophidian empire under the leadership of their god Draka will consume the soul of the universe. That is the future that the Eye of God now shows with almost certainty."

So, they're using this Eye of God to manipulate the future. If that's what they see now, then… she was about to acquiesce and say yes when she had sudden insight that left her cold. "Wait a minute…just how long have you had that crystal?"

"Since just after the destruction of the council of watchers… millions of years ago."

"And just how long have you been manipulating humanity's future?" she said, her mind thinking once again like a trial lawyer cross-examining a hostile witness.

Tau stared at her. A heavy moment of silence filled the air. Finally, he sighed. "From the very beginning."

"You mean since the dawn of our civilization? Is that why the pyramids in Egypt look so much like these snake temples?"

He smiled. "Much longer I'm afraid… We built the pyramids, not the snakes, and you owe us your very existence. We took over and controlled your evolution millions of years ago. Most sentient creatures evolve on their home planets in close tandem with other intelligent species all in close competition. Yet no one on your world ever questioned your total dominance and vastly superior abilities over all other life forms, thinking it to be simple blind luck of fate. It's all hogwash. You dominate over all other life forms on this planet because we bred you that way. Your evolution from primates to the beings you are now was a direct result of our meddling. We have been at it for millions of years. In a sense, you could call us your parents."

Today was proving to be another of those crazy days that she kept having ever since she had met Katrina. "Why are you meddling with our evolution?"

"The Eye of God. It shows us what we must do to defeat Draka and his empire. All other options fail."

"So, why did you allow humans, whom you allegedly bred into existence for this great savior, encounter the snake empire, now, before we were ready? You could have stopped the mass killing of billions of people," Linda said, now angry.

This time Tau's face became unreadable and an uncomfortable silence permeated the air again. "Once again, you have to understand we were simply following the path shown to us by the Eye of God …. First-contact with the Ophidians was no accident….. …We arranged it to happen. Otherwise, Sanctuary would never be built and Katrina would never be born…."

She slammed her fist down hard on the table, and she said her first cuss word in many years. She thought of Chicago now gone. Neal had told her that he had received a signal while in the cave that the Ophidians had taken out Chicago earlier that morning. She still had many friends there who had refused her offer to come here. No word about the Sparks and Lisa either.

And now this damn oversized plucked chicken had just admitted that it had not only allowed, but it had arranged for almost ninety percent of the Earth's population to be destroyed. Which aliens were truly worse, the snakes or these damn Fengani? "You tell me all of this and you expect me to submit to you now?"

"Once again, the Eye of God has shown us how to proceed. Only the truth works with you."

"That's right!" she said, slamming her fist again. She remembered the words of the oath she had heard every day in the courtroom for the last thirty years. …The truth, the whole truth… These were words that she had built her whole life around. She studied this alien creature in front of her. She sensed the truth in his words. She knew when she was being lied to. All those years in the courtroom and an uncanny sixth sense had taught her that. Whatever else she may think of him and his vile kind, he was being candid. She pointed her finger at him. "You know we humans have an old saying that fits you. The road to hell is paved with good intentions." She paused to let that sink in. Despite him being an alien, she could read guilt and remorse on his face.

"So, if I don't allow you to play with my memories, this will all be in vain. And everyone here dies?"

"Yes, Sanctuary will be destroyed within the next hundred years. Knowledge of your impending destruction in the far future will encourage the inhabitants of Sanctuary to attack first, but before they are ready. You humans instinctively believe that the best defense is a good offense. However, the only being in the universe that will have the ability and power to defeat Draka will never be born."

"Katrina's that important?"

"We have pruned all of the possible futures the Eye of God showed to us millions of years ago down to her. We did this by simply choosing the most probable to succeed each time we encountered a fork in the timeline. Draka has become too powerful. It's too late in the game now to change strategies and look for another path. She's now everything. Without her, Draka wins. "Not just here, but everywhere. Do you know what happens each time Draka absorbs a soul?"

"He adds their consciousness to his?" Linda said, guessing.

"Exactly. You've heard of atomic theory and critical mass?"

"Of course."

"Well, consuming souls and consciousness works in a similar manner. Once Draka consumes enough souls his consciousness will reach a critical mass and he will become a living Eye of God, having the omniscience of a real god, but not the loving God in your bible, rather his nemesis.

She considered what he was telling her. The stakes were too high not to. She wanted to call the guards and have him bodily thrown out of camp, but it would serve no purpose except to make her feel better. He had been right. Only the truth worked with her. She thought fast and hard. "Ok, I'll let you do this, but I want you to promise me to stop manipulating people's lives and begin showing more compassion…."

* * *

Neal walked quickly through the maze of tents. Linda's tent was just up ahead. As he walked he mentally reviewed the lists of supplies he had given her. He thought that was why she wanted to see him. Just before he entered her tent, a private with a nondescript face stepped out and passed him without making eye contact.

"Who was that guy?" he asked Linda after he had stepped inside. He thought he knew everyone by face, but his face was unfamiliar. Funny though, the more he thought about him the less he could recall any distinguishing characteristics.

"Who, dear?"

"Why, that private that just left."

Linda made a blank look as if she was having trouble remembering. "Oh him, it was nothing important, but I'm glad you're here." She motioned him to sit down.

By the time he sat down, the soldier that had just left was completely forgotten.

After he finished making himself comfortable, Linda said, "Neal, I want you to take over the sanitation project."

Neal just looked at her. There was so much to do. He had no idea how he would be able to handle all the added responsibility she kept handing him, but instead of trying to come up with excuses or find fault with her giving him more, his problem solving, and can-do intellect already began working on solutions....

TWENTY-FOUR

Through the port window of her shuttle seat, Katrina's eyes examined acres and acres of blacktop interspersed here and there with large hanger buildings for various types of aircraft. She concluded the airport looked very similar to the landing terminal for the space elevator in Ecuador. Nothing to indicate that she was about to land on an alternate Venus that had a moon and wasn't an inferno.

She heard laughter across the aisle. Jan and Anthony held hands, totally immersed in each other. She was happy for them; they were both obviously in love.

Her own love, Jeb, was upfront with Iaghi, going over strategies and brainstorming a plan on how to rescue her dad. Iaghi seemed most impressed with him. Linda had been right. He was the best at what he did.

She hoped that Linda and Lisa had made it safely to Sanctuary. Yet she felt a heavy sadness knowing that she would never see them again, for surely they would be long dead now. She worried that something may have happened to Linda, for after their Vanwanung, she knew exactly how and when Sanctuary would someday be destroyed; wouldn't she have tried to change the future or at least send a warning? If she ever made it back to Sanctuary she planned on searching through the archives and discovering what had happened to them.

Her thoughts returned to her dad. She remembered his gentle nature and the unending patience he had always shown with her and Anthony. He had always encouraged them to think and ask questions, "observe and learn," had been his motto. She missed him so much.

She wanted to go to prison at once and pay him a long overdue visit. However, Jeb and Iaghi both strongly discouraged this and said that would not be wise. They also advised her not to seek out her mother unless she wanted to find herself in the same predicament as her dad.

"Katrina, please be patient for just a little while longer. You'll see him soon. I promise. Jeb and I are working on a plan to rescue him, and I have a dedicated telepathic team working on restoring your mother's memories. It's just taking a little more time than we expected with her. She has a very strong mind and a determined constitution; she's stubborn." He smiled. "Kind of like someone else I know. But my good friend, Dr. Humli, says his team is making remarkable progress. Her unconscious mind truly believes that you and Anthony were both killed during the attack on Sanctuary, and it's this part of her that is fighting us. It doesn't want her to remember."

Two seats in front of her, the ingenious hacker Maureen sat glued to her holo-laptop, studying technical material prepared for her by Xelana, who sat beside her. They had become fast friends after he had designed and built a new power supply converter so she could recharge her holo-laptop from any modern power receptacle. They rambled on endlessly together in technical jargon that everyone else around them barely understood. Katrina remembered when she asked Maureen if she liked living two thousand years in the future, she said, "Thank you so much! This is the best thing that ever happened to me."

Even the kidnapped receptionist from the teleporter had managed to find a place. After the initial shock at discovering that

178

everyone and everything she ever loved was long dead, she decided since she must start a whole new life somewhere, she would go into the wilderness with the other newly released slaves.

A large jolt rattled Katrina's teeth together signifying that they were on the ground. She sighed; she had discovered that she didn't really enjoy flying. Perhaps, there were some things best left to birds and other such creatures that could fly on their own volition. Outside the shuttle, the hot, midday sun almost blinded her even with dark sunglasses on to protect her eyes from the strong ultraviolet rays that were stronger one planet closer to the sun. She pulled up the gray hood of the laity robe she wore as a disguise and as a precautionary measure to protect herself from sunburn.

They boarded several carrier wagons. "We don't use mechanized vehicles for travel inside our cities. We encourage exercise and living near our work," Iaghi advised them. The streets were full of Fengani and a small spattering of other races walking hurriedly to and fro.

Their destination, the great white temple of Raghu, looked eerily like how the ancient pyramids in Egypt once looked before their outer limestone had been removed. Inside the wagon, Katrina turned to Jan and asked, "What is the importance and significance of this temple of theirs?"

"The Great Temple of Ragdu is at the very heart and center of our religion. The ancient legends say that this temple is built on the very spot where the ancient one, a dying watcher, first revealed himself to Ragdu, the founder of *The Way,* and entrusted him with the Eye of God, our most sacred object."

At the two-story doorway into the temple, they were met and escorted inside by a dozen master priests all wearing their distinctive indigo blue robes.

The walls of the stone cobbled hallway were covered with hieroglyph pictograms interspersed with large clear quartz crystals, in regular intervals, in the walls. "These clear crystals are memory crystals, aren't they?" Katrina said to Jan.

Jan smiled. "Yes, each crystal contains short key memories of Ragdu. They're lessons and instructions on living according to The Way. Rather than using books, Ragdu recorded his actual memories. They work just like the memory crystal you used to access your father's memories. At the center of this pyramid, there is the holy of holies that contains the most sacred memory crystal of all, the Eye of God."

"Why is the Eye of God so special?" Katrina asked.

"When you connect your mind to it, you link directly with the very "I Am" presence of the universe. The past, present, and future become one to you. It contains the living memory and thoughts of everything that has lived, is alive and will live."

Katrina's face lit up. "Can I see that?"

"I'm afraid not. Only the high priests, the masters, and the grandmaster are allowed inside the holy sanctuary. For all non-believers, lay people, and acolytes like me that room is off limits." She paused. "We are taught that it's for our protection. For the untrained mind, attempting to connect to the mind of the Eye of God would drive you permanently insane."

They soon entered a large auditorium. Inside there were several hundreds of Fengani, several dozen humans and a smaller mixing of other alien races. Several large Stanchions, looking like giants compared to the others stood in the back, too large to fit in the chairs provided.

Katrina and her group took seats up front while Iaghi walked on to a large dais with a podium in the center of the room. He waited until everyone seemed settled in their seats and fully acquainted with their neighbors. Then he blew into a long twisted Orshank horn that produced a deep rumbling grunt that reverberated throughout the room.

Everyone focused on him and became quiet. "We are all here today to plan and discuss the rescue of our dear friend, General Kyle. Now, I've been working the last several days on a plan with a human named Jeb Parsons, who comes to us from the Earth's past, a time just before it was attacked and conquered by the Ophidian Empire. But please don't think of him as backward, because you would be very mistaken. He has extensive training and experience as part of a special tactical strike and rescue team for hostages held by superior forces behind enemy lines."

Iaghi paused to let what he had just said to sink in. "Unlike most of the military personnel here today, who are used to thinking in terms of moving and wielding superior forces and numbers in the field. Jeb, would you please step up here and briefly explain your plan?"

Jeb reached over and gave Katrina's hand a quick squeeze. They made brief eye contact, and then he walked carefully up to the podium. "A small, highly trained strike and rescue team will have the best chance at success rather than a large frontal assault. Stealth and quickness will be our best weapon…"

❋ ❋ ❋

After the meeting, while Jeb was busy answering questions, Katrina and many of the others left and headed for Iaghi's private study. There would be no time for her and Jeb to relax and spend some much-wanted down time together with no worries or deadlines. Her dad's execution was only two weeks away, and they had to begin training tonight. Katrina secretly had her doubts any kind of rescue was even

181

possible, but what other option did they have? A direct assault on the prison and Mega-Corp would begin systematically killing prisoners. They could be coldly efficient when it was necessary for them.

Once in the chambers, Katrina found an empty chair and sat down. She was exhausted; too much had happened to her in the past several months. Everyone was just comfortable when the study door opened and a Fengani wearing a blue robe of a master came in. He walked directly up to Iaghi, and they exchanged greetings. Katrina couldn't tell what they were saying as they spoke to each other in their guttural native tongue.

They then walked over to Katrina. Iaghi seemed very pleased, as he wore that funky grin that to humans looked more like a threat. "Katrina, this is Dr. Humli; he's the man that I assigned to work with your mother to restore her memories, and he says he's making excellent progress."

"Yes, I believe we have made a significant breakthrough. We've managed to siphon from her psyche weak copies of some of her lost memories. Memories are holographic. Even though the Ophidians thought they had erased all traces of her past, our psychic science has managed to locate traces of latent memories still stored at a deep subconscious level. We've now externally copied hundreds of these memory bites and we are working on restoring and enhancing them for later reintroduction into her conscious psyche. This should initiate a rapid and complete Recall of her former self."

"Excellent," Katrina said.

Dr. Humli's face darkened. "Yes, but please be aware there is a real danger. She will not like the person she has become or many of the things she has done working for the empire. The truth may destroy her."

TWENTY-FIVE

Rocky, hilly, and lifeless terrain continued without a break into the far horizon, a real no man's land. A walk on this worn out trail would be rough going for someone healthy, but for a woman about to give birth, it was proving impossible.

"My water just broke," Emily said. *The spreading dark stain down on her khaki pants confirmed this. She shuddered; the baby was coming now at the worst possible time.*

"We can't stop now! We have to go on. They're not far behind," Kyle said.

Emily wiped tears from her eyes. "Go! Leave me." Her face filled with pain. "…Just go!"

Kyle wiped his own eyes. "Not without you. I don't want to live without you."

"Go… They won't kill me. I'm young and pretty; I'm too valuable. They'll want me for the sex trade. They probably won't even harm the baby. They'll use it to control me…." She doubled over with another contraction.

At first, she insisted on walking unassisted, but soon she began to lean heavily on Kyle, who soon was practically carrying her. After more than two hours of hobbling along, they had managed to go at most maybe a half a mile. Between ever-increasing contractions, Emily continued begging Kyle to leave her and go on alone. But Kyle steadfastly refused and assured her that there was a village not far ahead and when they reached it, they would be safe.

Emily's next labor pain was so great that she lost all sense of who she was and where she was at. She said through gritted teeth, "Kyle... please...stop..."

Kyle set Emily gently on the hard ground. She reached out and clutched his hand. She squeezed so tight that their fingers turned white. When Kyle checked his watch, she managed to gasp, "How long?"

"They're less than a minute apart now."

When the next contraction began, a frantic Emily began to unbutton her pants, "Kyle... this baby is coming now. I feel the urge to push. Help me"

Kyle pulled her pants down, but instead of taking her boots off, he used his sharp knife to make slits up the legs of her pants so that they slipped off easily over her heavy hiking boots.

"I can see hair. The baby's already in position to come out," Kyle said peering between her legs. He encouraged her to push. The head popped out. He reached down and nuzzled his clumsy fingers under the baby's armpits still inside Emily, and ....

Kyle wrapped the baby in the remnants of Emily's work pants and gave Emily the baby to hold while Kyle severed the umbilical cord and tied a knot.

An elated Emily watched as the beautiful baby face of Katrina smiled at her. She returned the smile. At that moment, a squad of human slavers rushed in. Kyle jumped up, ready to defend his new family to the death, but before he could get out his pistol, one of the slavers from behind clubbed him....

Several large and dirty men dressed in rags and animal skins surrounded her. They seemed disappointed. They had been hoping to have some fun, but none of them were interested in a woman who had just given birth. But what she had told Kyle was true; they didn't try to harm her or the baby in any way. She was a very young and beautiful woman, and her beauty would bring them a small fortune. And for now, it would buy her and the baby safety among these ruffians.

When a man kicked Kyle, he came to and tried to jump up again, but this time he was stopped by a heavy noose wrapped around his neck. It was attached to a long pole, and the slaver that kicked him laughed, exposing a mouth with only half of its teeth. "You can't escape, slave."

When several ruffians escorted Kyle away in a different direction he tried to lunge again at the man with missing teeth, but he just pulled on the stick, tightening the noose and cutting off his air supply.

"He's not worth the trouble," the one that seemed to be their leader said as he pulled out a pistol.

Emily cried out, "Oh… please noooo…," as a warning red dot raced up across Kyle's chest until it settled in on the middle of his forehead and…

Emily woke up covered in sweat. The nightmares they kept getting worse and more vivid. They were almost every night now.

Where did she ever come up with the name Katrina for a baby? The mention of that name unsettled her. *Why?* Funny, she didn't remember ever having any children… but it would explain the many faint, spider-like stretch marks across her abdomen. She had always meant to ask a doctor, but never thought it mattered… or … was she afraid? Something in the back of her head had warned her not to.

For a moment, she entertained a sense of doubt, but she quickly remembered who she was, a high executive in the Ophidian military intelligence. High executives didn't have the convenience to entertain doubt.

Emily's tired thoughts returned to Kyle. What a nasty trick of fate. Why is it that the one man in the universe that she falls in love with turns out to be a traitor and a rebel? She knew she should hate him, but she couldn't get his handsome face out of her mind. He had become practically an obsession. *Why did I allow this to happen to me?*

Emily tried going back to sleep, but Faraday's raucous snoring kept her awake. Disgusted, she sighed and pulled herself out of bed. He was really beginning to play on her nerves. Why did she ever accept moving in with him in the first place? *To get back at Kyle?* Thank the eternal one, he was scheduled to leave in two days for headquarters and it just couldn't happen fast enough. Every night it was the same ritual. He'd stay up late with his goonish friends drinking and partying until the wee hours of the morning.

Afterward, he'd crawl into bed, smelling heavily of beer and whiskey and soon that horrible snoring would begin.

He certainly had a self-inflated opinion of himself; he drank too much and said all the wrong things. The man had no sense of imagination or adventure and having a conversation about anything that didn't center on him was not going to happen. What a selfish, mindless clout. And a romantic evening? Forget it. His idea of a special evening was beer and pizza during happy hour. She planned on telling Faraday that she was moving out as soon as they had some time alone together.

His goon buddies bothered her too. Especially the young Ophidian, Xletru. He gave her the creeps. He took special delight in tearing innocent people's minds apart until their intellect was if they survived the ordeal, reduced to the level of a small child's.

She checked the security system to check for messages when she discovered that Faraday was still logged in. She was about to log him out when she realized that he had just given her a wonderful opportunity. There might be something in here that she could use against him in case he tried to renege on that big promised promotion after he finds out she was walking out on him.

But when she opened his personal files, she discovered a folder with her name on it. Hmmm…what? Spying on me? She thought. The folder contained hundreds of files; she opened the first and began reading. An hour later, she read the final file. It was all here, everything. So, the life she was now living was a lie. Everything she thought she knew to be true about herself had been planted in her. *Kyle really is my husband.* And I have two children, Katrina and Anthony, who are the two

186

most wanted people on Earth. Funny, she had no memory… but something deep inside her told her this was true.

She wiped her eyes and closed the file. *So, that SOB knew who I really was from the beginning.* No words could describe the deep hatred that brewed in her mind at this moment. She wanted to go back inside the bedroom with a butcher knife and stab him where he slept. Killing him now would be too easy. She'd deal with Faraday later… Her head hurt. Faraday's snoring was changing pitch. He would wake soon. She needed time to work things out and she didn't want to be here when he woke. *Kyle, please forgive me…*

She left the hotel and walked through the bustling morning streets of Hoshama. She had no destination in mind. She walked around in deep thought trying to grasp the gravity of what she had just learned about herself.

Denial and disbelief of this new revelation were strong. If what she had just read was all true, then why didn't she have a single memory to support it? After an hour of self-interrogation, she found herself in front of the Hoshama library. On a whim, she decided to go in and have a look around. Her mind needed a break. Just before she walked through the front door, she remembered at the last minute to perform the Fengani appeasement ritual before entering.

A Fengani with very green complexion, marking her as a fertile female, sat at a desk facing the door. She looked up from a yellowed scroll that she had spread out on her desk and smiled with that disturbing toothy grin and the lipless smile that all Fengani had and introduced herself as Satira, the local librarian. She wore the familiar gray robe, the mark of the laity in *The Way*. Emily had a strange notion that Satira had been expecting her. *Absurd.*

"I'm pleased that you remembered to give homage to the soul of this building before entering. It's always a relief to meet non-believing foreigners that are willing to show respect for our culture."

"Feel free to browse and help yourself to any of the books in the shelves. The bookcase by the window contains a small collection of books from your Earth. Just be careful with them, they're very, very old and very valuable."

"Of course," Emily said smiling.

The room was stuffed with memorabilia and art collections from many cultures and races. All the walls had built-in bookcases and every row was stuffed with books. She took a deep breath and inhaled the delicious smell of a room full of books.

She discovered she liked the feeling of standing in a room that smelled of old books and filled with antiquities. She felt at home here. *Why? Maybe she should quit the bureau and take up being a simple librarian.*

She walked deeper into the room towards the window. A blue quartz crystal that sat on a table just before the earth collection caught her eye. It was egg shaped and translucent. She had a sudden urge to pick it up. She hesitated. The Fengani sciences and their religion had something to do with quartz crystals. The rumors she'd heard suggested that the Fengani knew how to store people's memories and possibly even imprison one's very soul inside these harmless crystals. She dismissed her doubts as superstitious nonsense and picked it up. It felt like holding an ice cube in the palm of her hand. But when she squeezed it, she felt a sudden jolt like she'd just grabbed a bare live wire...

... *What just happened?* The librarian, Satira, was staring at her from her desk. She had the unnerving sense that a fair amount of time had passed since she had picked up the crystal. *How long?* She put the crystal back on the table and walked over to the shelf by the window.

There was a sign above the bookcase and it was written in modern Universal.

It read a collective history of Earth's culture. Upon closer inspection, she saw that the books themselves were written in many different languages. These books were ancient and all originals she suddenly realized. Most of the title covers she couldn't read, but there was one in archaic English, and it read the complete works of William Shakespeare. She pulled this one out and opened it at random and read the title at the top of the page, *Anthony and Cleopatra*. Wait, how can I read archaic English, how did I even know that this is archaic English? She had to fight to keep from trembling. On the verge of a panic attack, she was just about ready to bolt for the door when she became aware of the most pleasant fragrance lingering in the air.

It was the strong smell of roses. She quickly located the source. There beside the bookcase and directly in front of the window were several pots of exotic lavender roses in full bloom. "Oh, I haven't seen this variety since just before the inv... *When had she seen this variety?* For a brief second, there had been a real memory at the tip of her consciousness. It had something to do with Lavender roses and Kyle. But when she tried to focus on it, it had vanished.

Frustrated that this memory had eluded her, she pulled out another book in archaic English. She opened it at random and read, "The book of Job." Another memory came to her consciousness. This time instead of trying to grab it; she let it play in her mind...she remembered... *sitting at a desk reading this title on a computer screen in another library... she was trying to decide if this story was worth making into a hard copy... when the evacuation alarm went off...*She dropped the book and the noise of it landing on the floor startled her.

Flustered she said, "I'm sorry, but I'm not feeling well... I'll come back again...," and without waiting for a response headed quickly for the door.

TWENTY-SIX

After running out of the library, she began to remember. Bits and pieces of foreign memories kept flashing through her mind. She held her throbbing head in her hands. It was like a dam bursting and it was happening all too fast.

She recalled different parents and relived their deaths during a slave raid on their scientific camp and the abandonment and cowardice of her sister Harriet during that raid. She re-experienced her capture and her emancipation by a group of Earth rebels lead by Kyle. The first time she glimpsed at Kyle through the iron bars of her slave wagon, the births of their children, the attack on Sanctuary and its destruction... Her resurrected self didn't like or approve of who she had become.... Her head seemed like it was about to explode. She so wanted it to just stop. She believed she was on the verge of losing her sanity.

She began walking through the congested streets of Hoshama reliving her true past as if everything had just happened to her all over again. When she found herself standing in front of the Yingzutan restaurant, she dipped her fingers into the ceremonial ashes and said, "*Noyami*".

Once inside, the Fengani waiter, without speaking, escorted her through the restaurant and outside to the picturesque veranda and seated her at the very table where Kyle had first taken her. She ordered a

Sangria and sat sipping it while she relived every precious moment of that day with Kyle.

They certainly must have been meant for each other. To fall in love twice in one lifetime with the same person, how often did that happen, she wondered? She wasn't normally a drinker, she liked being in control, but today, she made an exception. Several hours later and way too many Sangria's later, she decided to go home to her old apartment. The waiter when he saw her staggering up to leave called a carrier for her.

The carrier was a small coach wagon on two wheels that connected to a bicycle powered by a young alien creature. It had bird-like face and mannerisms with powerful thick crocodilian legs and a naked, seven-foot body wrapped in black leathery skin instead of feathers.

On the way home, the bouncy ride in the runner's wagon proved too much for her and she had to have the driver stop while she emptied her stomach. Once home, she fumbled with the key to the door to her apartment for several minutes until she managed to get it in the lock.

TWENTY-SEVEN

Wide-awake, Kyle got out of his dirty cot and began pacing in the dim cell-light to kill time. He walked in a tight circle inside his tiny four by six-foot room. Alone, in solitary confinement, he had nothing but his thoughts for entertainment. He began to doubt himself and the decisions that brought him before a terrible fate.

Kyle coughed up phlegm. The musty smell of damp concrete attacked his nostrils. In the time that he'd been down in this underground hole, between the cold dampness and the tiny, once-daily portions of colorless, tasteless gruel the heartless guards served, his health was beginning to fail. It would be poetic justice if he came down with pneumonia and died before the authorities could have their way with him.

He had to grab his pants while he walked to keep them from falling. His belt needed more notches, but there was nothing available to do it with.

"Oh, Emily!" Kyle pined. He just couldn't accept she felt nothing for him. Her eyes gave her away; they glowed whenever she had looked at him. Kyle stopped pacing. His broken heart ached. If only she had remembered…. Filled with dejection and despair, he just wanted to get the execution over with. A life without Emily in it didn't seem worth living.

He recalled the utter confusion on Emily's face at his speedy mock trial when he told her that she was, in fact, his wife. None of those fond memories of her wonderful childhood or her loving parents were real…. And that the life she was living now was a complete lie.

A noise, what was that? He stopped pacing to listen. His bowl of gruel lay untouched by the hole through the door. He picked it up. It felt warm. He guessed the guard must have delivered it not more than an hour ago.

Was today his big day? Buried deep in this underground concrete dungeon without his watch, he had no idea what day it was. He never saw the sun, and the weak bulb that dangled in midair overhead was always on.

He heard footsteps followed by the rattling of keys, and the door swung inwards. Flashlights blazed into his face blinding him with their brilliant lights.

"Someone's here at the base and they want to question you. We'll be taking you there," the callous voice of the lead guard, a big and burly man, rang out. He toyed with a Billy club in his hand like he was itching to use it. "Don't you try anything funny, or you'll wish you hadn't. Get on the bed and lie on your stomach with your hands over your head."

The metallic clicks of a dozen pistols cocked simultaneously, no doubt aimed at him, were the next sounds he heard. Kyle complied. They attached chains to his wrists and ankles.

When they finished, the guard who spoke earlier said, "Now get up and come out slowly."

The wary guards escorted him out, and they headed up concrete stairs. The chains on his legs seemed like they were made from lead. In his emaciated state, he found himself tiring easily; it seemed to take forever to reach the top.

By the time he reached the surface, he was panting heavily and the bright sun, his eyes accustomed to his dim cell light, caused him to squint so hard he couldn't see.

As his daylight sight returned and he could make out the sign of the Ophidian Empire, a large indigo-blue circle, against a ruby-red background blazoned the side of the pyramid-shaped building they walked towards.

They entered a door, and he stepped into a large modern conference room. At one end of an oval conference table sat Emily, just as lovely as ever. His heart skipped, and he had trouble breathing as if he had asthma and had just breathed in contaminated air.

She looked at the guards and screwed up her face as if she was looking at a mass of cockroaches and said, "Leave us."

Kyle stood there and just stared.

"Come sit down," Emily said smiling, pointing to a chair beside her.

Kyle remained stone-faced but complied and sat across from her. A variety of breakfast foods laid spread out on the table. There were scrambled eggs, toast, home fries, and even a glass pitcher of orange juice. A full glass urn of hot coffee sat within arm's reach of Emily. She sipped from her mug and her face lit up in that familiar way. *She always did love coffee.*

Emily then filled up a plate with eggs and home fries and placed it before him. Hot, delicious, breakfast aromas wafted his nose and his empty stomach churned in response. He picked up a fork and began eating with gusto. After finishing his plate, the best food he'd tasted in weeks, his senses returned. "Aren't you going to have any of this delicious food?"

"No, my stomach's still a little queasy from the food and drink I had last night." She paused. "But the coffee's staying down just fine."

"I don't understand. Is today my big day?"

"No, your execution is two days away," Emily said. She got up from her chair, came over to Kyle, and put her hand on his arm. "But that's not going to happen if I can help it."

Kyle looked at her. He saw recognition and tears in her eyes. "What are you saying?"

"I remember… everything… who I truly am…who we are…and Katrina and Anthony…it all happened yesterday." "I'm so sorry…Will you ever be able to forgive me? I kind of made a mess of things, didn't I?"

"This isn't your fault… If anyone's to blame, it's those SOB's at Mega-Corp that toyed with our memories."

Before he knew what was happening he found himself holding and kissing Emily, his body no longer interested in food.

Finally, they came up for air. "I'm getting you out of here," Emily said.

Kyle's heart dropped. "No, Emily, you'll just get yourself killed too. Please… just go. I can arrange it so the resistance will contact you. In your privileged position within Internal Affairs, you could become invaluable to our cause."

Emily's eyes hardened. "But you don't understand. I don't want to live a life without you in it, I'd rather be dead," she said, pulling herself away.

There it was. That same fiery determination that he saw the first time he met her. He smiled inside. *She's Back!* This was the Emily that he'd fallen in love with so many years ago. "OK, so when do we leave?" he said, knowing that it was pointless to argue with her when she had her mind made up.

Emily's eyes ran up and down Kyle's emaciated body. "As soon as you're done eating, and you need to eat as much as you can. I can't guarantee when or where we'll have a decent meal again anytime soon."

Two more fast plates later, they left. Outside, she had the prison guards who had been waiting for them outside escort them to a helicopter parked in the front lawn of the building that they had just come out of. When they reached the copter, several men, members of her personal security team, gathered around Kyle who walked like an old and feeble man with his arms and legs still in chains.

Her superior rank meant none of the prison guards dared try to stop her or question her intentions, but Kyle saw the confusion on their faces when Emily told them they were dismissed. Surely, they would be alerting their superiors as soon as they left. He mentally prepared for the worst, just in case. He didn't know how much assistance he could provide if things melted into a firefight, but he reached down deep inside and called up his last inner reserve. It worked, for he felt stronger, surer of himself. His chains seemed lighter.

The copter took off and after they were in the air, she produced a key and removed his wrist and ankle chains. Kyle rubbed his wrists. The chains had been tight, and it felt good to feel the blood flowing freely through his hands and fingers.

They landed at Hoshama's airport, and she ordered her men to take off again. She handed him a travel bag. "There's an electric razor, soap and a change of clothes inside. Do you know any place we can hole up long enough for you to clean up and lay low?" She said making a face and holding her nose.

He laughed. He did feel ripe. "Do you have a destination in mind?"

"Not really, and there is no elaborate escape plan. There was simply no time to make one and to be honest, I didn't really expect to get this far. If you were going to die, I wanted us both to go out in a blaze of glory. Suddenly, the most important thing I had yet to do in this life is to boldly show you that I know who I am and that I still love you." She smiled. "Did it work?"

Kyle Smiled. "Absolutely! And I know a place. Let's go."

Outside the airport, Kyle waived down a carrier wagon, and after speaking to the driver quickly in Fengani, they boarded and headed away from the airport. They traveled for almost half an hour and finally stopped in front of an old warehouse building.

"Come on let's get inside. There's no one here. It's a mothballed storage facility and it's unguarded."

Inside, Kyle pulled a flashlight out of a fixture mounted to the wall. The flashlight revealed row after row of neatly stacked empty military pallets. Kyle walked down an aisle to the back of the warehouse to a small enclosed office area.

He opened the office door and turned on a light. "Hopefully, the water is still on. There's a small shower in the restroom." He walked across the front conference room and around the large conference table and entered a short hallway on the other side until he stood in front of a door marked restroom. "I'll be out in ten minutes."

Kyle removed the rags that he'd worn the last several weeks after he turned on the shower. The desire to feel clean again was overwhelming, and with hot water flowing freely, he attacked his dirty body with fresh smelling soap with gusto. If he had the time he would have loved to soak in a hot bath for at least an hour, but this was the next best thing.

Ten minutes later, and on schedule, he came out of the bathroom fully dressed in fresh clothes with his hair-dripping wet running a cordless electric razor through his weeks-old beard. He stopped at once.

Emily sat bound and gagged in a chair. He dropped the razor, and on instinct, his hands flew to his sides. *Damn, I'm unarmed.*

Two large men with handguns drawn and a young Ophidian, maybe fifteen feet in length, emerged out of the shadows. The Young Ophidian slithered in front of the men.

"Please have a seat. Mr. Armstrong," the Ophidian said telepathically. Kyle obeyed and while one of the goons tied him up, the other removed Emily's gag.

When Emily's gag came out she said, "Xletru, What the hell are you doing here? Release us at once. I'm taking this prisoner over to internal affairs. He's offered to cooperate and provide names and locations of the enemy's whereabouts. You have no right to hold us."

"Really? You know next time you start snooping around in someone else's files; you should make sure no one else is in the room.

Emily made a funny face. "Yes, last night when you got up you failed to check the couch. I was sleeping on it." Emily turned white. "Yes, you woke me when you began typing. You were so absorbed in what you were reading, I was able to tap into your mind without you detecting me, just enough, to telepathically see what you were reading." His forked tongue began darting in and out of his mouth rapidly. "And I must say that was an interesting read. I was most curious to see what you would do with this astounding revelation about your past, so I followed you. In fact, I've been following you, or people secretly working for me have been following you at a distance ever since."

The Ophidian turned to Kyle. "Allow me to introduce myself, my name's Xletru. Emily and I have been best friends for a long time."

"Cut the crap, you're no friend of mine. Just get to the point. What the hell do you want?" Emily said.

Xletru pretended shock. "Why: to do my job, ferret out traitors."

"What I told you is the truth. Kyle is willing to share vital information on the rebellion. Cut us loose."

The table made a sharp crack when Xletru slammed his tail down hard on the table and he stopped flicking his tongue. "You should have allowed me to extract that information from him in the beginning when he was first arrested."

"You know it was a military court Marshall and we had no jurisdiction in their internal affairs. His superiors decided against it."

Xletru sneered. "They were cowards and afraid that their own incompetent mind control experiment might be exposed."

Emily's eyes hardened. "Regardless, you have no authority to hold us. Let us go."

"Not until I learn everything he knows about the rebellion." Xletru began flicking his forked tongue again. "And when I'm through with him, I'll know him better than he knows his own self. Xletru paused then stared hard at Emily with predatory eyes. "But first, I think I'll sift through your mind. You don't know how long I've wanted to see just how much it'll take to make you crack. You, humans, have a saying that goes, 'you should always save your dessert for last.' But, I'll make an exception in your case."

A presence. Emily felt her outer thoughts being probed. Then without any warning, Xletru attacked and tried to ram his presence inside her head. With all her might, she wretched against her bonds and tried to pull away. The thought of sharing her intimate consciousness with that abomination terrified her. Helpless, with nowhere to run, she did the only thing she could. She screamed.

TWENTY-EIGHT

After Iaghi placed Jeb in charge of the rescue mission, Jeb carefully considered the potential candidates for the strike team. He decided to go with the team that he already had with just a few new additions. He chose Iaghi, Katrina, her brother Anthony, his girlfriend Jan, Maureen, and her new best friend Xelana, and finally Bernie Paxton and Ed Bruce.

He pushed the rescue team hard. They trained in an abandoned military compound located in the wooded wilderness many miles outside of Hoshama that Iaghi said was very similar to the compound where the Ophidian army had Kyle detained.

In the early hours of the morning two days before Kyle's scheduled public execution, they loaded their gear into four carrier wagons. Each wagon was hitched to a paired team of elephant-sized beasts. Each beast stood upon four man-sized chicken legs supporting a reptilian body connected to a bird-like head with a basketball-sized beak. They had long, leathery whip-like tails that constantly flicked their alligator skin to drive off insects.

On a cue from Iaghi they departed. They traveled at a walking pace and arrived at the outskirts of Hoshama about three hours later and stopped at an old abandoned storage building to make their final preparations.

They went inside and ate lunch at a broken cafeteria table and drank coffee while listening to Iaghi and Jeb go over the plan one last time when Katrina exclaimed "Oh my…! Anthony! Quick!" She held out her hand to him and when their hands met, they both collapsed and passed out.

Jeb caught Katrina who was sitting to his right before she slid out of her chair and fell to the floor. Anthony collapsed forward with his head making a thud when it hit the table. Katrina's pendant stone began pulsing bright blue flashes like a heartbeat.

Iaghi took command at once, and he had them both placed on the table. He placed his hands on their foreheads. His face clouded over, and he went into a trance.

After a minute or so, he began chanting in that strange guttural native language of the Fengani. Xelana, who stood nearby, seemed alarmed and quickly pulled out a small phone where he barked several quick orders in Fengani and hung up.

"What's going on?" Jeb asked Xelana.

Xelana studied him with a grim face as if choosing his words carefully. "Remember that the pendant that Katrina wears makes her a very powerful telepath. She just heard her mother's soul telepathically cry out in frantic desperation for help. An Ophidian with immense telepathic abilities is, at this moment, is trying to forcibly penetrate her mind. She and Anthony have formed an emergency Vanwanung to reach and help her. Iaghi has joined the Vanwanung to make it even more powerful, and now I must go too." He stopped talking, placed his hands on top of Iaghi's and went into a trance.

Jeb turned to Jan for answers. She looked at him, and she saw the confusion on his face.

"A Vanwanung is a temporary joining of their individual consciousness to create a more powerful being with a higher state of consciousness. The more minds joined, the stronger it becomes. Hopefully, it will have sufficient strength to protect their mother from her attacker. But it is very dangerous to do this. This consciousness that they're creating won't have the identity of Iaghi, or Xelana, or Katrina, or Anthony. It will be a new being with a sense of its own consciousness and a will of its own and therein lays the danger. It may decide not to help Emily at all, or it may help her but decide not to disband when it's no longer needed, which it would perceive as its death."

At that minute, Dr. Humli and his assistant, Satira, the young female Fengani receptionist, entered the briefing room. He went immediately over to the table and placed his hands over Xelana's.

Satira stood back and held her three-fingered hand palm out and entered a trance.

With her eyes closed, she said, "I will remain outside of the Vanwanung."

Jeb didn't like any of this. This was all new territory. He would have preferred a direct fight, not all this telepathic stuff. Everyone in the room was tense. They had just prepared to go into harm's way and now this just put a whole new twist on everything.

Suddenly, Satira came out of her trance and headed at a fast pace towards the door. "Quick, grab your weapons and follow me. We must hurry. I know where they're being held, and it's less than a fifteen-minute walk from here."

"Maureen, you stay here and keep an eye on things. Everyone else, follow me," Jeb said.

When the Vanwanung first became conscious, it delighted in being alive. Its first formed thought was, "Who am I?" It reflected and discovered it possessed the memories from each of the lesser beings that had joined their minds to create it; in a metaphysical second, it learned it was created for a specific purpose. For a brief instant, it entertained the notion of discarding its intended purpose and living for itself, but it quickly discarded this idea for the creature had also inherited from those lesser beings their same deep inner-sense of duty.

It expanded its awareness outward across the telepathic realm and soon located the glowing good-soul of Emily and the dark-soul attacking it.

Emily had managed to create a rudimentary shield made of her strong will that offered a temporary barrier keeping the dark-soul from gaining control of her being, but the dark creature was relentless in its lust to force his will upon her. It rammed itself into this shield relentlessly. Cracks were developing in Emily's shield and it would soon fail.

The dark soul was so preoccupied with attacking Emily that it failed to notice the creature's approach.

The creature lashed out at the unsuspecting dark-soul with psionic limbs shaped like claws, ripping and tearing at its essence.

The dark-soul turned then to defend itself. This gave Emily the necessary seconds to restore her shield and then she joined feverishly in the counterattack.

The dark-soul, sensing danger, tried to withdraw. But Emily and the creature pursued it on the psychic plane and they continued with assault after assault until the dark-soul mortally wounded turned and made a vicious last stand...

The Vanwanung seeing that Emily was now safe and its mission was successfully completed, sadly willed its existence to cease...

Xletru fell to the floor. His cold, dead eyes stared vacantly into space, misting over even as Kyle watched. Emily sat unconscious in her chair with her head bowed down. Kyle breathed a sigh of relief for he could make out the slow rise and fall of her chest indicating her body still held life.

One of the human thugs gave Xletru's body a rough kick and jumped back in fear. A surprised look came over his face. "He's dead," he said aloud. "How did you do that? You bitch. I've had enough of you." He pulled his pistol.

The thug next to him grabbed his arm. "What are you doing? Do you know what the boss will do to us if you kill her?"

He scratched his head. "So what? She's a powerful witch! She just killed him, using only her mind. Until her, no one's even been able to resist him."

"So, we call the boss, get a squad of telepaths over here and let them handle her."

"Are you sure?" But the thug grudgingly lowered his pistol and pulled out his phone.

At that moment the office door burst open and a man with a pistol in his hand side rolled into the room. The thug holding the phone and the man rolling into the room fired at the same time. Tied to a chair, Kyle couldn't see if the thug's bullet had hit the unknown invader, because he was on the other side and below the table, but the thug beside him dropped the phone and discharged his weapon several more times harmlessly into the floor as he fell dead a growing red stain appeared in the center of his shirt.

The other thug who had just stopped Emily's execution had his back turned from the door. Instead of turning and firing, he dropped down in between Emily and Kyle and hid behind the table and out of sight. Kyle became horrified when the thug, apparently convinced he was outgunned and outnumbered, pulled out his pistol and lifted it to Emily's unconscious forehead. Kyle's foot was untied, so he kicked out with all his might and managed to strike the unsuspecting arm of the murderous thug, causing the bullet to pass just above her head, striking the back of the conference chair and blowing bits of upholstery everywhere. Before he had time to compensate and fire again, a woman suddenly appeared around the side of the table and fired into him several times at point-blank range.

* * *

When Emily came to, she felt Kyle's arms wrapped around her. His hand was softly stroking her hair, it felt good and she remained still for a time not wanting it to stop. When she did finally move, she opened her eyes and saw the lifeless body of Xletru and both bodies of the dead thugs spread out on the floor. She turned her head and saw two strange men standing by the door and a strange woman holding a pistol at ready standing guard.

"What's happened?... Who are these people?" She asked.

They're our saviors, and they're friends of Anthony and Katrina, our children."

The names of her children sent a shiver down her spine. "You know before our memory swipe, I had convinced myself that our children were dead. I no longer wanted to live... Maybe that's why I never started to recall any of my past...I want to apologize to you for so much."

She looked again at the strangers. "How did our children know where to send friends to get us?"

"They knew because they're here on Toyama. The first image she had in her mind when Kyle had mentioned her children were of an adolescent boy and girl, but she realized that the image was outdated. Katrina and Anthony would both be young adults now. She tried to think of a response to this new information, but her mind simply froze. This had never happened to her before. She felt elation, anticipation, fear and trepidation, all at the same time. The whirlwind of life-changing events for her was now on day three and her mind needed some down time to absorb and digest all that was happening.

As if sensing her confusion, a handsome young man who seemed to be in charge smiled at her. "Ma'am, my name is Jeb, would you like me to take you to see your kids now?"

Those words thawed her tongue. "Yes... I would like that more than anything in the world."

✳ ✳ ✳

A short time later, Jeb accompanied a jubilant Kyle and Emily back to the cafeteria of the abandoned warehouse. Instant paternal concern crossed the faces of Emily and Kyle when they saw their still unconscious children.

"How are they?" Jeb asked, also concerned but trying hard not to show it. He thought that they'd already be awake by the time they had made it back.

Satira turned and said, "They'll both be just fine in a short time." She made a quick s-shaped motion with her hands. "Thank the eternal one, the Vanwanung was successful and their souls were not lost."

Emily and Kyle rushed to where Katrina and Anthony lay stretched out, still unconscious, on the cafeteria table. This family reunion had been years in the making and he couldn't wait to see the happy expression on Katrina's face when she woke up and saw her parents.

Emily picked up Katrina's hand and began to rub it. The affectionate stimulation seemed to work, for Katrina began to stir, and her eyes popped open.

"Mom?" a groggy Katrina gasped when she saw her mother standing over her. They grabbed each other and cried then.

Jeb waived discretely to the others and they all followed him out of the cafeteria and into the small kitchen to give the Armstrong's a long overdue private moment together.

While Jeb made a fresh pot of coffee, Iaghi told them about their next hideaway. He described it as a private place deep in the heart of the wilderness where they wouldn't be bothered. Within the hour, everyone climbed into the same transport wagons that had brought them into Hoshama that morning. Jeb climbed into the back and sat next to Katrina. Her mom sat down on the other side of her. They all sat in silence to maintain a level of stealth. Katrina, who seemed exhausted from the Vanwanung, laid her head on her mom's lap and soon went to sleep with her mom stroking her hair.

For several hours they traveled on a narrow, stone road. Their hideout turned out to be a cave deep in the mountains surrounded by old forests of native trees that looked very similar to Earth's conifers except for the color of the needles on the trees had a bluer tinge to them than any conifers Jeb had ever seen on Earth.

Built deep inside the large cave, hidden from view, was a very modern multi-room facility complete with electricity, running water and restrooms. There were enough private rooms in the facility to house hundreds of people. Jeb's favorite room was a large library stocked with thousands of books from Earth, many from his time period and written in English. He soon spent most of his mornings sitting in a comfortable chair reading Tolkien.

For the next two weeks, Jeb tried to enjoy the long-needed downtime. This was his first real vacation since he had been a boy in middle school – where he worked part-time to help his parent's out with their bills, for right after high school he had joined the army and after that, he had been caught up in one war after another. After a few days with nothing pending to do, no emergencies or crises to rewrite the day's plans, life did seem to become a little more carefree and upbeat. In the afternoons, he and Katrina would go for walks in the surrounding woods. They soon discovered an exotic, furry animal that looked everything like a hairless squirrel that collected acorn-sized nuts from the blue-tinged trees. And they watched a cross between a wasp and a dragonfly buzz around collecting nectar from the purple flowers of a plant whose stems had thorns on them like roses. This was what life could be like when you weren't constantly fighting or drinking yourself to death while on furlough trying to forget the atrocities you had done in combat.

During these walks, he told Katrina more about his life growing up in the twenty-first century and what it was like knowing that one of the few available opportunities for a successful career was in the military. She, in turn, told him of acquiring a deep sense of responsibility to humanity, instilled in her by her parents, while growing up as a citizen in humanity's last free city on a hidden alternate Earth.

About the third week of their restful stay at the quiet hideout, Jeb's active sixth sense kicked in, and he knew that his wonderful respite in paradise would soon end. This sense was something that he had learned to trust. It had saved his life countless times from just knowing that an enemy combatant was hiding just around the corner to when to immediately head for cover. This time it was telling him there was a new dangerous mission brewing in his future, but what could it be?

Later that same afternoon Iaghi announced that tomorrow morning there would be an important meeting and he needed everyone to attend.

The next morning, Jeb and Katrina marched into the library where all the reading tables had been removed and replaced with several dozen rows of folding chairs.

Once the library was full, Iaghi walked up to a podium equipped with a microphone.

He made his famous lipless grin but it seemed different, unusually serious. He was not projecting the usual positive force that Jeb had come to know.

"It's time to tell all of you exactly what Draka is so you will know exactly what we're up against. This may take a while; I need to start at the beginning."

He paused to catch his breath. "Long ago, when our solar system was much younger, the first intelligent races began to emerge in this timeline and the surrounding alternate realities of the multiverse.

"After a time, these developing civilizations became cognizant of one another and discovered ways to communicate across the alternate dimensions, and they formed friendships. They created a loose confederation where they shared knowledge of their different sciences, technologies, and most of all they shared their advanced knowledge of the universal consciousness that pervades all things.

"Even by Fengani standards, their shared technology was very advanced. They worked together and they perfected the technology of what you know as memory crystals.

"As more civilizations evolved and they became aware of the existence of this confederation, they too wanted to join. The members of the confederation saw no reason to deny anyone access to their elite club. The confederation welcomed everyone to join freely who became cognizant of their existence. Unfortunately, this policy proved disastrous to one newly-joined race, for shortly after joining the confederation they used the new technologies they acquired upon joining to make war upon inner factions of their own civilization and they destroyed themselves completely. The confederation felt guilty about this and its leaders realized they needed to be selective in granting membership and sharing technology.

"The confederation created an inner council of twelve members, called the watchers, who were given the task to seek out, discover, and observe all new emerging civilizations in the local multiverse and determine if and when their civilization was mature enough to offer membership.

"However, there was some disagreement in the council as to just how deeply involved they should be with the development of these emerging races. Two of the members felt that a totally hands-off approach, aptly nicknamed the Right of Self Determination, was the most appropriate. While the other ten members believed that they should not only be involved but try to manipulate and control the evolution of these young civilizations to assure they were on the proper road of development.

"This led to some very heated arguments, and no agreement could be reached. Finally, the ten decided to meet in secret and take matters into their own hands. They began to experiment on a race of slightly telepathic Ophidians by introducing selective genetic modifications for enhancing intelligence and telepathic abilities.

"Remember I told you that these first civilizations of the Confederation created the technology of the memory crystals. One of the watchers of the renegade faction was a brilliant scientist and he secretly experimented and continued to expand on this amazing technology until he secretly created the most wonderful memory crystal of all: our precious Eye of God. Connecting your consciousness to it grants you access to the memories of creatures that once lived or are living now." He paused. "And sometimes you can even catch glimpses of the future memories of creatures that may come to live in a possible future. The possibilities are only limited by the power of the intellect that connects to it, for it is a gateway to the total collective consciousness of the universe.

"The ten-member faction of the council decided to test the Eye of God's forecasting abilities on the young emerging sentient Ophidian race they were genetically experimenting on. Unfortunately, the Eye of God revealed nothing but disaster for all possible futures for this race. Perhaps if our consciousness was more powerful we might be able to see a solution they reasoned since the ability to see into the future through the Eye of God was only limited by the power of the intellect that connected to it.

"In desperation, the renegade watchers chose to create a special Vanwanung consisting of them and the collective consciousness of the race of Ophidians whose future they were trying to change, without the consent of the Ophidians by the way, while attuned to the Eye of God.

"This experiment was a complete disaster for the Vanwanung they created we know today as Draka. Yes, Draka is not a flesh and blood consciousness such as you and me.

"Draka rejected outright the purpose of its creation, for the Eye of God revealed to it that it could maintain its essence of self, independent of the council, by simply binding its essence permanently into the DNA of the Ophidian race to which it was telepathically joined. It did this at once, and then it consumed the souls of the renegade watchers so that they could never be a threat to it.

"After this infusion of Draka's essence, the Ophidians became fully sentient and powerful telepaths with advanced telekinetic powers. However, they had no technology and no ability to develop one as they had no limbs. Using the Eye of God, Draka tricked a developing race of space-faring creatures, who we all know as the grays, to land on the Ophidian's home planet. Having no telepathic abilities themselves, the grays minds were easily taken over and they became the Ophidian's first possessed slaves. Draka and the Ophidians then took over their entire civilization and used them as their army and he began to make war on and to systematically destroy all the member races of the confederation.

"Unfortunately, at first, the leaders of the confederation were hesitant to take action against Draka and only too late when their worlds faced imminent annihilation did they grasp that the creature Draka was not bent on just destroying their civilizations but their complete extermination.

Sometime after Draka began his butchering campaign, the two remaining members of the watcher's council discovered, by chance, the log of the renegade watchers' secret meetings and learned of the Eye of God. They understood that they must take the Eye of God from Draka at all costs. So, they rallied the surviving forces of the defeated confederation and led a desperate attack.

"The confederation army fought bravely but Draka's forces sorely defeated them and took no prisoners and gave no quarter. However, during the heat of the battle, the two watchers did manage break into the council room and to steal the Eye of God and escape.

"Sadly, while stealing the Eye of God, both of the watchers were severely wounded. Shortly after their escape one of them was so weak that it died within minutes. It was then that the last remaining watcher made a fateful decision, for if it died now, it knew that Draka would simply find and retrieve the Eye of God making their efforts in vain.

Seeing no other way, it began to draw from the life force of its own soul to keep its body temporarily alive at the cost of its own soul's immortality. Knowing that it could only cheat death this way for a short time, it took it's dead partner's pendant and the Eye of God and teleported to our world, for we were now the most advanced race in the cosmos after the extermination of the confederation and we had already made First-Contact and had submitted a petition to join the confederation.

"The dying watcher appeared to Ragdu, the founder of The Way. It shared with him the technology of the memory stones, and then it then gave Ragdu its pendant and instructed him on how to attune his soul to it.

"Finally, it tasked Ragdu and all of the Fengani with guarding and protecting the Eye of God and the other pendant until its owner was reborn. Not long after, the watcher died.

Ragdu then followed the dead watcher's instructions and attuned himself to its pendant and began to experiment with the Eye of God. He discovered that by linking to it while also attuned to his pendant he could with effort, access the memories of anyone who had ever lived in the past just by naming them. He could also access the thoughts of anyone now living. But when he turned his thoughts to the far future, he discovered Draka ruling the universe as a dark and cruel lord."

Iaghi paused to get a drink from a glass of water that sat on a table next to the podium. "Let me explain something. Each time Draka consumes a soul his consciousness levels and prescient abilities incrementally increase, and the power of the Eye of God decreases. And at some point, Draka's consciousness will reach a critical mass and it will instantly transform into a living Eye of God, and making it a god."

"So, Draka is a Vanwanung that eats souls like we eat flesh?" Katrina said speaking her thoughts aloud.

Iaghi smiled. "Yes."

"How long before Draka reaches this critical mass and becomes a living Eye of God?"

"Not long, now. It's taken many millions of years and trillions of souls to get to this point – A few million more souls, a few months at most. The Eye of God has already revealed to us that if we fail in what we are about to do, we won't get another chance, which brings us to our next guest."

Iaghi called General Kyle to the podium and stepped away to give him access to the microphone.

"Iaghi and I have come up with a plan so bold and brazen, it just might work. What do we all know about Ophidian battlecruisers?"

Jeb raised his arm. "They're the backbone and strong arm of the Ophidian Empire. Any planet that tries to rebel and break away from their empire winds up with an armada of them in orbit above their planet and faces total annihilation.

"Yes, their fleet of battlecruisers is the tooth and claw of the empire and their fleet has many such ships. However, it always costs the empire too much to man all of them. Therefore, most are mothballed for just when they need them.

"Now I just happen to know there is a fully operational battle cruiser that is mothballed and stocked with full armaments parked in geosynchronous orbit above us.

"It has only a small security force on board and I'm thinking that a small special ops team could steal us that ship."

Hushed murmurs broke out from all quarters of his audience, so Kyle stopped talking briefly to let the audience absorb what he had just told them. After nearly a minute, he waived the audience to silence.

"Well, that is a bold plan, but then what? What are we going to do with it? Try to get the Fengani people to rebel? They'd send an entire armada here and destroy everything." Anthony said aloud.

Kyle smiled. "Once we take command of that ship, we head to the Ophidians' home planet. And when we arrive, we launch a full-scale attack on their temple."

"But even if we took out their home world, the empire will still exist. What about their god Draka, this runaway Vanwanung?" Anthony added.

Iaghi moved up to the microphone. "That is the point. The true purpose of our attack will be to bring Katrina and me, face to face with Draka so that we can engage him in a winner take all battle. Once he is destroyed, the Ophidians will lose their sentience along with their telepathic powers. Their empire will cease to exist.

Any more questions…"

TWENTY-NINE

Jeb crossed his fingers as he watched the shuttle approach the battlecruiser through the shuttlecraft's main view screen. "This has to work," he chanted under his breath. Two days ago, ingenious Maureen had successfully hacked into the mothballed battle cruiser's main computer and had caused several of the ship's sensors in key locations to indicate a malfunction. No doubt about it, with Xelana's crash-course modernization training and her uncanny hacker ability, she was proving once again to be invaluable. She sat now with her holo-laptop perched on top of a bulkhead next to her good friend Xelana. Together they attentively monitored the ship's navigation systems.

The plan was simple. When they docked at the battle cruiser the on-duty guards were expecting an ordinary repair crew. They would split up into teams and go to those locations in the ship where the sensors appeared faulty. They would then replace the faulty modules with a new module that secretly contained a small canister of a very powerful nerve toxin that would render anyone who breathed it unconscious. Everyone in the assault team had been given an antidote injection so that they would remain unaffected.

"Everyone keep your eyes open and wits about you. We need to reconnoiter as we move about." When the docking doors opened everyone exited in pairs.

Bernie Paxton and Iaghi made one team, and they headed for Engineering, while Jan and Anthony took off for life support. Kyle and Emily's target was living quarters. Maureen and Xelana were to stay on the shuttle, coordinate all teams and hack into the ship's weapons and navigation systems once a direct connection was made to the network.

Katrina walked beside Jeb and helped him carry their trunk-sized suitcase of tools and spare parts towards the bridge, their target.

His senses were on overload and every nerve in his body was on edge. Nothing was too trivial to notice, their lives and the fate of the mission depended on this. The bridge doors opened and he looked around. The layout of the bridge was exactly how he had pictured it. Lights flicked on and off on the large instrument panels of several workstations spread around the room. The main viewing screen was presently turned off. It was uncanny how all of those sci-fi TV and movies he had watched as a kid had got some things dead right.

The room was vacant except for a duck-billed sentry. The creature stood about the average height of a man. Its entire body, except those parts that were covered by its gray fatigues, was covered with a soft tawny, baby-chicken down. Since traveling into the future, he'd managed to meet over a dozen alien species. But he didn't recognize this one.

Jeb walked over to the main console, where a red light blinked and began to remove the cover while Katrina worked on the navigation controls on the other side of the room. They both knew just enough, thanks to Xelana's in-depth instructions, to appear like they knew what they were about.

The truth was he never was good with fixing things. His dear dad had tried to teach him; he'd been computer repairman and had made a decent living at repairing computers, cars, and just about any appliance, after society's collapse of '37 and there was nothing new to buy in stores anymore. Handymen who knew how things worked and could fix them suddenly became invaluable. It was a handyman's dream come true. But, it didn't take. He had no interest in fixing things. Instead, as soon as he turned eighteen he enlisted in the army and never looked back. There he soon discovered, he had a sixth sense about fighting and an uncanny ability at staying alive. He quickly became an expert with the rifle, and at his drill sergeant's recommendation; he became a ranger. Before he knew it, he had become part of an elite assault and antiterrorist strike team.

His thoughts returned to the present and he focused on the task-at-hand. He installed the replacement module and placed the panel back on. The red light on the control console returned to green. "I just needed to replace the power supply module. Everything should work fine now." He said glancing at the guard, who just stood there unmoving.

He looked over to Katrina who had her replacement module in and was working on getting the panel back on. She glanced over at him with the just the smallest hint of nervousness. He noted the time on his twenty-first-century watch complete with, even then, old-fashioned dial hands, right on schedule. Iaghi and Kyle had both strongly advised he not wear it while on this mission as no one from this time wore dial watches, but he had steadfastly refused.

Luck charms were real. He believed that if he didn't wear it he might jinx the mission. The only mission he didn't wear it went down badly. The poor hostage they were supposed to rescue and half of his team that day was killed.

He sadly remembered Harold, a guy on his team who had a fixation on yellow #2 pencils. He had to carry one in his shirt pocket on every mission. Whenever he became nervous, he'd pull out the pencil--he nicknamed it Penny- and just play with it and talk to Penny like it understood him. It was his security blanket and best friend. Just before Harold's last mission, someone played a very ugly practical joke and had hidden all his #2 pencils. Harold went frantic and tore the barracks apart looking for one. In the helicopter on their way to the hostage rescue, Harold's face became ashen, and his eyes took on that distant look of a man who knew his time was up. Poor Guy took a bullet from a sniper the minute they stepped out of the copter. Coincidence?

Katrina gave him a thumbs up from across the room. "Team 3 Modules are in place," Jeb said aloud.

"Roger that," he heard in his ear. "Restoring power to all systems."

As Jeb and Katrina repacked their tools, a light on the navigation console began to blink red, and an overhead alarm sounded. Smoke began pouring out of both repaired consoles. "Guard! We have an electrical fire. Quick! Bring us the fire extinguisher." Jeb and Katrina both moved quickly to remove the screws from the panels they had just reassembled.

The duck-billed guard grabbed the fire extinguisher, which hung beside the door to the bridge and rushed over to the smoking panels. One whiff of the gas and he coughed once and fell to the floor unconscious.

✳ ✳ ✳

Hours later, Maureen worked diligently beside Xelana as they brought the battle cruiser's weapons systems back online. Maureen was getting a little antsy. So far, everything had gone without a hitch. None of her missions had ever done that. Something always went wrong. She feared that when something did go haywire it would be big. A green light on the console lit up; she smiled and turned towards Xelana. "Weapons systems are online." He gave her the high five she had taught him.

Bernie, Ed, and Jan walked through the ship's armory section inspecting the weapons cache. The armory was well stocked with thousands of laser rifles, laser pistols, pulse grenades and a large cache of fully charged power packs. They had all just spent several hours practicing and familiarizing themselves with these new weapons in the ship's practice range. With the weapons stashed here, they could arm a very large army.

Ed returned the laser rifle he'd just spent an hour shooting to an empty spot on the rifle rack. "You know, I'm getting to like these modern laser weapons. They're lightweight and ergonomic, no recoil, more accurate, very quiet, have a longer range and general Kyle says that one fully charged power pack the size of a six-volt battery is equivalent to thousands of rounds of ammunition.

"They're ok," Bernie said pulling a laser rifle off the rack and bringing it up to his shoulders. "I still like shooting a weapon with boom and recoil, lets me know I am shooting."

"Well, you don't have much choice. Jeb wants us to trade in our cache of ballistics weapons and replace them with these. That includes that antique sidearm you're so proud of," Jan said, pointing to his side

Bernie pulled out an ivory-handled 1911 and stroked it. "No way. Not this," he said. He removed the clip, opened the slide, then handed it to her.

The pearl handles felt worn from use. She took imaginary aim and played with the safety several times using her thumb, then quickly pulled and locked the slide back before handing it back to him. "I see you're already familiar with it."

"Some of the weapons we practiced with at the monastery date from your time. I have logged several hours shooting a pistol almost identical to yours.

Bernie seemed impressed. "You do know your firearms, lady. Anyway, this stays with me. It belonged to my great-great-grandfather. He carried it in WW2 and each succeeding generation of Paxton has carried it into battle since." He stuck his chest out and pointed at it. "I'm not breaking tradition, especially not before the most important battle of all times. He inserted the magazine and cycled a round into the chamber, and clicking on the safety before returning it to its holster. "I'd be willing to trade my life to give this baby an opportunity to take out one of those mind controlling Ophidians."

Jan raised her finger. "Do be careful what you wish for Mr. Paxton."

THIRTY

The large viewing screen on the bridge of Nemesis, the name they had given their stolen battle cruiser, showed nothing but the black void of empty space until a small point of light appeared and within seconds it grew until it filled the screen with a swirling, turbulent dark mass, illuminated by erratic peals of lightning. "Move the ship towards the forming vortex," Kyle said, sitting in the captain's chair.

The ship nudged forward. When the ship met the vortex's outer edge, it shimmered briefly and then disappeared...

Kyle's stomach felt like he'd just rapidly dropped several stories in an elevator, and he had the throbbing headache of jump sickness coming on. He knew from painful experience the coming nausea and headache would last for several hours, and that he'd just have to live with it.

When he looked up at the viewing screen it was black again. The entire bridge watched it with him, prayerfully waiting. Vortex teleportation was considered a very safe means of transportation, but there had been accidents in the past. No one wanted to materialize inside or very close to a planet. Thankfully, after thirty seconds or so, the screen came back online and a familiar blue planet with continents and deep-blue oceans appeared on the giant screen.

On a cursory glance, Kyle saw that it looked very much like his Earth. Upon closer inspection, however, he did detect a few obvious dissimilarities such as South America was no longer joined to North America; the narrow land bridge had a gap in it joining the Atlantic and Pacific oceans about where Panama should be. An examination of North America revealed the Great lakes were missing too. This was his Earth but in an alternate timeline, and in this reality, it was known as Djaftafe - the Ophidian home world.

"Captain, we're being hailed by Teleportation services," the telecommunications officer, an alert, young human-lieutenant Trudy announced. "They're angry that we just made an unscheduled jump and they want us to explain ourselves."

"Begin transmitting our surprise package and move us out of the teleporter ring towards the planet," Kyle said.

"Sir there's another cruiser, less than twenty thousand kilometers off our port bow and it's powering up its weapons."

"Have they raised their shields?"

"No, sir."

"Power up our weapons but keep our shields on standby."

Kyle reached down and clicked on the intercom, to Maureen and Xelana who had relocated to ship's communications. "We've begun transmitting the virus." He paused to read a gauge. "Estimated time to completion is ten seconds.

"Excellent, in another twenty seconds they should begin to have some real problems," Maureen said.

Twenty seconds later, "Captain the teleporter's just lost power," Lieutenant Trudy said smiling broadly. "The entire power grid of the teleporter has gone out."

Excellent, Kyle thought. With the teleporter out thanks to that virus Maureen wrote, they wouldn't have to worry about more ships teleporting in. The remaining threat was that other cruiser across their bow.

"Quick, raise shields and target that ship's main power supply and propulsion systems. Prepare to fire on my command."

'Sir, Power supply targeted... Sir! They're raising their shields too."

"Fire"

"Sir, we scored a direct hit on their propulsion system with our forward laser cannons," officer Trudy announced.

"Any effect?" Kyle asked.

Officer Trudy glanced at the screen on his workstation. "Sir, their propulsion system is just a pile of rubble, they're dead in space, but their shields and weapons are still operational."

The ship rocked violently as it took a blast from the enemy's laser cannon.

"Shields?" Kyle asked.

"Maintaining full strength, sir." Officer Trudy pushed several buttons at his workstation. "Sir, they're locking on to the attack-vessel."

Kyle's mind raced. There was no time to consider. They couldn't afford the attack ship to be damaged, and the attack ship's defenses were no match for a sustained firefight with that battlecruiser. "Move the ship in the line of fire of the attack ship. Then bring her alongside and prepare boarding parties."

"Aye, aye sir."

When the cruisers came within a thousand yards of each other, they both ceased firing. They were too close now to use cannons. For if a shot managed to get through either ship's shields at this close proximity, the resulting explosion would destroy both ships.

✳ ✳ ✳

Katrina sat in the belly of the cramped cargo hold of the attack ship, which had launched from the dock of the battlecruiser just after teleportation. The entire strike team of over three hundred of their best troops waited with her. Her mother was sitting up front in the cockpit with the pilot, Bob Jordan. She was officially in charge with Jeb as the second in command.

"Everyone fasten your seat belts and grab onto something. We're about to take some heat," her mother announced over the intercom.

Jeb sat beside her and they held hands. Anthony and Jan sat across from them looking grim. They all knew that the fate of the universe depended on the success of today's mission. But most importantly, she knew everything depended on her and Iaghi. For the only way to stop Draka and end, once and for all, his mad scheme of becoming a living Eye of God and consuming everything conscious in the entire multiverse was to get inside the pyramid on the Ophidian's home world. But this would not be easy as a small but elite human-force of the best troops in the Ophidian Empire guarded that temple.

The ship rocked hard and she bumped against Jeb's shoulders. Jeb turned towards her. "I love you."

As she glanced into his eyes, the strong sense of prescience filled her. Her ability to see the future became clearer each time she used the pendant. This time she had a vision and saw Jeb in two very different futures, simultaneously imposed over each other; one with his face full of anger and sorrow, and the other where he's happy and smiling. Someone, --was it her?—had a decision to make that would make one of those futures a reality? She grasped his hand and squeezed. "I love you too," she told him. She didn't say anything more. She just enjoyed their moment of closeness.

She glanced again at Jan and Anthony. She tried to see into their future as well, but the evasive power of prescience had abandoned her. She hoped that they would both survive this day unscathed.

The voice of her mother over the intercom pulled her out of her thoughts and back to the mission. "Everyone, grab hold of something. We're coming under fire. There's another battlecruiser engaged with Nemesis. It may get a little bumpy." After that warning, the ship experienced several sharp bumps.

Amazingly, no one on the surface fired at them. Kyle and Emily had anticipated this. The Ophidians in their hubris had considered defenses against a direct assault as unnecessary. This was Draka's lair. Who would dare attack?

The blazing white peak of the temple pyramid could be seen in the distance. It was the exact copy and in the same location as the great pyramid of Giza on Earth. The landing near the pyramid was uneventful, and they exited the landing craft.

They split into three teams and advanced unhindered toward the temple. Emily oversaw team Alpha and spread out on her left flank. Jeb's team Beta was on her right flank and Katrina's team Gamma came up in the center.

Iaghi and the rest of the master Fengani priests followed close behind her. The priests had insisted that they must be present when she and Iaghi confronted Draka. Their prophecy said that it would be necessary for them to be present or all would be lost. They huddled now all in a group and walked in unison chanting softly and holding prayer beads in their hands. Each bead was a memory crystal and contained the reverent memories of a deceased master.

Finally, when they were within two hundred yards of the temple they encountered their first resistance from the temple guards along the ten-foot-high, ebony-black wall that surrounded the great pyramid. The wall's composition was the same material of the wall that surrounded New San Diego on Earth. Nothing in the universe was known to be able to penetrate or damage that material. Their attack crew came with hooks and ladders to cross over.

At one hundred yards out, her team came under heavy laser cannon and small arms fire halting their advance and they began to take casualties. They dug in and returned fire. The sky around the temple lit up looking like a harmless laser light show.

If they tried to advance against that magnitude of firepower, they would suffer heavy casualties, and even risk total extermination of her team. Katrina willed up the power of her pendant. Power flowed into her. She quickly conjured up her familiar blue shield and stepped into the open with her shield of light in front of her. Nothing that the defenders fired at her could penetrate it. She willed it to increase in size until it covered her entire unit and she began walking forward. Her troops stood up and followed her. When they reached the black wall, she touched it with her hand and commanded it to separate. The wall responded and began to groan and buckle. A large crack from top to bottom appeared directly in front of her. The crack made a boom and fractured.

A ten-foot gap in the wall now existed. She stepped through it and entered the outer temple courtyard. She made a beeline for the great pyramid followed closely by her troops.

When they stood before the entrance to the great pyramid, she turned and said to her troops, "You must stay outside, and make sure that no one but the Fengani priests follows us." She then walked into the entrance of the great pyramid with only Iaghi and the Fengani priests following behind at a distance.

The dark narrow hallway soon opened into a rectangular room large enough to hold a small crowd. Illumination came from hundreds of small votive-black-candles that burned in the four corners around stone statues of Ophidians wrapped around a stone tree that stretched all the way up the twenty-foot ceiling. The walls were plain-white with no markings of any kind. Across the room there stood a large wooden door with hieroglyphic Egyptian style runes carved into it. She walked warily across the polished black stone floor. When she reached the door she grabbed the brass handle. The door opened, and she peered into another long narrow hallway that ended at another wooden door. She hesitated as the hair on the back of her head began to stand up. She sensed the pendants of the dead watchers were just on the other side of that door. In the ethereal world of her mind, they glowed like a giant fire. She sucked up her courage and was about to step into the hallway when something black and smoky coalesced, materialized and took the form of an angry Draka standing before her.

THIRTY-ONE

Kyle fell out of his chair as a third explosion rocked the ship. He swore under his breath. This was not going well. Both ships were now infested with boarding parties and each engaged in heavy hand-to-hand combat with the intent of taking out the other's Engineering and Command Centers. He didn't have nearly enough men for this kind of fight; the simple law of attrition was against him. All he was doing was buying time for Katrina and Iaghi and hoped that they succeeded in their quest on the surface.

"Where was the location of that explosion?" Kyle asked Lieutenant Trudy.

"On level three, Engineering. There's at least a squad of an enemy boarding party that just shot their way through our defenses on level five and they're now heading to the bridge."

"How long before we have visitors?" Kyle asked.

"They'll be here in less than three minutes."

"Everyone! Take defensive positions and draw your weapons. Make ready!" Kyle said as he took position behind a large support column. He pulled out his laser pistol and flicked off the safety."

The locked double door to the bridge exploded inward, and before the smoke cleared several alien grays appeared in the doorway. They were the first casualties. Next came several humans and they died too. They were all possessed; they had no sense of fear. An enemy combatant threw a pulse grenade through the doorway but a quick-thinking Lieutenant Trudy caught it in midair and threw it back towards whoever had thrown it. However, by doing so he exposed himself and before he could get back undercover, he took a laser blast to the chest and fell to the floor.

Kyle rushed over to him and tried to stop the bleeding while a solid wave of possessed troops came through the doorway. They couldn't shoot them fast enough and they were simply overrun.

Several possessed soldiers came over to Kyle while he nursed Lieutenant Trudy and menacingly waived their firearms in his face. Kyle started to object but Lieutenant Trudy who was still conscious grabbed his arm. "It's OK sir, I'll be OK."

The bleeding had seemed to have stopped. A reluctant Kyle raised his hands and joined the rest of the survivors. He counted five including him.

The possessed troops stood unmoving but with their weapons poised ready to shoot at the first provocation. They seemed to be waiting for someone, Kyle thought.

✳ ✳ ✳

Maureen and Xelana monitored the fall of the bridge still nestled in ship's communications. Several large screens showed ongoing battles taking place in various corridors of the ship, and they were about to lose Engineering too, for there were only a handful of soldiers returning fire in that sector.

"We don't have much time; we need to go into hiding at once. Soon the entire ship will be flooded with possessed troops," Xelana said.

Maureen turned off her holo-laptop and clutched it closely. They were about to leave and take their chances in the hallway when Maureen noticed a large bulkhead overhead with an access port directly above them. After moving a desk underneath, and with Xelana standing on the desk and Maureen on top of his shoulders, she managed to reach the lattice access door and open it. A squeaky hinge screeched as it opened. After climbing in and Xelana handing up her laptop, he then jumped up and grabbed the opening and climbed in too.

The shaft inside the bulkhead was about three feet by three feet. They shut the door behind them, and then they crawled quickly but quietly on their hands and knees for about fifty feet until they rounded a corner where they would not be seen by peering eyes. They stopped then to catch their breath. While they waited, Xelana raised his three-fingered hand and motioned for her to remain quiet. A short time later, she heard voices, and then Maureen's heart pounded as she heard the familiar screech of the squeaky hinge, but she relaxed when she heard it screech a second time and the voices moved away.

She glanced at Xelana across from her who seemed to be in a trance. She was wearing her thought band, so he couldn't talk to her telepathically. She reached out to touch his hand, remembering him telling her that if they made physical contact he could still make mental contact with her, even if she was wearing her thought band.

"I'm monitoring the corridor for possessed soldiers. I've also detected the presence of several Ophidians on the ship and I must be very careful that they don't detect my presence and give us away."

"What are they doing?" She asked without vocalizing her question.

"They're very upset, and they want answers. No one has ever dared to attack them like this before," she heard him whisper in her mind.

232

"I also am in and out of contact with Iaghi. They're inside the temple; they're close behind Katrina and they're making their way to the altar now. We will soon know if they succeed or not."

Maureen activated her holo-laptop. She had access to the cameras throughout the ship. Engineering had fallen, and enemy forces were now manning the technical stations trying to bring the weapons and propulsion systems back online. She prayed that Katrina succeeded soon. Otherwise, she had one final order to follow. Just Before leaving the orbit of Toyama, the crew and officers had conducted a vote, and everyone had unanimously agreed that death would be preferable than surrendering to the Ophidians.

Kyle had given her and Xelana access to the self-destruct codes for Nemesis and ordered her to engage them if all looked lost. "Gladly, sir!" she had told him. "I'm tired of being someone's patsy and used."

She stared at the skull and crossbones icon hovering in holo-space in front of her. She looked to Xelana for hope and waited while her finger quivered ready to pluck the icon from space. *Next stop, the hereafter.*

* * *

Lieutenant Trudy was looking very pale. Kyle guessed the bleeding must have started up again. He was about to demand that he attend to his wounded when the largest Ophidian he had ever seen slithered through the doorway and onto the bridge. This was the mother of all Ophidians. It was at least sixty feet long and twice the thickness of a man. It wore a funky headdress, which surprised Kyle. He had never seen an Ophidian wear anything before.

"Who's in charge here!" the snake roared out with its mind. The Ophidian studied them with its forked tongue darting rapidly in and out of its mouth. Then its eyes settled on Kyle. "You!" Its slit pupils locked onto Kyle's. "Your surface thoughts betray you. Your concern for the welfare and safety of these men dominate your thoughts."

The Ophidian paused and looked down at a very pale yet still conscious lieutenant Trudy. "Especially for this poor wounded man here. Oh, I'm afraid he doesn't look very good, does he? He needs immediate medical attention... which he won't be getting by the way...." The Ophidian's head bent down and did a quickie-touchy-feely with its forked-tongue of Lieutenant Trudy's body from head to toe. "You know it's a shame to let such a good meal go to waste. I prefer my dinner alive and kicking. I so enjoy experiencing their last few thoughts of terror. It makes dinner so much more palatable."

Kyle watched with horror as the snake's mouth began to widen and... *Oh my god!* Then it began to swallow the poor lieutenant Trudy head first. Kyle tried to move but found he couldn't. His legs wouldn't respond to his urging and he found himself locked in place. He couldn't even turn his head to look away.

When the Ophidian finished swallowing Lieutenant Trudy it said, "That was most enjoyable. I can't decide whose emotions I enjoyed more. The horror poor Trudy felt as he was swallowed alive, or your sense of helplessness and feeling responsible for his fate." The Ophidian turned towards the rest of his men and with its tongue flicking rapidly in and out. "But, I'm still hungry. I think I'll eat the rest of your men now... Yes master...?" The Ophidian's eyes suddenly became out of focus as if it had gone into a trance, and its face made an unreadable emotion.

Several minutes later the Ophidian returned to its self. "Fools! What have you done? You shall all pay for this with your lives when I return...." Then the Ophidian just disappeared.

The possessed guards suddenly came back to themselves, they seemed confused. One said, "How did I get here?

Kyle wasted no time. He picked up his thought band and put it on while his men did the same. Then they took out spares from a cabinet and passed them out to the former possessed. After several precious minutes explaining to almost seventy former possessed soldiers what was happening, he had them swear allegiance to him and they took off for Engineering, to try to take it back.

THIRTY-TWO

For the second time, Katrina battled Draka and with more confidence. She had bested this creature once in a direct assault and she knew she could do it again. Continuous bolts of blue and red lightning bounced off of their protective shields of power and danced at random up and down the stone walls of the pyramid's narrow hallway, pulverizing and vaporizing large chunks of stone.

After several minutes of this sparring, the air became so thick with rock dust in the confined space of the hallway that Katrina found it difficult to breathe. She began to cough and she had to stop her attack to cover her mouth with a handkerchief, hoping to filter out most of the choking rock dust.

On seeing her plight, Draka seized on this. He didn't breathe air as she did, so the accumulating rock dust in the air had no effect on him. Shear hatred lit up his face as he attacked without relent, forcing Katrina, who was already down on her knees and still coughing, to throw her entire will into just maintaining her shield. For if it collapsed now, she would be vaporized at once from the magnitude of power Draka was throwing at her.

Sadly, she felt her shield begin to buckle, and she began to desperately consider turning back and abandoning the mission when, thankfully, Iaghi stepped up beside her and sent his own lightning bolts at Draka.

The surprise of a second attacker caused Draka to back off slightly his attack, and it was enough for Katrina to restore the damage to her shield. Though coughing, she proudly stood up again, raised her hand above her head, and created a blue ball of flame in her open palm and began to feed it power while Iaghi attacked and kept Draka occupied. She let it build while painful, raw power of the universe surged through her. When she felt she couldn't contain the ball of flame any longer, she released it and sent it at Draka.

Upon contact with Draka's shield, it exploded and the force of the blast knocked her and Iaghi down.

She quickly regained her feet with all her senses alert for any danger and quickly recreated her shield, which had been extinguished from the blast of the explosion. She searched frantically for Draka who was nowhere about.

She panicked then, remembering how last time he had tricked her. "Quick! Let's get back-to-back before he materializes behind one of us," she told Iaghi who had just now regained his feet. With their backs to each other she reached into her pendant and increased her sense of awareness many times higher than that of a normal human, but she still could not sense him. She reached even deeper. There, she caught a distant sense of his essence in a nearby alternate reality, but he seemed very weak, just a shell of his former self.

She prepared to teleport there now and finish him off once and for all while he was weak when Iaghi spoke to her telepathically, "Katrina don't; it's another trap. Draka cannot be killed that way. He's not a normal creature like you or me. We must go into the next room and finish what we came to do while he is still weak and won't be able to stop us."

They walked together, then over to the door that Draka had stood in front of just moments ago, opened it and stepped inside.

*　*　*

Katrina stared into solid blackness except for the dim glow of two burning candles that were about twenty-five paces into the room. She raised her arm and on command a cold, blue flame engulfed it, turning her arm into a large torch that didn't burn or harm her in any way.

She looked about, utilizing the added light. She stood inside a large amphitheater, maybe fifty yards across. *"This must be the center of the pyramid,"* she thought.

Iaghi pointed. "The altar of redemption is between those two candles. Let's go. Quickly, we don't have much time. Draka could return at any moment." They approached the altar with other Fengani priests all following close behind, still chanting prayers in unison in singsong fashion in their guttural language.

When she arrived at the altar, she saw that the two six-foot high identical candle stands were adorned with the carved image of a hissing cobra wrapped around a central pole. The black altar of redemption sat between them.

Revulsion and terror filled her heart when her eyes fell upon it. How many countless victims' souls had been consumed by Draka on its surface? She walked up and touched its cold marble surface. There was something engraved upon it. She raised her flaming arm and increased the intensity of the cold flame. The increased light revealed the wheel of the zodiac etched into the marble top.

"Yes, it's the zodiac," Iaghi said. "Those ancient symbols are far more ancient and universal than even you realize." He placed a comforting hand on her tense shoulder.

She saw that in the center of each zodiac symbol was a jewel, except for the symbols of Leo and Cancer, which were absent. She looked at the missing symbol for Leo, as she touched her pendant. "But I have no memory of this place."

"It was another life," Iaghi said telepathically interrupting her thoughts. "Our memories and our experiences are not normally carried into our next existence, only the soul's state. Some religions call it karma."

"So what do we do now?"

"The Fengani priests with us will each pick up a pendant and perform the tuning ritual and then we will sit down to form our own Vanwanung, the first one involving the entire council in many millions of years.

After the last priest finished the attunement process and everyone was seated, Iaghi placed the Eye of God in the center of the altar and they joined hands…

THIRTY-THREE

"Quick! You must get ready to make for the pyramid." Jan heard the voice inside her head say. "This is your moment; the reason for all of your training. You must protect Katrina and the Fengani priests. They must not fail at what they are about to do. You must move when I tell you."

The sudden appearance of the voice inside her head now at this moment surprised her. She had not heard from it in months. She had even begun to doubt and wonder if it had been a creation of her imagination. She turned toward Anthony. "I need to get into the temple. Can you cover me?"

She peered over the top of the mortar hole that she and Anthony had hunkered in. The entrance to the pyramid door that Katrina had passed through only moments ago was about thirty yards ahead. It was sure death to cross that distance now; heavy crossfire zipped back and forth through those thirty yards.

Anthony grabbed her shoulder and turned her around, so he could stare directly into her face. "You're talking madness. There's no way you can cover that ground. You'll be dead before you take two steps."

She patted his shoulder. "I'll make it, trust me."

"If you're going, then I'm going, too."

"No! You must stay here and guard the entrance."

"But I don't want to be separated from you…. I love you."

Jan grabbed his head and pulled it closer. They kissed. The desire to make love, battle or not, was intense. They continued kissing until she heard, "*Jan, quick go. Now hurry!*" She didn't hesitate. She pulled away and rushed out of the fox hole putting her trust in the voice once again. It had always guided her and protected her. *Why stop trusting it now?* She ran as fast as she could towards the entrance to the pyramid without looking back. But if she had, she would have seen Satira had jumped out of a nearby fox hole and was following her.

She was about halfway to the pyramid entrance when the voice said, "*Quick duck down!*" She felt the hot air and hiss from a laser bullet as it sang by where her head had been a microsecond ago.

Miraculously, she reached the entrance unscathed. She ran through the stone hallway, where Katrina and Draka had battled only moments ago, and passed through the open doorway. She continued running towards the burning candles until she came to a round stone table with Katrina and the Fengani priests all sitting holding hands with their eyes closed and in a trance.

She heard footsteps behind her then and flipped around and made ready with her laser pistol. When she saw it was Satira running towards her, she lowered her weapon and said, "How did you get in?"

"I followed you," she said. Her face made an alien expression that Jan couldn't read. "You aren't the only one who hears the voice. It told me to follow you. I need to be here too."

This revelation surprised her. So, the voice was talking to others as well. If there had been more time, she would have pursued this news with questions, but for now, she'd have to ignore her burning desire to learn more and stay focused on the task at hand.

Jan turned and studied the altar and everyone sitting at the table. Everyone wore a pendant like Katrina's except in color. The colors ranged From Katrina's royal blue, to white, green, orange, and yellow. The pendants all radiated a pulse of colored light in unison with each other reminding her of the heartbeat of a single organism. There was also a violet crystal-ball sitting in a pocket in the center of the table that pulsed a bright purple-violet, several magnitudes brighter than the others, but in sync with the pendants.

"Do you know what they are doing?" She asked Satira.

"They've formed a special Vanwanung and are using the pendants and the Eye of God to amplify this consciousness. This Vanwanung now prepares to do battle with the abomination Draka, which is also a Vanwanung. Our mission from the voice is to protect them from Draka's servants who will try to enter this room and kill them and thus kill their Vanwanung before it succeeds in destroying Draka for they are totally helpless and defenseless while they are in this state."

So, the purpose and reason for all her combat and self-defense training had led up to this moment… the voice of Anthony barking on her walkie-talkie interrupted her thoughts. "Jan Get ready you're about to have company. A moment ago, all of our laser weapons stopped working and the possessed troops broke through. Bernie still had his ballistics sidearm, and Bernie and Ed tried to stop them, but a large wave assault overran their position and about fifty possessed troops led by several Mega-Corp soldiers got inside the pyramid."

While she and Satira scrambled to take up defensive positions Anthony added, "By the way, it's totally nuts out here. It's almost like they're being driven. The possessed and even some of the Ophidians themselves are attacking in waves by the hundreds trying desperately to get inside. Everyone is fighting hand to hand and we can't kill them fast enough…." She heard running footsteps in the distance. Jan turned the walkie-talkie off.

She pulled out a flare gun and shot it into the air. The spreading light showed enemy soldiers beginning to pour into the amphitheater. She saw that many were human but there were also some rare grays and even a few stanchions. She took careful aim and squeezed the trigger of her laser pistol, but nothing happened. She turned to Satira for help.

"I suspected something like this might happen. As you know this is no ordinary Vanwanung. The unleashed power of the crystals and the Eye of God must be affecting the crystals in your laser pistols."

"Are there any more surprises? I need to know quickly if I'm going to properly defend them."

Satira shrugged. "I think that's it"

Jan moved quickly. In one fluid motion, she whipped out two large, double-bladed short swords out of her thigh high leather boots and produced a metal pole that telescoped out to about three feet. Working quickly she screwed the ends of the hilts of the blades into each of end of the pole. Within seconds she had armed herself with a simple dual bladed staff. She raised it spinning above her head and attacked.

The enemy soldiers she encountered were all likewise armed with laser weapons that didn't work either. They tried using their weapons as clubs. However, their coordination and reflexes were slow, and Jan moved quicker than seemed humanly possible. She dodged in and out of the advancing combatants, swinging her double staff with deadly accuracy until she met a Mega-Corp soldier who was armed with an old fashioned, ballistics, semi-automatic pistol. Fortunately, Jan saw him raise it just in time, and she called on all her skills and all her training. Suddenly, Flashes of images appeared in her mind showing her where he was pointing his weapon and when he would squeeze the trigger. It must be the voice she reasoned. She followed the visions. It worked. Using this knowledge, she moved lightning fast out of harm's way each time the soldier fired his weapon. She moved hurriedly towards him and crushed his skull with a quick head butt to his forehead and took the pistol from him. Before he fell dead to the floor, she grabbed the familiar pearl-handled 1911. She knew without looking at it that it had the name Paxton engraved on it. She collected a handful of spare ammo clips from the dead soldier's web belt. Newly armed with Paxton's pistol she turned then and quickly used it to kill all of the remaining enemy combatants.

She checked the last clip in the pistol as she walked back to Satira who had remained just in front of the altar. She had three rounds left, one in the chamber and two in the clip.

"Is that the best you can do Draka?" Jan said aloud to no one. Almost in response to her exclamation, the room shimmered and the largest Ophidian she had ever seen materialized about forty feet in front of them.

It wore a headdress adorned with many multicolored beads and a tangle of braided leather strands with feathers.

Satira screamed and fell down to the floor. A wave of pain crossed her alien face and she covered her head with her hands and writhed on the floor.

Returning her eyes to the Ophidian Jan said, "What's wrong?"

"It's their high Ophidian. Its mind is directly linked to Draka's. Their thoughts are one. It's their most powerful telepath, and much stronger than anything I've ever felt before…it's even stronger than Iaghi." Her face wracked with pain. "It's trying to penetrate my mind."

Jan weekly felt the mental attack then too, but she took comfort in knowing she was wearing her thought band. She raised her pistol to fire at the head of this leviathan as the creature turned its head towards her. She planned to squeeze the trigger and place the bullet right between its snake eyes as soon as she had the shot. But before the creature's head made a full turn, its forked tongue began to flick rapidly out of its mouth, and her thought band flew off her head of its own accord, landing just in front of the giant Ophidian.

"You didn't expect that one. Did you! You didn't know that the most powerful of us possess the powers of telekinesis. How foolish. But now, you know." With the Ophidian now staring directly at her, she tried to squeeze the trigger, but at that moment her arms went limp and fell uselessly by her side and refused to move. Her only consolation was that, through some stroke of luck, she still held the pistol in her limp hand. She tried to take a step forward, but she was totally paralyzed, frozen in place.

Then Satira screamed again while the Ophidian slithered closer. "Your telepathic friend here can no longer help you. Stupid Fengani, they believe that their mental powers are a match for us. Only now, too late, she knows just how powerful we really are. I'll save her for last, so she can enjoy watching me consume her friends, starting with you."

The Ophidian slithered over to Jan and its tongue flicked rapidly in and out touching her body each time as it tasted her.

"You do have a very strong mind my pretty, much too strong to make a good possessed servant, you would have made an excellent slave, perhaps. Too bad though, I won't let you live."

Tears flowed freely now down Jan's cheeks. Unable even to raise her eyebrows, the sudden insatiable urge to just give up and surrender to despair was almost overpowering, but she refused. No way! She thought. It must be projecting these dark thoughts into my mind, she guessed. She mentally screamed at her limp arm to obey her will.

The Ophidian reared up above her. She watched, almost detached, as it raised its head above her and its jaw seemed to unhinge, and it opened its mouth wider than she would have thought possible.

At that moment something touched her foot. It was Satira's tail.

While the snake had been preoccupied with her, Satira had scooted slowly closer to her until her whip-like tail was able to wrap around her leg. "Jan, just listen," she heard in her mind. "Make your mind go blank. Don't think anything. The Ophidian will read your thoughts. I can access your mind directly while I'm touching you without the Ophidian knowing. I think I can free your body. Try to move your toes."

Jan did, her toes wiggled easily inside her boots.

"Good. Now listen we only have one chance at this. You still have the pistol in your hand. Be ready. You must move faster than you have ever moved before, for if the Ophidian discovers what we are about, he will immediately take command of your body again and stop us."

The Ophidian's open mouth began to descend.

"Get ready."

Just before her head entered its mouth, she heard Satira scream in her mind, "Now!"

She snapped the pistol up and fired the last three rounds of the 1911, boom, boom, boom into the roof of the Ophidian's open mouth just above her. The .45 caliber bullets traveled through the roof of its exposed mouth then into its brain, and out the back of its head leaving a hole large enough to stick a basketball through. It died instantly.

The body of the giant snake jerked involuntarily backward, and the lifeless, huge head slammed hard to the floor beside her and on top of Satira.

THIRTY-FOUR

A wispy essence similar to a small patch of fog coalesced out of the air above the altar. "Where am I?" was its first conscious thought.

It sensed the presence of other beings connected in a deep trance sitting with joined hands around the altar. Using its mind's eye, it recognized and knew each of them by name.

There was the young beautiful woman Katrina, the master priest Iaghi, and all the others. It knew with certainty each one's darkest fears, the kind that leads to the dark night of the soul, as well as their most private thoughts.

It understood that it was all of them rolled into one, but none of them at the same time. It remembered then the reason for its creation. To destroy another creature like it who had become an abomination.

It sensed then the great evils and atrocities that had been done to keep Draka alive on the altar below it. The horrible memories of each sacrificed victim's final moments were burned and etched into the altar's essence.

It understood what Draka had done to survive. Such horrid deeds would have required a special cunning and callous ruthlessness. It knew that if it wanted to, it could do likewise and continue its existence independent of its creators.

It toyed with the idea for a moment and imagined itself becoming like Draka, a god to these lesser creatures demanding living sacrifice for regular sustenance. But at what cost? For unlike Draka, it had an ingrained sense of compassion and genuinely cared for these lesser beings. It would have to routinely feed on the souls of helpless others to just maintain its existence. Eventually, it would become just as evil and twisted as Draka. It rejected such an existence. Instead, it chose to embrace its mission, to live a brief life and destroy Draka.

It reached out with its mind using the Eye of God and sensed Draka's location and transported itself there.

It now hovered above a barren plateau. There were no forms of life about, just barren rock and reddish sand everywhere. It took a solid form then and chose to martialize as Katrina for of all the souls that constituted the Vanwanung, she had the strongest sense of will and the strongest desire to succeed and her soul was the most ancient.

She also gave herself the name Zakia. She wore a long white robe with a gold sash tied at its waste.

An angry Draka stood about a dozen yards away. He no longer wore a pendant, for when the lesser beings had performed the attunement just prior to performing the Vanwanung at the altar of atonement; their powers were taken from him.

He looked weak and his body appeared translucent for the process of disintegration had already begun. There was no longer a need to destroy him. Without the powers of the pendants to prop him up, his soul was beginning to disintegrate.

"I hope you're happy," Draka spat at her. "My consolation is that you won't live long to enjoy this victory. For you know that when you terminate the Vanwanung, you will cease to exist.

"And what about all of the poor innocent souls that you consumed to continue yours? They deserved more. You stole eternity from them."

Draka smiled a wicked smile. "Not forever, for as soon as I cease to exist, all of the souls I consumed will be free once again."

Using the powers of the Eye of God, Zakia immediately saw the truth of its words and all the horrors and havoc of releasing many trillions of twisted and ruined souls into the greater cosmos.

Those poor ruined souls were all now hopelessly insane and could never be allowed to re-mingle with the universal consciousness. The event would poison the soul of the universe and risk driving the very, I Am, essence of reality mad. The dissolution of Draka was now almost complete. Any second now trillions of ruined, twisted, and broken souls would be assimilated back into the greater universe.

Alarmed, she brainstormed for a solution and her mind conceived a plan almost at once. But it came with its own risks to carry it out; she would have to draw upon the life forces of the creatures that created her. If she drew too much, it would kill them. There was no more time to consider alternatives. Several souls, those of the most powerful and demented, had already separated their consciousness from Draka and were already unleashed. They would have to be hunted down, later.

Attuned to all the pendants, she used her will to combine all of their powers into one and a white wand appeared in her hand. She raised it and waving said something in the ancient forgotten language of the watchers. Waving the wand above her head, a thread of white light issued out of the end of the wand where it floated through the air over to Draka and began to wrap itself around him. In just a few minutes, a cocoon of white light formed around the dissolving Draka.

"What are you doing?" Draka asked when the only part of him left exposed was his head.

"You're right. The ruined souls that you consumed cannot be allowed to poison our universe. Therefore, I'm creating a separate reality, an Abyss, just for them. Perhaps, given time, they will heal. And if they do, then the fabric of this prison will no longer hold them, and they will freely pass through it to rejoin with the greater universe.

No sooner had she completely closed the cocoon of reality around Draka when his essence completely dissolved and now countless souls began to beat on the walls of their new prison desperately wanting to be free. The cocoon of light held, but it turned color from white to ruby-red.

Zakia knew that she had made the right decision. She continued working with the wand and when she finished, the cocoon disappeared and a ruby-red, egg-shaped, quartz crystal the size of a chicken egg appeared at her feet. She picked it up. With her mission accomplished, she sighed. She returned to the altar of redemption, placed the egg containing the souls of the lost next to the Eye of God, wiped sad tears from her eyes, took one last deep breath and willed to terminate her existence.

THIRTY-FIVE

Emily and her team Alpha scaled the walls with hooks and ropes. They encountered little resistance and soon her entire team was over the walls with no casualties.

Emily picked up her radio. "Anthony, we're inside the compound, tell me what's happening?"

"Great! Can you come and reinforce us?

"Roger that, what's your location?"

"We're just outside the entrance to the great pyramid."

"What's the status?" Emily said.

After Katrina and the Fengani priests went inside the pyramid, about a half an hour ago, all hell broke loose. We managed to fight them off, but we killed, and we killed but they kept coming. Then, right in the middle of this fight, our laser weapons just stopped working and we had to switch to hand-to-hand combat. Fortunately, Bernie still had his ballistic sidearm and he and Ed took a position in front of the entrance to the pyramid and at first managed to stop anything that broke through our defense line. But there was a heavy push a few minutes ago, and several hundred enemy combatants broke through our position. I witnessed Bernie and Ed make a last stand in front of the entrance. But they went down and at least fifty possessed troops and Mega-Corp soldiers managed to make it inside the pyramid. After that, the fighting just stopped, but it looks like it was only a temporary respite for they appear to be regrouping, preparing for another assault. Please get here ASAP. I don't know how much longer we can hold out."

"Roger, we're on our way." She gave the command and they began to move, fast.

At first, they encountered no combatants, but when they were within two hundred yards of the Great Pyramid, they encountered the regrouping possessed troops. When Emily and her soldiers tried using their laser weapons, theirs failed too, so they fought their way forward using their combat knives and laser rifles as bludgeons for weapons. Her team fought like there was no tomorrow, for they were expendable, their only mission was to buy Katrina and the Fengani more time at all costs. For the fate of the universe depended on Katrina and the success of her mission.

The last hundred yards to Anthony's location was complete chaos. The possessed troops attacked with complete abandon, many armed only with their fists or whatever they could find to serve as a club. Finally, though, after almost an hour of continuous hand to hand combat, she reached Anthony.

The possessed troops, like a hive of angry bees defending their home, continued to attack without a thought or concern for their personal safety, desperate to reach the entrance to the pyramid. But with her troops and Anthony's fighting together, and then, a short time later, Jeb's team joined them. They went on the attack and pushed the possessed troops back several hundred yards farther away from the pyramid.

Maureen continued to stare at the skull and crossbones icon hovering in front of her. *One minute left.* If the time ran out and still no word came, then by God, she would follow orders; she was a soldier, she had given her personal word to General Kyle and the others that she would do it. There was nothing on this side of hell that would cause her to back out on that promise. Her tense thoughts raced. The last two months of her life had certainly been interesting. Beyond her wildest dreams would be an understatement.

After her complete disenchantment with the corrupt world she had grown up in and the power-hungry people in Mega-Corp running it, she traveled two thousand years into the future and discovered a real cause worth dying for. And finally, she meets the love of her life, her soul mate, wearing a thick brown alligator skin looking like something out of a cliché sci-fi flick. But she had something amazing with him that she never had with any human. He completely understood her and accepted her for who she was, and he considered her quirkiness and intellectual interests a form of brilliance instead of a turn-off.

Thank god for the Shanfin stones that made making love and a chance for a real relationship with him possible. She remembered again with fondness her first night on Toyama when Xelana had shown them to her…

She looked out of her shuttle window at the harbor below, as they approached to land in the city of Hoshama, she just couldn't believe it. She had just traveled in space, and now she was about to land on an alternate Venus that was much cooler than the one in her reality. This Venus supported a rich diversity of life.

Everything that had now happened to her since she met Katrina was way beyond her wildest dreams. Imagine me an astronaut. This was like living in one of those great sci-fi television shows of the late twentieth century, the classics, she thought.

She tried to take it all in as she gazed out of her passenger window at an alien city that Xelana told her was millions of years old. The alien city buildings below came in many different sizes, but every building she saw was pyramid shaped and white. "Why is every building a pyramid?" she asked Xelana sitting beside her."

"We believe the shape of a thing determines its power, and the one shape that exudes the most power to its occupants is the pyramid."

Ok, but why is every building also white? Don't your people believe in colors?

Xelana smiled enjoying the opportunity to talk about his beliefs. "Once again, white is the combination of all colors. As such, it's a visualization of how the One exists in our lives and it resonates with a simple purity, being made up of all the colors giving it the highest power."

She didn't understand their preoccupation with power; Xelana had begun to explain earlier that they believed Power to be some kind of a life force that was in all things to some degree. She found their ideas and mystical approach to understanding the world interesting, and she really did want to learn much more, but she knew she could question him later at her leisure. However, in a few minutes, the spectacular bird's-eye view of an alien city in her passenger window would be gone forever and she didn't want to miss it.

They were close enough to the ground now that she could see the people of the city. She saw mostly Fengani and a few humans hustling about. She also saw a few buggy carts, and some wagons, all pulled by creatures that looked like an alligator with the legs of a horse.

"So, what do you think?" Xelana asked after they landed. "Do we really look like alien monsters? He made that unsettling toothy grin that they all seemed to make when telling something they considered funny. "Hmmm, you do look tasty." He said squeezing her arm."

"Hey, are you reading my mind?" she asked with a hint of sarcasm in her voice and wearing a disarming smile.

"No, it's not considered polite to do so and it's not quite that easy. I would have to concentrate a lot harder on you than I am. And besides, it's usually not comfortable getting inside someone else's head; it can leave me with a headache. This time I did it the human way, I read your face, and I'm seeing a complete sense of awe splashed all over your face."

That was true. The word awe was probably an understatement. She patted his arm. Xelana was really proving to be a wonderful, dear friend and he was the most interesting creature she'd ever met. Thanks to him, her holo-laptop could now recharge as often as needed. She sighed. Too bad he was an alien and looked like something out of a childhood nightmare. Still, she found herself wanting to spend more time with him, but he probably had a family and friends waiting for him when they landed whom he'd be wanting to spend quality time with and catch up on their lives.

"OK, I admit it. I just read your thoughts, please don't be mad."

"I'm not," she said.

"Truth is, I don't have any family. There's no one special waiting for me when we land at the airport wanting to catch up on my life. I never chose a mate. My work has always kept me too busy." He scratched his chin with a claw-like finger as if he was trying to reach a decision. "Say, there's a restaurant in downtown Hoshama called the Yingzutan that caters to off-worlders like you, and it has a hotel, the Rasmutan - just for humans, right next to it. I could arrange to get you a room in there and I'm kind of hoping that we could have dinner together. What do you think?"

"Are you asking me out?" She smiled. "Sure. I'd love that."

Jeb, on seeing that she was enjoying Xelana's company, suggested, "Look there's nothing for you to do here while we make plans, take some well-earned downtime and get some R&R. I mean it. Get out and enjoy. It might be a long time again before you get any time off. See you bright and early tomorrow morning soldier."

So she did. When she told Xelana she just got the day off, he offered to show her the best sites of the city. Their first stop was the Fengani's own great pyramid that was the center of their culture and their religion. He explained to her that it was built during the time of the Way's founder, Ragdu. Inside the great hall that led to the center of the pyramid, he showed her the many egg sized memory crystals embedded in the stone wall every few steps down the main hallway that lead to the interior of the pyramid.

"So, you say these crystals contain memories?" She said not quite understanding how that could work.

"Yes. In fact, each crystal is a lesson on how to live according to The Way. If you open up your mind while touching one, the short memory contained in each crystal will become yours."

"Will it hurt me or change me in any way?" she asked thinking of it as a mind-altering substance and remembering how unscrupulous pushers back in Chicago would sugarcoat the effects of their drugs to the city's many homeless hoping to get them addicted so they would hand over what little money or possessions they had for their next fix.

"No, it won't hurt or harm, and the memory is pleasant by the way. "Just listen and reflect on what he says."

She still wasn't sure about this, but she was learning to trust Xelana.

"Here touch this one," Xelana said, pointing to a blue egg-shaped crystal embedded in the wall at eye level. "It's the first stone in the series and it contains the first lesson."

She reached out but still hesitated.

"It won't hurt, I assure you. You won't disappear. Or lose your sense of self. You will just absorb the memory from one of his first readings, that's it."

She reached out and...... The room disappeared. She found herself standing in a different room and instead of Xelana standing before her, a smaller Fengani, much older than Xelana stood before her wearing a black robe with deep mesmerizing eyes much like Iaghi's.

"So, you have come here to learn how to live your life according to The Way. Excellent choice. My philosophy offers the universe hope for a better future.

"I have seen one possible very dark future, and I have learned that the only thing that will prevent that future from enfolding is to teach as many of us as possible to learn to live out our lives according to The Way. That said, I'm sure you've prepared yourself before coming here to hear me eschew some boring loquacious speech meant to share with you a long list of moral do's and don'ts. Instead, I offer you this one thought.

"Realize that we are all–everything animate and inanimate--One. Whatever deed or transgression you do to another you are also doing to yourself...."

She lookup up and Xelana stood before her once again.

"What do you think?"

"That was most interesting... I'll have to get back with you. I do need to think about what he just said."

After leaving the Fengani great pyramid, they toured the Ginlo, the grand museum and cultural-historical center in downtown Hoshama. There she learned that some Fengani even possess the powers of telekinesis and prescience.

When it became afternoon, they walked through the market center where local merchants sold their goods. In the streets near the market, she saw Fengani children for the first time. They looked much like miniature adults except their color was a mottled Gray not the dark brown of adult males, the pale green of females beyond their egg laying years, or the bright green of a fertile ovulating female.

The well-fed children were full of vitality and they appeared cheerful and happy as they ran to and fro in the streets playing a game of tag. She didn't see any adults guarding them. Not like the children she remembered back in twenty-first century Chicago, who were dirty, wore ragged clothes, looked undernourished, and never smiled. And always guarded by at least several adults, lest they get snatched up for the sex trade business.

Finally, they made it to Yingzutan. While the waiter escorted them through the bar area toward the dining terrace, she saw mostly humans on business and several groups of Mega-Corp human soldiers drinking and being loud. She ignored them and seeing that she was with a Fengani priest, they ignored her too.

The waiter seated them at a table next to the railing of the terrace that looked out over the lush surrounding hills and handed them each a menu.

"She looked at the pictures on the menu but every entre seemed to have parts of an Orshank added to it. "Xelana, can you help me to select my order? Don't forget I'm a vegetarian."

"Do you eat seafood?"

"As long as it's not something intelligent and it didn't suffer when it was harvested."

We have a native fish called sagte, very similar to the salmon on your Earth. They only have a rudimentary intelligence, nothing more. We take great pains to make sure that every creature we harvest never suffers unnecessarily. Trust me on this, we're all telepaths and we would know."

So, she ordered the sagte with a grain called quertara that Xelana told her was similar to the texture and flavor of fried rice on Earth. While they waited for their dinner he introduced her to a most delicious local beer brewed in the basement of the restaurant specifically for humans wishing for a taste of home. To her wonderful delight, it even came served in a brown bottle with a long neck. "Wow, even after two thousand years. Thank God, some things never change," she said aloud. Her mouth watered in anticipation. Oh please let it taste as good as it looks, she prayed. She just couldn't believe her good fortune, getting served a beer here on an alien world in an alternate reality.

The bottle came with a black label, with the name Adele in bold white letters across it. To her delight, it tasted perfect, very similar to a bud-light. If she closed her eyes, she could imagine she was back on Earth drinking at a sports bar watching the football game. She drank several more and Xelana got her to open up about her past, and she told him why she had joined the army instead of getting a higher education when she had won a full scholarship to the University of Chicago. "I was in love with a jerk, fricking Craig, my high school sweetheart, who dumped me for who at the time I thought was my best friend, Chloe." She wiped her eyes, even after all this time some memories always hurt. "I was devastated, and I went into a destructive mode. I just wanted to die, and at the time, joining the army seemed like a nice way to get yourself

258

killed. Better than slitting my wrists open, at least my parents would have gotten a nice settlement from the army if I was killed in action."

Tired of the conversation centering on her she asked, "So, what made you become a priest?"

Xelana made a toothy grin. "This sounds so simpleton, but the truth is a felt compelled to. Remember that some of us are prescient, so, I just knew from the time I was very young that someday I would wear this robe," he said pointing to his blue master's robe. He paused, and his eyes became far away. "Just as much as I knew that someday I would meet you, Maureen and that someday in the far future I will wear the black robe of the high priest."

Before she could ask him about his revelation that he knew he would someday meet her, their waiter brought their food. It smelled and tasted delicious, the quertara did have the flavor and texture of fried rice, maybe just a little nuttier.

They ate in silence. Conversation limited itself to comments about the delicious food and neither seemed ready to pick it back up where they had left off, but all the while she kept thinking, damn I wish he were human.

After dinner, they had several more drinks together where Xelana seemed to want to hear what Earth had been like before the Ophidians had come.

At her hotel room, she made coffee and they finally picked back up their conversation about themselves and talked until four in the morning.

She yawned, "I'm sorry, but I need to get to bed." She got up to show him the door and said, "I sure wish you were human, I'd be all over you right now."

Xelana looked at her and smiled. "There is a way."

"How?" she asked. "Are you people shapeshifters too?"

"No, but we have something similar. He pulled out a marble-sized, red crystal.

He made a lipless grin. "This is a Shanfin crystal," he said.

"Is it another type of memory crystal?" she asked.

"Not exactly. This is another crystal technology altogether, very different. We can connect with it to create a mental world of our choosing, a kind of virtual reality.

259

For lack of a better term, we'll call it a dream. In some ways, it's not unlike a waking dream where we're fully conscious. However, it has at least several properties that make it very different than an ordinary dream. For one, and the most fun, we can mutually share our experiences in this reality with anyone who links with us through the Shanfin stones."

"Ok, so, how does it work and how does it help us?"

Xelana had them both sit on the floor. He placed the Shanfin stone in the center between them. "Before we begin, a few words of caution. When we go into this dream that we imagine together if something happens where you are killed, in almost all cases the person dies in this world too. Or, if you are seriously wounded when you come back to this world, you will wake up with the same serious wounds here as well."

"That's bizarre."

He smiled a toothy grin. "There is one thing more. If for any reason you should become pregnant while in this virtual world, then when you return here, you will be pregnant here as well. So, as I said, the reality of the Shanfin stones is not really a dream. Even we do not fully understand it yet. Although we do have several possible theories."

"Is there anything else?" she asked. This sounds like fun she thought.

"Just one more thing. You can become any creature you imagine yourself to be when the reality of the Shanfin stones first begins. But once it's begun you must remain that creature for the duration of the time you're linked to the Shanfin stones. There is no shapeshifting in this dream world either.

Never afraid to try something new, she said, "Ok what do we do now?"

Let's choose a place and a time," he paused. "You choose. Pick a place where you were always happy and felt safe.

"Sure, but how will I find you?"

"I'll meet you there and tonight I will be human."

"Really? How will I know you?"

"Just look for the man of your heart's desire. I can tap into your subconscious, remember. I will look exactly like him, except the soul inside will be mine."

"Ok," she said. They touched hands together, and they both stared at the stone. A place where... she remembered her most pleasant memories as a little girl were when her family used to visit and stay with her grandparents at their summer cottage in Traverse City... yes, she was always happy there...The Shanfin stone seemed to grow brighter. She closed her eyes. She could almost see her grandparents cottage. She heard seagulls and...

She thought of the many hours spent with Xelana and their minds linked to it in a tiny reality of their own making. Who cared if it only existed in their heads? When you connected to the Shanfin crystal, the reality you created was *so* real, the touches feelings, smells, the lovemaking, everything.

Sometimes she would become a female Fengani, but mostly Xelana, tapped into her unconscious and become the perfect physical man for her, they made love as humans. Xelana confessed that he preferred the gentle mutual sharing sexual experience of mating as a human. She heartily agreed. Fengani mating was a violent, catlike aggressive affair, done more out of a need to continue the species, than an act of intimacy.

She softly placed her hand on Xelana's shoulder and caressed it. He still didn't move and remained in his trance. "Any word?" she asked telepathically. Nothing, no response.

She returned her attention to the clock on her screen. When the clock got down to ten seconds she prepared mentally to push that button and then she would wake Xelana and they would both flee into the Shanfin crystal together. If they died in this world would they die in a Shanfin dream as well? We'll just have to find out she decided. Oh well,

261

living in the future sure had been a fun ride. Time to pay the band she decided as she watched the clock count down to five four…

"Hold! You don't need to push that button," she heard in her mind. Xelana stirred and smiled at her. "It's over, we've won."

✳ ✳ ✳

Kyle led his troops comprised of the remnants of his command and liberated souls to Engineering. On the way, they encountered more former possessed lurking in the corridors, looking lost and forlorn. His men passed out thought bands to protect them from being enslaved again in case any Ophidians remained on the ship. But they didn't meet any and they retook Engineering without any conflict. They must have all transported elsewhere like the SOB that ate Trudy. He couldn't wait to meet that one again, that's one Ophidian he'd personally enjoy making into purses.

Katrina and the Fengani priests must be having some success on the surface. One could only hope.

✳ ✳ ✳

"Look at that!" Anthony said standing up in front of the great pyramid. Every one of the Ophidians had collapsed and the possessed troops had stopped fighting and stood looking lost and confused. They ordered the possessed troops to throw down their weapons, which they did willingly; all desire to fight was gone.

They rounded up all the comatose Ophidians they could find and placed them in special faraday prisons blocking their telepathic abilities, making them as dangerous as a tiger in a cage in a zoo.

✳ ✳ ✳

Jan stared at the broken body of Satira. Her legs were bent backward at an odd angle, while her left arm was broken in at least three places. When the snake had slammed its head down, Jan who had been standing up and had the reflexes of a wild cat had easily jumped out of the way, but Satira, who had been lying on the ground, didn't have time to react and the head of the giant snake had slammed hard into her body.

Satira's eyes opened. "Jan we've won. I can sense it. Draka is gone."

Jan bent down and inspected Satira's body for more injuries.

"Jan, don't bother it's too late. My body is broken. I can sense that I only have a few minutes left. We're prescient, remember?"

Jan wiped tears from her eyes. If hadn't been for Satira, she'd be in the belly of that ophidian she just killed.

"Jan, there's a blank memory crystal in my right pocket," She said through fits of coughing. Red bright blood leaked from the corner of her mouth.

"Got it!" Jan said holding it up.

Good. Please hold it steady about six inches from my face, and help to get my good hand on it.

Jan held the stone and Satira's good hand together while Satira stared hard.

The stone came to life and radiated a soft violet light. After about two minutes, Satira stopped staring and said, "You can stop now. The stone contains all my memories from my earliest childhood to this moment.

"Jan…" Satira said. She paused coughing up blood. "Can you please see that Dr. Humli gets it?"

"Yes of course," Jan said wiping her eyes.

"Jan... Than..."

Satira's eyes froze and Jan knew that she was gone. She reached into her backpack and pulled out a lightweight emergency blanket and used it to cover Satira's face and upper body.

She stood up then stared at the mammoth dead Ophidian that almost had her for a meal. She walked over to the altar. The pendants and the Eye of God no longer glowed. Katrina raised her head and opened her eyes.

"Are you OK?" Jan asked.

"Yes, I'm fine."

"What now?"

"We must help the former possessed and the slaves. Many of them have lived their entire lives in servitude to the empire. They won't know what to do or even how to think for themselves. They'll be like lost and little children."

"Help me up," Katrina said. "I want to do something before the others waken." Jan helped her. Katrina stood like she was weak as a kitten. She had Jan fetch the Eye of God from the center of the altar and place it on the ground before her feet.

Then she called up the power of her pendant, and she seemed full of strength once more, gone was the exhaustion that filled her face moments before. Her eyes glowed again with strength and determination. A blue, cold flame engulfed her foot as she raised it and then she slammed it down as hard as she could on the Eye of God. "Never again!" The stone shattered from the force of her foot into tiny pieces and then the pile of pieces began to burn with a blue flame and turn to ash.

"What have you done?" a surprised Jan said. "That was the Fengani's most sacred crystal."

"Hold Jan," Iaghi said, who was now coming around too. "If I had come around first I would now be doing the same thing. It's unfortunate, but a necessary loss. The Eye of God was simply too powerful for any mortal creature to possess."

At that moment they heard footsteps coming towards them. Jan launched another flare into the air as the previous one had gone out. She then reached down to pick up her double-bladed staff.

"Relax Jan you don't need weapons, it's your friends who are coming," Iaghi said.

THIRTY-SIX

When the Armstrongs and their friends returned to Sanctuary, they returned to a hero's welcome and they became instant celebrities. The populace of Sanctuary sorely wanted one of them to run for mayor. However, they all graciously declined and tried to explain they would never be happy living the settled life of an administrator sitting behind a desk the remainder of their lives.

The re-born city now had a growing sizable population. Many more thousands of people had resettled here during the few months that Anthony and Katrina had been gone thanks to the resistance. And the residents had been busy too. Many of the automated systems such as lighting, traffic control, running water and sanitation had been restored and were fully functional once again.

However, with no one officially in charge, the resistance was trying its best to manage things. But they were out of their league and many were becoming frustrated. They had joined the resistance to fight slavery not to become city administrators. After several days of meeting with various grassroots organizations, Kyle and Emily met privately with several citizens that showed excellent promise with the necessary leadership skills and the drive necessary to manage the growing city. They convened an emergency council where the previous city's constitution was ratified and reactivated and then the council approved an emergency election of new administrators on the last day of the month.

Shortly after that, Kyle and Emily had a teleconference with the entire city where they announced they were planning on going back to Earth, but this time with a sizable army to end slavery in all its evil forms once and for all. They reminded everyone that on Earth the rigged cast system created by Mega-Corp was still rigidly enforced. They advised that this would be a formidable task as Mega-Corp would not give up without a fight.

Their planned first destination was a series of small towns where Mega-Corp ran a cluster of slave factories about a hundred miles south of Lovington where their friends the Pickfords lived. They then asked for volunteers and to their delight the next day they had many thousands requesting to sign up.

Several weeks after the special election and their lives began to return to a somewhat normalcy, Katrina began searching through the archives on what had happened to Linda and the little girl Lisa. She delightfully discovered that Linda had ruled Sanctuary with an iron fist the first thirty years of its existence and only retired just before her death at the ripe old age of ninety-six. *What a woman she was.* That would have been Linda all right, strong and resourceful. She would insist on remaining in charge. Those first years of Sanctuary with her at the helm would be its own story.

But it bothered her that she could find no mention of Lisa Sparks anywhere – nothing, not even so much as passing mention in the archives. Surely, Linda would have insisted that Lisa would be there with her. Linda had adored her.

She spent several obsessed days looking through the archived records. Jeb came in to see her several times and offered his help, but she insisted that she do it alone. Not finding anything out about Lisa had put her in a very dark mood. She knew Jeb was just trying to help and normally she was pretty level-headed, but she strongly feared for the worst and didn't feel like talking about it yet.

A short time later, her mother Emily stopped in and asked, "Why don't we both take a coffee break and talk. Tell me what you're doing. You have us all worried sick."

Katrina beyond exasperation quietly agreed. On their way to the cafeteria while her mom doted on her disheveled hair trying to make her look semi-presentable. "What is it that's bothering you?"

Katrina said, "Funny, I never did tell you about my journey back through time, did I?" So, she did. She told her the whole story, about appearing in the streets of old Chicago, meeting, Linda, going to the homeless shelter, the good people she met, and then she talked about Lisa.

At the mention of Lisa's last name, her mom's face became ashen. After Katrina concluded her story, Emily said, "I have something back in my office that I think you should see. I believe it will answer your questions." Twenty minutes later sitting at her mom's old workstation, Emily opened a drawer to her desk and pulled out an old pink diary. "This belongs to your father. Your father showed it to me when we first got married. He couldn't read it as it was written in archaic English and he only spoke Universal at the time. He said it was an old heirloom in his family that has been handed down for many generations. It is so old that his family no longer remembered its history or meaning. They only valued it because of its age. Since I could read it, your father gave it to me to keep. I never thought too much about it until you mentioned the name Lisa Sparks. This is her diary and it was given to her by a woman coincidentally by the name of Katrina."

Katrina recognized the book at once and just stared at it. With her hand shaking, she took the book from her and began to read. She read for the next half hour. Unfortunately, the book had once been in a fire and the last pages were missing. The final page talked about them being stuck in a traffic jam during their escape from Chicago. Did she die there on that road? She could accept that Lisa was now long dead, she had expected that. But she had hoped that Lisa had had a good long life, and she felt angry and upset that she may have been denied that privilege. She didn't sleep at all that night.

The next morning Katrina had decided to spend the whole day in her room, sulking. She put a do not disturb sign on the outside of her door. She refused all calls from Jeb or either of her parents. But then about noon someone began pounding on her door. At first, she decided to ignore it hoping that they would just go away. But they continued to knock. This made her angry thinking that it must be Jeb or her parents, but then she heard a gruff, familiar voice say "Katrina! Please open up."

It was Iaghi, what was he doing here? "What do you want? Can't you see I don't want to be disturbed?"

"I know what you're upset about, but there is more to the story, trust me. I know what happened to Lisa. Please allow me to come in?"

What news could he have that was going to make her feel better? She thought about telling him to just leave her alone, but she decided she might as well hear what he had to say. So she opened the door even though she really didn't want to.

She was sure she looked a fright. She still wore the same clothes as yesterday and hadn't slept in over thirty-six hours. "Tell me what you know and then be on your way."

Please allow me to come in. "It's very good news actually, I promise." She opened the door wide but before Iaghi stepped through the doorway he sprinkled ashes on the doorstep and said the familiar word *Noyami*.

He waited until he was seated and comfortable before he spoke. "Lisa Sparks didn't die on the road out of Chicago."

"And... how do you know that?"

"Because we saved her."

"But why would you do that? I thought the Fengani didn't normally interfere in people's lives. Why would you save her?"

"You're correct that we don't normally interfere with the time continuum, but sometimes it is necessary, especially when the Eye of God showed us that we must."

"You're beginning to confuse me. Why would the Eye of God care so much about Lisa?"

"When you stepped back into the past you made several modifications of the time continuum. One was Lisa. She was meant to grow up and someday have a family Otherwise you would have never been born and Draka would never be defeated."

"But there is no record of her ever being in Sanctuary, how could she be my ancestor?"

Oh, she's your ancestor all right, but not on your mother's side, but your father's. We couldn't take her to Sanctuary, or once again, you would never have been born. She was the great, great, many times removed grandmother of your father. I can honestly tell you that she had a long life. She was never a slave. In fact, when she grew up she had formed the first resistance, became their leader and fought the Ophidians and their slave trade in any way she could. She lived free, and she had seven children and she lived to be ninety-three. After all, she had you and Linda as mentors how could she have done anything else."

Iaghi pulled out a green quartz crystal the size of a lemon. "The head of our religion, Tau at the time, visited her and convinced her to allow us to make this just before she died. She agreed on the condition that someday we would give it to you. We promised her that we would give it to you when you were ready. See, she always remembered you and it made her very happy knowing that someday you would have this. She really loved you. Anyway, here it is. It's a small gift to you for all that you have done for the universe from all of the Fengani. We will be eternally in your debt."

Iaghi placed the memory stone on the coffee table. "You know how to use it I'll leave it here for you to use when I'm gone."

Suddenly, all the anger and disappointment she had felt for the last several days boiled away like wispy morning fog when it comes into contact with a bright, hot sun. She saw Iaghi out the door, returned to the table. With trembling hands, she picked up the memory stone and began to concentrate.

✳ ✳ ✳

As Anthony and Jan walked through the cobbled stone streets of the Way missionary, Anthony could see why the Fengani had taken over this old Catholic monastery deep in the mountains. The place was naturally defendable as it was built on the top of a plateau with limited access.

They were returning here, so, Jan could finish her training as a missionary, which could take up to almost a full year. She had long ago given up her idea of becoming a full-fledged priestess and living celibate the rest of her life, but she still wanted to earn the right to proselytize *The Way* to all who would listen. She hoped to share a way of life centered on peace, love, and harmony with the universe to a world that so badly needed it.

After graduation, they had originally planned on hooking up with his parents and Katrina and Jeb and join the liberation movement, but now plans had changed again he thought as he looked over at Jan's growing belly. "Just think, they were about to become parents and he wanted everything to be perfect for them. He would have preferred that the baby would be born in Sanctuary, but she assured him that the doctors here were very competent.

They hadn't been able to come up with any names that they liked. They still didn't even know the sex of the baby, but she told him there were prescient Fengani here that would know and would even give them a reading of the child's future if they asked. For now, they had both agreed to wait to find out and enjoy picking out a name for both sexes and see what they came up with.

As they walked in the quiet streets of the monastery, they saw Maureen and Xelana come out to meet them. They had both moved here a few weeks ago and planned to live here permanently.

"Congratulations you two," Maureen said when she saw Jan's belly. "Do you have any names picked out?"

Jan smiled and winked at him, "no but we're working on it"

"Come in, come in, I'll show you to your rooms," Maureen said motioning them inside.

Just before they stepped through the doorway, they all dipped their fingers in ashes and together said, "Noyami."

Without any modern roads and no cars, it had taken them, and the thirty guards her father and mother had insisted they take as an escort, weeks to get to what was once known as the state of New York. "Those highways are infested with many thieves and bandits who would be delighted to fleece a couple of lonely travelers," her father had said. They saw a few passersby, on the journey here, mostly peddlers of goods in large caravans traveling heavily armed like them.

They held hands as they walked the shore along the top of the falls. They wanted to be even more intimate, but they were self-conscious of their armed escort that followed them everywhere. The roar of the falls here was deafening. They found a rock that they could both sit on and just enjoy the spectacular view.

"I can see why people would want to come here on a honeymoon. The view is stunning," Katrina said talking into her hands that were cupped over Jeb's ear. "Just imagine, we're the first honeymooners to come here in almost two thousand years."

When Jeb had suggested Niagara Falls for their honeymoon she had asked, "Why there?" and he had explained that it had been very popular as a honeymoon resort in the time he had grown up. She had considered it and thought, *why not*. The Ophidians had robbed them of all links to their past when they had destroyed civilization. Maybe, they could re-bridge a piece of that past by restoring some lost traditions.

She silently thanked fate for bringing them together. He was such a kind and gentle man. She loved him so much; she could no longer imagine a life without him.

For now, she just wanted to enjoy this moment, to delight in the caring touch of his soft, warm hand, to bask in his aura of kindness, and taste the sweet smell of his breath when he whispered in her ear, so he could be heard over the noise of the falls. They might not have the luxury of growing old together. That was for people who lived in peaceful gentle times, and to people who didn't go up in arms when they encountered inequity in the world and couldn't turn the other way.

After their honeymoon, their lives were about to become hectic again, and they would be soon stepping back into harm's way.

When Katrina had suggested to Jeb that they join her parents and take up their quest to liberate the Earth and put an end to slavery and the draconian caste system created by Mega-Corp, he loved the idea. "I have no problem fighting for a cause I can truly believe in."

"What are you thinking about honey?" Jeb asked her while putting his arm around her shoulder.

She scooted closer to him. "Nothing important, I found myself worrying about tomorrow... why?"

"You seemed distant all of a sudden."

She smiled. "Well if I do that again you make sure you do this, and she pulled his face into hers and kissed him."

When they came up for air, Jeb found Iaghi's face not more than two feet from theirs staring at them with that frightful lipless grin. "Iaghi, what the hell are you doing here?"

Katrina turned and frowned with anger written all over her face.

Iaghi said through that eerie toothy grin of his. "We need to start the emancipation of humanity tonight."

"Iaghi, we are on our honeymoon. Besides, you don't even have the Eye of God anymore. How could you know that?"

"True, but you forget that we Fengani are prescient. I can see that if we are to successfully liberate humanity, we need to start tonight. Let's go. I already have a portal prepared to take us to your army. I took the liberty of having the troops assembled. Everyone is waiting for your orders."

Katrina and Jeb looked at each other and sighed in tandem as they got up to follow Iaghi on their next adventure.

Thank you so much for reading! If you enjoyed this book, I would really appreciate it if you went to amazon.com and left me a short and honest review. That would really help others find my book.